I0682207

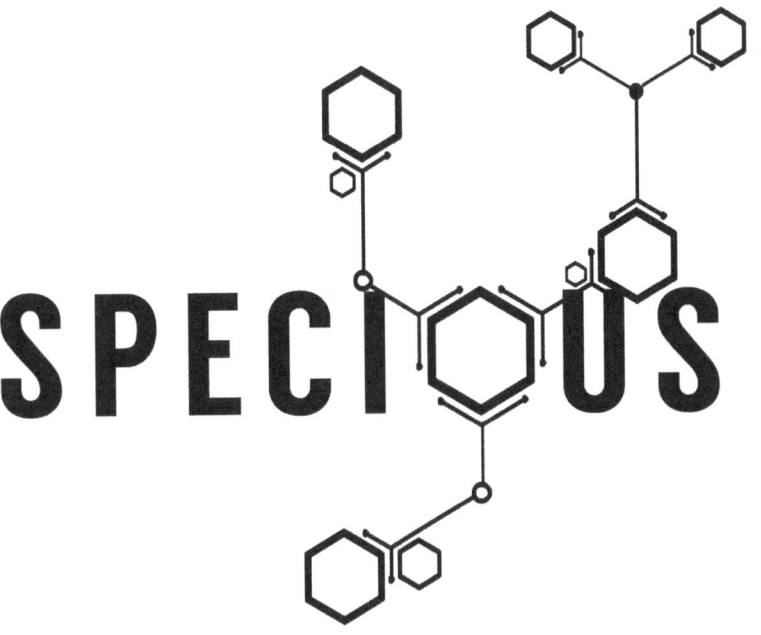

SPEC   US

ROBIN BERKSTRESSER

Book cover design by The Scarlett Rugers Design Agency www.scarlettrugers. com

Specious/Robin Berkstresser–1ˢᵗ edition

For Printed Copies ISBN 10: 069259552X 13: 978-0692595527

DEDICATION

To my mom for always giving fantastic advice, such as "it's probably not a good idea to get in the habit of drinking a whole bottle of wine by yourself." To which I promptly ignored and wrote this book.

CONTENTS

ACKNOWLEDGEMENTS

I have to give thanks to everyone who has supported me (and a big middle finger to those who didn't). Though my name is on the front cover, I couldn't have done it without the help of so many. Before formal editing, I enlisted a select group of people. I cringe whenever I think how rough the draft was when y'all saw it, so thank you for sticking with me.

Mom: You gave me the courage to initially share the story. To be fair, as my mom, I think you're obligated to believe in me, but, nonetheless, thank you for being the first and last eyes on the story.

Dad: Even though you tried to get me to change the whole premise of the book in the final stages of editing, it came from a place of excitement for the story. Plus, you had other much better ideas.

Sean: Thank you for being a better brother to me than Dominic is to Elliot, despite trying to get me to name the Letum "the Stinkies." Really, Sean?

Amanda: Your tiny writing was the hardest to get through. More than once, I had to ask you to decipher your own comments, but I'm so thankful you wrote every thought you had while reading. It helped me tighten so much of the story.

Sam: I can't thank you enough for helping me come up with a "slightly plausible" theory for why the infection started–someone get that woman her doctorate already! Just so you know, you're the voice of Dominic. Take that as you will.

Emma: Out of everyone, I think you connected with and understood my characters the most. It was way cool to talk about them with you. Also, thanks for putting up with seemingly endless random questions as I've finalized this story—and beyond. Girl, you're my go-to.

Kathleen: As always, I could count on you to be blunt. I appreciate you telling me my initial Dominic was "so evil (you) were waiting for him to stroke his mustache." I hope you think he's more believable now.

After I got through their feedback, I enlisted outside, professional help. I have so much gratitude toward everyone at KM Editorial for helping me clean the story up to a point where I feel comfortable sharing it with everyone. Specifically, I would never have made it this far without the help of my lovely developmental editor, Katie McCoach. You took my hand and guided me through the crazy world of self-publishing. Thank you so much for everything you've done.

CHAPTER ONE

The alarm clock vibrates in warning. I curse under my breath as I reach across my bed to turn it off. I stare out the window into the abyss of all of the living quarters. Massive, grey buildings cloud the view. Everyone must be waking up right now. It seems bizarre that one person can have such a big impact on the entire territory. I yawn loudly and prepare for a day surrounded by judgmental society members.

Being that I'm only on the thirtieth floor, the other buildings block the sun so I turn on the light. I let out a deep breath to calm my nerves. Even though I'm not looking forward to the day, I need to be the son my mother believes in. The thought of her pulls me out of bed.

As with every morning, I walk down the hallway, drawn in by our family portraits. The evolution of the pictures hypnotizes me. A happy couple transforms to a family of three once my brother is born. I enter their lives and it's four of us. Then, our patriarch leaves and it's back to three. I examine the last frame and my older brother's smug face stares back at me. I enter the kitchen and come face-to-face with the same look on the older version.

"You are out of bed later than anticipated. You need to speed up your morning process if we are going to be on time, Joe," my brother says as he gulps down his breakfast.

He's been calling me this nickname for as long as I can remember. Joe, short for "Average Joe," is his method of making sure I always know how mediocre I am.

"Leave Elliot alone, Dominic. There is no need for that, especially today," my mother says. She pushes a lock of her blonde hair back behind her ear while she rushes around the kitchen.

I look back at my brother. He's still in his pajamas, his light hair tussled from sleep. Our eyes meet, his blue matching my blue, and he stands up quickly. At six foot four, he's always been an intimidating figure.

"My apologies, *little* brother." He offers a sarcastic bow and moves his bowl over to the sink.

The best response is to remain silent. I open the pantry in search of my packet of food. I briefly consider taking Dominic's morning allowance, but a brief glance at Mother's smaller packets stops me. As our food is portioned based on age and weight, being twenty-two allows me much more food than my mother's older demographic. I turn to get milk out of the refrigerator and accidently bump into Dominic.

He sighs heavily. "Another member in my training program and his family have a kitchen that is almost twice as big as ours. It is much less likely that they have these problems." He stares pointedly at my mother.

I glance to see her reaction. Her mind is elsewhere as she looks toward the hallway. Our most recent family portrait is visible.

She responds, "I've done the best I can."

Dominic's eyebrows rise. "This could have easily been avoided." He shifts his gaze to me before stalking out of the kitchen.

I cringe and look around at our kitchen. It isn't grand by any means, but my mother has always kept it immaculate and clean.

"I don't think our apartment is too small," I say.

My mother's attention breaks away from the hallway and her hazel eyes refocus on me. With Dominic out of the room, my mother and I visibly relax. Whenever my brother and I are in the same room, tension is a close companion. Besides the color of our eyes, we have practically nothing else in common. From the old family portraits, it's obvious that he strongly favors our father, whereas I have the softer characteristics of our mother.

"I really wish he would stop calling you that name. It's a terrible nickname to give someone…" Her eyes widen in alarm when she realizes what she's about to say.

I quietly finish her sentence. "Someone like me?"

"You know that isn't what I meant, Elliot. The world might not know it yet, but you have been given such a gift. You're who you are because of fate, not because of some scientist. You're going to do something so important with your life. You may not know it, but I do."

My mother puts a comforting hand on my shoulder. "You really should have gotten up earlier. You're going to need to hurry. I don't want us to be late today."

"Don't worry, I'll be ready. I promise, Mother."

She runs her hands through her hair anxiously. "I know you will. I just can't believe we have to go to another one of these." Her eyes drop in grief.

I nod in agreement. This time, it's my mother leaving the room.

I sigh and take my next bite. She's right. It really is shocking we're in the same situation, especially so soon. This isn't supposed to happen in our society. It's not like we live in the outer regions or even Acroisia. We've evolved from that.

I finish my breakfast and bring my dishes to the sink. In a hurry, I head toward the bathroom to take a shower. To my disappointment, Dominic passes me in the hallway. My foot catches on the floor when I try to get out of his way. I'm forced to put my hands up against the wall in an attempt to catch myself. His cruel laughter echoes through the hall, even after he closes the door to his room.

I rush through my shower routine and hurry to my bedroom to get dressed. Years of scuff marks cover the grey walls. I grab underwear from my dresser, then pull open the closet. The monotonous grey outfits stare out at me, evidence of the years of structure I've been subjected to. A structure I've never been able to truly fit in.

Solemnly, I pull the formal attire hanger from the rack and get dressed, careful not to wrinkle the fabric. It fits loosely around my chest and shoulders. I straighten my posture to try and hide that fact. I don't want to let Mother down by looking unkempt. Just as I'm tying my shoes, her raised voice calls out.

"Sons, we have to leave now if we want to make it in time."

I quickly comb my dark hair down, one of the few traits I inherited from my father.

I hurry out to the front room. Mother spots my uneven tie and smiles a little as she corrects it. "Remind me next time we visit my parents to have your grandfather teach you how to tie a tie. Your father should have..." She pauses a moment before continuing. "Well, it just seems you missed that lesson." She pats my chest and takes a step back to admire her work and nods in approval.

Dominic finally comes out of his room looking impeccable. I'm not surprised. There are going to be a lot of highly ranked officials at the town hall. Impressions are everything to Dominic.

"What are we waiting for? Let's go. We do not want to be late. The whole community will be there." Dominic's fingers drum lightly on his thighs. He eyes the motion, takes a deep breath, and steadies himself.

"Let's go to the elevator," Mother says. She lets us walk out in front of her. The beep of the front door announces she's locked it. It seems like an unnecessary motion, as our society doesn't have a problem with burglary, but Mother has always done it. I've always assumed it was because she grew up outside of our territory.

We walk down the community hallway and wait for the elevator to bring us to the vehicle storage area. My mother takes advantage of the time. "We need to be on our best behavior for this. Can we just get along for a couple of hours? You two are brothers. Please act like it." As she finishes, her stare lingers on both of us, ensuring the message gets through.

Of course, I know she's right, but I doubt my brother will listen.

Another family walks toward us and prevents Dominic's reply. He instantly squares his shoulders in reaction and makes small talk with them. I tune them out due to habit. I'm not interested in listening to Dominic brag about himself. I've heard it all already.

In contrast to Dominic's emotional disconnect to the situation, my mother can't hide her worry. If we don't understand what's causing this, how can we prevent it from happening to anyone else?

The elevator beeps in arrival and we all cram in. I steady myself for the quick drop. Within seconds, we arrive on the bottom floor, my ears popping.

Wordlessly, the three of us enter the public vehicle. Because we're one of the last families to step on, the space is limited. Dominic eyes the lack of seating options and walks toward the back, leaving Mother and me. The ride passes without conversation. The building density decreases steadily as we drive away from the jungle of living quarters.

Everyone seems to be lost in thought. I picture my mother fretting over the implications of today and my brother focusing on impressing the right people. As for me, I just want to get through the day without being noticed.

We arrive at the community center and join the mass of mourners dressed in black. Away from the density of the living quarters, the building's large windows allow sunlight to fill the entire location. Black drapes cover the walls in respect for the dead. A sea of silver, backless benches covers the entire room.

Dominic catches up to us so we can all sit together. We find our seats close to the back of the giant room, with my mother between us. I try in vain to get comfortable even though I know it isn't possible. The seating was made purposefully hard to help ensure everyone stays awake during the various territory meetings.

Movement in the center of the room catches my attention. A large holograph screen shows the image of the deceased. A young girl beams into the camera. Her green eyes light up in amusement. My heart drops when the hologram transforms to the next image. A newborn baby fills the room now. It's customary for the slideshow to document the deceased's life. Normally, these shows last several minutes and end with pictures full of grey hair and evidence of a long life. Medicine has advanced to a point where death normally doesn't occur until old age. Recently, more and more children have been dying and the government hasn't offered any explanation.

Mother leans over. "Is that her family?" She nods in the direction of a group of people bound in sadness.

I recognize one of the men. I don't really have any friends at school, but he's always treated me with kindness. Once we were old enough to realize that I was different, most of my classmates either avoided me, which I've always preferred, or treated me with complete disdain and disgust.

"Yes," I whisper in an attempt not to disturb anyone. I strain my neck to get a better view of the family. Grief is carved into all of their faces. "The tall blonde in the back is one of my classmates. His name is Ian."

"I can't imagine the pain of losing a close family member like that. He's going through a terrible loss." A tear falls down her cheek. She hastily wipes it away.

Dominic nudges my mother to get her attention. "See, over in the corner?" He points subtly. "That is the Territory Leader and the rest of the council. The male with the striped tie is the representative for the genetic engineers. Do you think I should speak to him about my latest genome isolation? I have not had a chance yet." His voice is full of excitement and possibility.

"This is hardly the time for that, Dominic. Show some respect for the situation. You'll have plenty of time to present yourself later," Mother says. She looks kindly at him in order to soften her scold.

She refocuses her attention toward me. "Please be sure to offer him," she pauses to nod at Ian, "our deepest condolences."

"Of course, Mother," I say. She doesn't notice it because her attention is concentrated on the family, but Dominic glares at me. I swallow down my fear.

The Territory Leader steps up to the podium and ends the tense moment. Instantly, all conversations in the room stop. For a moment, the only noise is the solemn grief coming from the child's family. Then, the steady, deep voice of a man echoes throughout the hall.

"Too soon, the life of young Melanie was taken from us. Nine years old is much too early to be gone. Do not despair in her death; rather, celebrate her life..." He continues on as someone, perhaps Melanie's mother, lets out another agonizing wail as she succumbs to her pain.

Melanie's funeral is the fifth we've attended in the last three years. Until recently, this has been completely unprecedented. Barring any major accident, everyone can expect to enjoy a very long, healthy life. This string of young deaths throughout the territories has been troublesome for everyone. Without warning, the young fall ill and within a few days, they're dead.

The government has assured us that they're working on a solution, but they haven't provided any answers on where the problem originated. Luckily, my family has been spared from whatever is causing this fatal illness.

"And now," our Territory Leader begins, snapping me back to the present to take in his words, "let us take a moment of silence for Melanie and her family."

No one dares to make a sound. A drop of sweat falls down my back. Even though the windows are open, the sheer amount of people in the room has raised the temperature. The only noise is the misery of the family. Once the Territory Leader deems the silence has gone on long enough, he motions for us to stand and leave.

I'm shorter than the other men and some of the women by several inches. Other members of society have always taken pleasure in making fun of me for this. Because there are a lot of people, I grab my mother's hand so she doesn't fall behind as we make our way out of the community center. Despite the situation, she smiles appreciatively and we push our way to the public vehicle.

For once, my brother doesn't throw any insults my way. Instead, he simply ignores me. Even though Melanie wasn't a family member, her death still impacts us and we all spend the commute in silence contemplating this newly realized mortality.

CHAPTER TWO

The next morning, I sit in my usual spot on the public vehicle. Even though Dominic and I ride the same bus every day, he sits by his colleagues in the back while I find a seat to myself.

Over the years, our life expectancy has increased to the point where it's now rare for people to die before reaching one hundred. Because we live for such a long time, we go through schooling until we're twenty-eight.

We're given our specializations at twenty-four but until then, we focus on every subject equally, unless our educator recommends an alteration of schedule. Dominic got his specialization three years ago. Since then, he's been studying at a different facility that's close to the main campus. I still have another two years until I receive my assignment.

I stare out the window to pass the time. I always breathe a sigh of relief once we drive out of the shadows of the living quarters. The buildings there all contain around fifty floors. I find them extremely stifling and look forward to leaving their oppressive nature every day. However, the clouds prevent the sun from greeting us today.

Rain falls gently and beads on the window. The water drops seem to race each other down the glass. I always root for the smaller drop to reach the bottom first. But, every time, the bigger one wins.

A high-pitched, nasally voice interrupts my thoughts. "Oh, dear me. Is that Annalise's youngest?" In recognition of my mother's name, I jerk my head away from the window. The voice is attached to a lady, probably in her mid-fifties, with large, buggy eyes. She's standing in the aisle with another woman, similar enough in appearance they're probably related.

The second voice gasps in excitement, "I'm not sure. You," she points to me. "Look here." I do as commanded and their eyes light up. "It is. What's your name again?"

"My name is Elliot. Do I know you?" I ask. They're both wearing the red coloring associated with the medical field.

Both of them giggle and the first lady says, "We went through training at the same time as your mother. Of course, she was in a different class."

"It's nice to meet both of you," I say in an attempt to end the conversation. I have an idea of what they want and have no desire to speak with them.

They refuse to take the hint. The ladies sit down in the seats next to me and continue the conversation anyway. "Where are you going right now?"

The question catches me off guard. I thought it was obvious. "I'm going to school."

The first lady screeches and pats my shoulder. "That's just so inspiring."

The other one nods encouragingly.

"Despite your disability, you're still going to school."

My cheeks flush. A snicker erupts from the seat behind me. The women press on.

"And your mother! We haven't spoken in awhile, but she's a tolerant lady. Not many people would have carried you to term being well, you know, what you are," the one with the nasally voice informs me.

"I'm very lucky that she's my mother," I agree. I consider her one of the only good things in my life.

"Oh yes," Nasally Voice sneers, "I couldn't raise a child like you. In fact, I've terminated two pregnancies because I didn't want to bring someone with such disadvantages into the world."

The other lady nods. "Not everyone would put up with you."

I'm at a loss for words and don't know how to respond politely. What do they want from me? As much as I would like to, I can't change who I am and the circumstances that created me.

Luckily, someone else joins the conversation so I don't have to. "Excuse me. Do you mind if I sit next to Elliot? We're working on a school project and I would like to discuss it with him."

Before waiting for a response, he squeezes his way in and forces them to make room. They lose interest and lean away to gossip amongst themselves.

I look gratefully at Ian and whisper, "Thank you."

"Don't listen to them, Elliot," Ian replies. His right hand rubs his forehead as if he's trying to dispel a headache.

His sister's funeral was only yesterday. I'm surprised he's on the vehicle today. "I'm so sorry about Melanie. I can't imagine the pain you're going through right now," I quietly say so only he can hear me. I don't want to have the two ladies realize who he is. I can't make out their individual words, but I hear laughter coming from them every few seconds. They're oblivious to the situation.

Nothing but silence comes from Ian for long enough that I don't think he's going to reply. Our education building looms in the distance by the time he finally asks, "It really makes you think, doesn't it?"

His voice simmers in anger. I look around to make sure no one else heard him. It wouldn't be good for him if people heard his discontent. As a Planned individual, I can't imagine he means anything too rebellious by that statement. Surely he's just in pain from his sister's death and isn't thinking rationally.

We arrive at the education building and I exit the bus, entering the flood of students and educators making their way into the building. It's one of my favorite parts of the day. There are so many people focused on getting inside that nobody notices me. In the crowd, I'm just like any other student in a grey outfit. I can blend in anonymously.

I put my head down to avoid eye contact with anyone. At the same time as the rest of my classmates, I walk into our assigned education room and take a seat in my usual spot toward the back. Our educator interrupts my unpacking of my supplies and calls me to his desk. Nervously, I walk over to him. My heart beats in my ears. This is the first time he's singled me out for specific attention all year.

I shift my feet. "Good morning, Educator Haven," I say.

He glances up and eyes me severely. "Elliot, I called you up here to inform you that I'm recommending you skip the remainder of your education and start your work assignment at the conclusion of the month." He drops his eyes in dismissal.

Shock and disappointment course through my body. I look around to make sure no one else heard him.

"I don't understand," I whisper. "I still have almost two years left before my work assignment training begins."

He reluctantly returns his gaze to me. "That's an incorrect statement. That's your classmates' trajectory. Your time focusing on education is no longer beneficial for your career assignment. Everyone must serve a purpose in society and yours simply doesn't require further education."

I take a deep breath to try and release some of the tightening in my chest. "What function will I serve, Educator Haven? I was hoping to work in food distribution like my mother."

His left hand strokes his beard in thought. "No, we have stronger students for those careers. You will enhance society by focusing on its upkeep. You should be grateful you're a part of our society. You have family in the outer region of Accidia, correct?"

I nod in response. "My grandparents live out there."

"You have seen how backward that population is. Imagine a life where your sole purpose is to supply the territories: Potentia, Robur, and Vis…" He scoffs at the idea and lifts his chin. "And let's not even start about the savages living in Acroisia. The audacity of a group of people to turn their backs on all of the advancements our society has been able to offer." He shakes his head. "We tore this country apart in the Civil War so we could genetically plan and escape from those limiting themselves—the Barbarians," he finishes.

I struggle with the suggestion I should be grateful for being forced to devote my life on a career path I don't desire. My heart drops. I'm going to have to tell my mother that I failed. "How many of my classmates will be joining me?"

He looks surprised at my question. "This is only impacting you."

"When will this be final?" I mutter.

His attention focuses on the papers on his desk as he responds, "I anticipate by the end of the week. Please return to your seat, Elliot."

I nod and numbly turn around. My dreams of following in my mother's footsteps are shattered with my fear of working in the janitorial field taking its place. My gaze shifts upward and the startling green eyes of Ian stare back at me. Embarrassed, I lower my eyes and take my seat just as the bell announces the start of our school day. Right on schedule, our educator stands and begins our lesson.

"By the end of next year, most of you will receive your specializations for the careers you will be assigned. Everybody must serve as a productive member of society. I know for some of you, it can seem like a long way off, but it's important that you understand how relevant these jobs are to your life, today."

Just as my classmates straighten in their chairs, I slouch lower. None of this is relevant to me anymore. My future has been decided.

"As you all know, you will state your preferences for your job and that will be taken into consideration with the territory council. Let's begin by going over the most important job: Genetic Engineering." Our educator's voice drones on.

While the rest of my classmates listen in an attentive excitement, I lose interest. I've heard this description so many times and it's no longer relevant for me. Even though I never had a desire to be a genetic engineer, a seed of injustice smolders inside. That choice should have been mine to make.

"Before we could control the genes that were passed on to our offspring, so much was left to chance. Society was, simply put, overrun with the weak, vulnerable, sick, and those of low intellect. As such, many undesirable traits have been eliminated from our gene pool. They aren't an option for future generations. From handpicking a child's adult height to ensuring certain diseases, such as Alzheimer's and Parkinson's, are eradicated, this specialized science ensures these cruel ailments are eliminated via genetic impossibility. Our society today is stronger and continues to flourish because of the works of these genetic engineers."

He pauses and focuses his gaze on me. "Of course, there are still those in society who do not always take advantage of our modern genome and have children without these purified genes." Almost all of my classmates shift to stare at me.

My face burns and I look at my desk. I'm the only one in this class he addresses, a fact I'm painfully aware of.

"In the past, this was very common and no one really cared one way or the other. However, today it makes a very big difference if you were Planned or not. These relics of the era of humanity's weakness have been named the Unplanned. Planned children are born predestined for greatness. Each sequence of genetic code necessary to create these individuals is hand selected by this elite group of scientists. That being said, the Unplanned still have their uses," he says and nods in my direction. "We need people to clean and do the other less desirable jobs required to maintain a comfortable society."

The class poorly conceals their amusement. Someone in front of me cackles and says, "Elliot, it seems like you have a bright future ahead of you."

Like always, I pretend to ignore them; although their words take on a new meaning after my conversation with Educator Haven. There's no benefit to standing up for myself—I'll only regret it later. Instead, I reflect on the past.

When my mother discovered she was pregnant with me, my father was outraged. Although getting pregnant unexpectedly isn't uncommon, most often people decide to abort, like the two women on the public vehicle. Why bring someone into the world at such a disadvantage? In the past, this reasoning was used to abort when it was discovered a fetus carried disabilities. Now, natural conception is considered a major disadvantage, if not a full-blown disability.

My father wanted my mother to get an abortion and they fought about it for a long time, even after I was born. When I was eight, my father walked out on us. My brother blames me and has never let me forget it. I've always thought he was right. Plain and simple, I'm the reason he had to grow up in a broken home.

From the moment my mother refused to abort me, my father held my existence as a personal insult to him. Families are only allowed two children, so he transferred to another territory that would allow him to start over. When I was little, I would daydream that I would prove myself and he would come back and tell me he was proud of me. I know this isn't realistic and I tell myself I've stopped looking for his approval. But deep down, I know this isn't true. A parent's one job is to unconditionally love their children and I prevented him from carrying out his sacred duty.

"There are obviously other areas the genetic engineers control beyond the aesthetic choices that the parents control." The educator's voice brings me back from my past. "We must ensure that society endures through the healthiest, strongest units possible. That's why the government controls certain genes that are passed on to the next generation, such as sex of the child. Clearly, imbalance of males or females cannot be allowed." The educator clears his throat. "This careful manipulation of genetics is, quite frankly, the most important career that everyone should strive for. Genetic engineers determine virtually every aspect of who a person will become. That's why we need our best and brightest to pursue this path and help build a stronger, healthier tomorrow."

"How many people are chosen for this program?" A question rings out from the other side of the room. The excitement and enthusiasm for this role is palpable. I restrain from rolling my eyes.

"It's a very prestigious program to get into as only the smartest and most capable students are selected. The last entrant into the program was Dominic Greer, who graduated at the top of his class three years ago. Before him, there was a five-year gap between acceptances. The question is a good segue into our guest speaker for the day. Dominic is actually here today to speak to you all and share his personal story." The educator walks to his desk and says into the phone, "We're ready for you, sir."

Dominic didn't mention coming into class today. My chest tightens in anxiety. Some way, Dominic will use this opportunity to cause me unhappiness.

Maybe he didn't realize he would be speaking to my class. I sink down a little more in my chair hoping he won't notice me. The educator walks back into the room with Dominic closely on his heels.

"Oh," the girl next to me mutters in appreciation. He's always had this effect on the opposite sex. His eyes follow the voice to her and he shoots her a wink.

Looking rather pleased with himself, his gaze shifts and a look of gleeful anticipation sweeps across his face. He loves to watch me squirm, and right now, he's holding the magnifying glass and I'm the helpless ant.

CHAPTER THREE

"First of all, let me take this moment to thank Educator Haven for allowing me to speak today," my brother says. He was blessed with the gift of charisma. "We have been trying to fit this in the schedule for over a month now. I am glad we are finally able to do so."

My eyebrows involuntarily rise at his statement. How did I not know about this? Dominic looks back over at me and I try to hide my surprise, but it's too late. He's enjoying this.

"It's nice to have one of my favorite students come back to the class," Educator Haven says to us all. This statement doesn't surprise me. Dominic has always excelled at everything, so, of course, an educator would remember him fondly. They don't see the side of him that I do.

"Very bluntly, as a genetic engineer, we identify how to make everyone better. We dive into billions of sequences of amino acids and determine the precise combinations that produce desirable genes while eliminating disadvantageous sequences. We work with families to help identify what traits they want to be passed down to their children. This can range from a person's height, eye color, intelligence, or even his or her physical appeal." He takes advantage of this opportunity to nod at another one of my female classmates.

"What is extremely important, but sometimes not as appreciated, is our ability to remove the undesirable traits from the gene pool. As some of you may know, just last month, we isolated the genetic predisposition gene to cystic fibrosis. As long as children are genetically planned, cystic fibrosis will cease to taint our genetic blueprints." Several people in the classroom begin to clap and soon, the whole class has joined in, including me. I don't want to stand out.

Dominic allows the applause to continue for a moment before raising his hand to silence the room. "I could stand here and rattle off statistics and tell all of you how important it is to follow the route of genetic planning, whether that be in a career as a genetic engineer or planning your future children. But I will not. Instead, I want to show you." Dominic gestures toward me. "Elliot, please come up here."

My stomach drops. I knew something like this was coming. I sigh in submission and walk over to my older brother. I spend almost all of my energy attempting to make sure nobody notices me, yet here I am, at the center of attention.

"No need to be shy," Dominic says. I awkwardly wave. My classmates respond with laughter. Dominic pats my back, a little too hard, and continues. "So, class, this is what happens when you do not genetically plan your children."

Every face that stares back at me is filled with disgust, pity, or some combination of the two. It's like I'm contaminated. Standing next to my brother, our physical differences are exaggerated. His six-inch height advantage allows him to tower above me and he has a physical mold of which I'm a poor imitation. Every inch of his body is covered in lean, hard muscle that allows him to look strong without being too big.

Beyond that, though, every movement and word that comes from his body is filled with a confidence that I've never come close to replicating. I wish for a natural disaster, a hurricane or earthquake, anything to get me out of this situation.

"Elliot and I are brothers. While I am the product of the careful, thought-out process of genetic planning, my brother was not. He is what happens when you leave genetics up to chance. Tell them about yourself."

Shamefully, wanting just about anything else, I do as I'm told. "I wasn't supposed to be born. My parents didn't plan for me and I'm the result of that." My brother has punished me for these reasons my whole life so I know what he wants me to say. "I've always had a problem keeping up with schoolwork and other activities."

Out of the corner of my eye, I see my educator nod in agreement. I attempt to defend myself. "It isn't that I'm unable to comprehend the material or finish assignments, it's just that sometimes it can take me a little longer than others."

Educator Haven opens his mouth like he wants to respond to my claim. Before he can speak, Dominic relentlessly continues. "Do you feel like you are at a disadvantage because you are Unplanned?"

I know better than to lie in front of Dominic. It's better just to give him what he wants. "I do."

This is one of my nightmares. All the attention is on me while my brother ruthlessly points out my flaws and misgivings.

"Do you wish you were Planned like everyone else in this room?" he asks.

"Of course," I say. I've wanted to fit in my entire life.

"Genetic planning has allowed me to excel. Even in a society filled with other Planned, I finished school at the top of my class, was placed into the top career-training program, and am expected to lead that division one day. I am not trying to brag, but those are the facts. My brother's future on the other hand…" He pauses dramatically and motions at me again. "Let's just say it is not nearly as promising." Dominic chuckles good-naturedly. Most of the class joins in.

I stare down at my feet.

"Any questions?" My educator addresses the entire room. "This is a great opportunity to gain insight into the life of a person who's leading your generation. He's a phenomenal role model."

One of the students in the back raises his hand. Dominic nods at him in acknowledgment. "Why didn't your parents terminate the pregnancy? They clearly believed in genetic planning with you. Why the change?"

"That is a great question and actually something I have wondered for a long time. For my creation, my parents deliberated for months with their genetic engineer. The end result was a success: me."

Dominic shrugs, a motion I know is for him to appear to be modest. My brother is perfect at a lot of things, but humility isn't one of them.

"I believe my parents thought that since they were both Planned, their Unplanned child would theoretically have a higher chance to receive desirable genes and be able to function as a valuable member of society."

"So they meant to have an Unplanned?" another student asks.

Dominic scoffs at the question. "Of course not. Elliot was a mistake."
I shift my feet. I don't like the turn this conversation has taken.
"Then why didn't they abort him?" the original student presses.

"I can only speak for my mother as my father died many years ago."
Dominic tells everyone the same lie he's been saying for years. "Rather than looking at the facts, I believe my mother fell prey to a terrible weakness: hope. Hope can make someone disregard reality for how they want things to be. It is my understanding that they wished for the best but in the end, all of their hopes and dreams could not stand up to the variability of nature." He stares meaningfully at me to let the message sink in.

Silence spreads across the room like a fog rolling in before a rain. I look up from my feet to assess the class's reaction to his words. My classmates shift their gaze from me to my brother and back to me, clearly comparing the two of us.

I miserably make eye contact with Ian again. The same anger from earlier seeps through his entire being. I wish I could find that same fire in myself. Unable to maintain the eye contact, I blink away.

"Any other questions for Mr. Greer?" Our educator prompts once the quiet has gone on long enough.

"Yes, I have one," Ian calls out from the back, regaining my attention. His eyes are drowning in grief. "I want to talk about the recent children deaths. What do you have to say to the people who feel the genetic engineers are to blame? How many young people like my sister need to die before you do something?"

"Ian, that's inappropriate," the educator says. He casts a horrified glance at Dominic.

Melanie's alarmingly short slideshow flashes through my mind. How advanced can our technology actually be when people are dying so young?

"No, it is a good question, Educator Haven, and something I really would like to clarify for everyone here." Dominic's stern voice is much less carefree. My palms sweat in reaction to his tone. "We are in the business of preventing sickness and disease from ever occurring. The doctors are responsible for healing the people who have contracted illness. In fact, if you look at the numbers, compared to twenty years ago, there are thirty percent fewer doctors on staff than there used to be. That is because we can prevent sickness from transpiring in the first place. Quite simply, you are upset with the wrong department."

"So you're saying that there is nothing the genetic engineers can do to prevent these children's deaths?" Ian's voice rises in disbelief. A fire of anger overtakes some of the pain in his eyes.

Dominic squares his shoulders and I'm thankful his anger is directed toward someone else, even if it's on my only ally in the room. "We are working closely with the doctors to better understand what is going on. Once we are able to determine the cause, assuming there is a new genetic predisposition, we will be able to ensure this never happens again."

"Why is it taking so long?" Ian continues his questioning. I admire his bravery, but I don't envy him right now. My brother isn't someone to cross.

When Dominic responds, his voice is icy. Chills run down my spine. "Because examining miles of genetic code for a mutation that may or may not exist can take time, if it is even successful. It requires patience. Is the importance of taking your time not clear by looking at my brother and me? My brother took less effort to create than I did. But look at the difference."

Dominic stares down Ian. "Hard work and determination do, in fact, pay off. It is clear you would never have the ability to be a good genetic engineer. You share this trait with my far less achieving brother."

Ian's mouth is wide open in shock. His ears are bright red. He sounds embarrassed when he says, "I'm just worried, that's all. Melanie was my younger sister."

"It is understandable that you want answers. We all do," Dominic says. His tone is softer, but I can almost feel the tension radiating from his body. His anger bubbles just under the surface. "Assigning the blame for your sister's death is not going to benefit anyone. You must learn to control your emotions and approach situations by considering the facts. That is my advice to you."

The grief has retaken home in Ian and he drops his head in pain. Dominic offers one last look at Ian and then dismisses him to reopen the conversation to the class. "Are there any other questions for me while I am here?"

One of the prettier, snobby girls from the front raises her hand. Dominic slyly smiles at her. "Do you think Unplanned should be allowed to procreate with Planned?"

"I do not think there is ever an excuse for the birth of an Unplanned. Our society is worse when irresponsible individuals further detract from the gene pool by creating even more Unplanned. If this continues, our society will be back where it was before: less intelligent and much weaker. Does that make sense?" Dominic regains his composure and finishes full of charisma once again.

"Oh, yes. But I do have one more question," she says as she blushes.

"Feel free to ask me any question you have." He responds in a way that could be interpreted as flirting or just being friendly.

"Have you determined the individual that you will genetically plan your children with?"

Dominic smiles at her and noticeably checks her out.

Our educator jumps in to control the situation. "Ava, that's an unsuitable question. I'll speak with you after class to determine your punishment."

Her face falls in horror.

"No need, Educator Haven. It was a simple question. However, I do need to get back to my job training. It has been difficult to be away for this long. I thank you all for your time and I hope to see some of you outside of here." He pauses and makes eye contact with Ava. "Best of luck to all of you in your last two years leading up to the job selection."

The class claps in appreciation for his discussion. Dominic leans in closer to me so only I can hear. "You most of all, Joe. You are going to need it."

He maintains eye contact with me long enough for me to break it in submission. Dominic waves good-bye to the class and Educator Haven. Once again, he claps me with too much force on my back. He smirks knowingly and exits the room, full of smug satisfaction.

"To your seat, Elliot," my educator says.

I quickly walk back to my desk and stumble into my seat. The class laughs openly. Educator Haven watches on with a look of disapproval.

"Now that Elliot is ready for us to continue"—he gives me yet another severe look—"I hope you all learned a significant amount from listening to Dominic. Did you all find it beneficial?"

The girl right next to me says, "Yes, Educator Haven. I need to ensure the proper genes are passed down. I need to make sure my children are Planned. I don't want to end up with…" She tapers off as the entire class follows her direction of thought and focuses on me. "I'm just saying it isn't fair to anyone if an Unplanned is born into our society. I don't want that for any child of mine." Everyone nods in agreement, even the educator.

In this moment, I feel sorry for myself. This is how my entire life has been. I've always known I was second-class, but somehow Dominic manages to make it even worse. By driving such a sharp wedge between the two of us, he couldn't have made it more clear who I am. I'm undesirable and worth nothing. I shouldn't even exist.

CHAPTER FOUR

I pull the handle to our front door. It's locked. I frown and place my finger on the pad. It hums in recognition of my fingerprint and unlocks. I retry the door and this time it allows me admission into our apartment.

"Mother?" I announce my entrance to the empty house. My mother normally gets home before I do, so I expect to hear her answer. Instead, the only sounds are my footsteps bouncing off the walls as I set my backpack down in the front entry.

My movement triggers the lights to turn on. A light flashing in the corner grabs my attention and I walk over to it. I motion across the sensor and a hologram of my mother fills the space.

"We're swamped here at work," my mother's image informs me. There's still light pouring through the windows. She must have sent it earlier in the afternoon. Her hand runs through her hair. "I'll be home as soon as I can. I'll see the two of you when I get back."

Another message plays immediately after and this time, it's my brother's image. "I will be back later. I am busy. Do not expect me for dinner." A girl's laugh echoes through the speaker.

With that, I'm once again alone. After the day I've had, the idea of having some time to myself is very appealing. At this moment, all I want to do is forget about everything. Every time I close my eyes, the images of my classmates looking at me with complete revulsion fill my head.

I breathe out in frustration. I want to be somewhere where I fit in. I want to escape my body, but I can't. I'm stuck. This is who I am.

I slump into the bathroom and undress. My grey outfit falls to the floor and I wonder how many days left I have before I have to switch to the brown color of the janitorial career. How am I going to tell my mother about today's news?

The water heats up and I step into the shower. The feeling of warm water touching my skin soothes me. If I only focus on the sensation of the heat against my body, my life seems almost bearable.

I decompress and soon slip into a daydream. In my fantasy, I'm Planned. Dominic is graduating at the top of his class. His speech includes a touching memory of the two of us from our childhood. On one side of me is my girlfriend and on the other is my father, with my mother on the opposite side of him. His arm is around her. He glances at me and smiles proudly. We're a family.

The speaker in the bathroom beeps to let me know someone has entered the apartment, interrupting my thoughts of a life that was never meant to be. The messages are replayed and then footsteps get louder as they approach the bathroom. I hold my breath, hoping it's not Dominic. The footsteps stop and a light knocking follows. I exhale in relief.

"Elliot, is that you? I just saw Dominic's message." My mother's voice reaches through the door.

"Yes, I'll be out soon."

I take one more deep breath to enjoy the shower before I turn off the water. I cover myself with a towel and snatch my outfit off the floor. In my room, I dig through my dresser for fresh clothes. After I get dressed in the white, casual outfit, I make my way to my mother in the living room.

We sit in companionable silence. My mother's automatic acceptance of who I am is refreshing after today's lesson. I take one more deep breath and examine her. She's still in the green food distribution outfit and clearly distracted with her own thoughts.

"What's going on at work?" I ask.

"I'd honestly rather not talk about it, Elliot." She smiles at me tenderly and her eyes sweep my face. Her eyebrows furrow. "You've had a bad day."

I nod in agreement. She patiently waits for me to elaborate and when I'm ready, I oblige.

"Why did you choose not to abort me when you found out you were pregnant?"

"Why is this coming up again?" Her eyes race across my face as she tries to pick up on any hints as to why I'm asking this. I keep my expression unguarded.

"Please, I need to know."

"That was simply never an option. You're my son. I've loved you from the moment I knew you existed." She takes a deep breath. "Tell me why you're asking."

"Dominic came and spoke to the class about a career as a genetic engineer. He and the entire class made it perfectly clear that I shouldn't exist," I say.

"Elliot…" My mother begins but I cut her off and keep talking.

"They're right. Why waste space and resources on me? I can't contribute like the rest of society. I'm not good enough. I'm never going…" I fumble through my words while I try to think of a way to tell her I won't live up to her expectations of me finishing my schooling.

This time, it's my mother who cuts me off. "Stop. I never want to hear those words come out of your mouth ever again. You're so much more than you see yourself. When are you going to realize that?" She takes a deep breath. "Just because your father and I didn't specifically pick every single one of your attributes does not make you any less than Dominic or anyone else. I don't care what anyone else thinks."

My voice breaks as I say, "But I care."

My mother grasps both of my hands and holds them tightly. "Why?"

I don't have a good answer for her, so I respond with, "So you're saying every single one of my classmates is wrong?"

"Yes," she says. "They are."

In spite of everything, I chuckle at her determined answer. "Are you just saying this because you're my mother?"

"I'm positive. It's the truth." She studies me and then proclaims, "Now stop feeling sorry for yourself and cheer up."

I take a deep breath and allow her words to resonate. I consider sharing the news that I'm being released from my education, but I can't bring myself to do it. I want to have at least a little more time with her believing in me.

"Have you had dinner yet, Mother?" She shakes her head. "I'll get our food packets ready. Do you think Dominic will be home anytime soon?"

"I doubt it," she says. "He's all over the place lately. I need to speak with him about it." She frowns and follows me into the kitchen. "Let's go visit your grandparents at the lake this weekend."

"Can we?" I ask. The idea of getting away from Potentia and all of the judgment that comes along with it is tempting.

"It'll be good to get out of the territory for a little bit. I haven't seen my parents in four months." She looks out the window. "You'll be able to see Chris and Andrew," she adds as an afterthought.

I stop rummaging through the pantry and hug my mother. "Thank you. I love you." I want to add more, but I don't need to. She knows me too well.

"I love you too, son. You just need to work on your confidence." She smiles and lightly pats my cheek. "I'll put in the request for the vehicle. It shouldn't take more than a couple of days to get the approval."

The government controls the amount of traveling we can do via vehicles to reduce our dependency. Requests to visit close relatives are fairly easy to get approved. Plus, we haven't been out to visit them in so long, due to the loss of productivity from adding the five-hour drive.

In the past, every person in a family would have their own vehicle until the nonrenewable resources ran out. Our society pushed the boundaries to research new areas of energy and from this, expanded the collective knowledge base that led to genetic planning. A big segment of the population, now those out in Acroisia, didn't agree with this and about a hundred years ago, the Civil War started and split the nation

"Can I call them and let them know we're coming?"

"Of course," she says. "I'm going to change out of my work clothes."

I walk to the phone to dial my grandparents' number. It rings for a while and goes to the message machine. They don't have video capabilities with their phone, so I leave a quick message letting them know that we're coming this weekend.

The moment I hang up, I dial Chris and Andrew's number. On the second ring, their younger sister's voice answers. "Hello?"

"Hi, Carly. This is Elliot," I say. "Are Andrew and Chris available?"

"They're out on the water," she says in the slower drawl of Accidia, presenting a small pang of disappointment. "You want 'em to call you back?"

"No, that's all right. Just let them know that we're visiting this weekend," I say.

"Oh," she exclaims in exhilaration. "We haven't seen ya'll in a long time."

I chuckle a little into the phone. Her energy has always been infectious. "I'll see you in a few days. Have a good rest of the night," I say.

"You too, Elliot. I'll let 'em know. Bye."

"Take care." I conclude the conversation and hang up. The way my morning went, I never thought I would finish the day with a giant smile on my face. I walk back to the kitchen and finishing making dinner for us. My heart is so full of appreciation for my mother.

I can get through these next few days, I tell myself. Soon, I'll be in a better environment. I summon my strength and prepare myself for the rest of the week.

CHAPTER FIVE

Luckily, the next few days pass without incident. I've had a lot of practice ignoring the looks of my pitying classmates. The eagerness for this weekend overpowers any other thought.

By Thursday, I'm nearly shaking with excitement. We're going to leave the territory tomorrow and I anxiously await seeing my grandparents and friends again. We haven't heard back from my grandparents, but that's pretty normal for them. They always seem to get lost in their own world.

I arrive at school just in time and get ready for another day dealing with my near-perfect classmates. Normally, we start straight off with our lessons but today they make us go to the auditorium.

Once we're all seated, the Territory Leader comes onto the stage. I inhale sharply when I see how haggard he looks. In less than a week, he seems to have aged ten years. I can see the bags under his eyes even though I'm halfway to the back. Murmuring occurs throughout the room. Despite this, the Territory Leader still exudes a great deal of power and is able to silence the whispers by raising his hands.

"Students," he says. "I am here today to relay messages that have been given to me directly from the President. There is an illness spreading throughout the other two territories, Vis and Robur. While it has not reached Potentia, we are still going to be placed under some restrictions in order to reduce the chance of an epidemic."

My eyes widen at his last statement. The soft scuffles and intakes of breath from hundreds of students suddenly paying attention spreads throughout the auditorium.

"This illness—although the President assures me is completely curable—is highly contagious and appears to be spread through the exchange of bodily fluids. If you see anyone acting strangely, it is best to avoid all interaction and report them to the authorities immediately— even if it is a family member." He pauses to let the words sink in.

"Aside from school and work assignments, everyone should remain at their living quarters. Every other activity is canceled. This starts immediately. There is absolutely no reason to panic and the President told me she has the utmost confidence that this minor issue will be resolved shortly. I have discussed the matter with the Territory Leaders from Vis and Robur and we are all in agreement to follow this precaution."

There is some muttering at this last comment. The way our government is structured, if all three of the Territory Leaders disagree with the President, they can override the decision. Typically, there are disagreements between the four of them and it has historically been challenging to get everyone on the same page.

"Thank you for your time. I will let you continue with your studies." After he finishes his speech, he leaves the room and a blanket of silence surrounds everyone.

Finally, someone across the hall calls out, "What does that even mean? What's this illness?" He's quickly ushered out of the room by an educator. After this, the fear of punishment prevents anyone else from speaking. As I always avoid confrontation at all costs, I keep my mouth closed and follow orders.

Educator Haven says, "You heard him. Stand up and let's go back to class. I have an exciting lesson for you today."

Some students groan at this statement. The last time he said this, we spent the rest of the day learning the rules of organic molecules.

Some of my classmates remain seated, so he continues, "If you don't adhere to my instruction, there will be severe consequences."

Ian is the last person to stand, his shoulders tense with anger.

I direct my attention back to returning to our classroom when someone pushes me into an empty closet. This happens a couple times a year, so I close my eyes and wait for the attack to be over. My mother may think that my being different is a blessing, but the guys bigger than me sure don't when they feel like venting their frustrations.

When nothing happens, I peek through and see my brother. He runs his hands through his hair. This gesture reminds me of my mother so much it startles me. We make eye contact and dread courses through my body.

I've never seen an ounce of fear in my brother before—even when we were little and he got caught out after curfew. When he was returned to our house, he faced my father straight on.

Now, however, the panic that comes off of him is more contagious than any illness. "What are you doing here? What's going on?" My voice rises with anxiety.

"Something's wrong. I don't understand what's happening." He fades off and stares blankly at me.

My eyes widen in shock. I've never heard him make such a statement before. I wait for him to continue but after a few seconds, my patience wears thin. It had to be something serious for him to leave his training and be in such a state of terror.

"Dominic, listen to me. You need to tell me what's going on. Maybe I can help," I say in an attempt to get information from him.

"Maybe you can help?" He utters a humorless laugh as he repeats my words. "There's nothing you can do. There's nothing any of us can do, Elliot."

The hair on the back of my neck stands up at his use of my name. I can't remember the last time he used my actual name.

"We need to go find Mother. We need to go home. We need to get out of here. We need...we need..." And shockingly, my older brother, who I've never seen show any sign of weakness, starts crying, his entire body shaking. Not knowing anything else to do, I reach out to hug him. Once he senses what I'm trying to do, he freezes.

"Do not touch me, Joe." His jaw clenches, regaining control. "Despite everything else about you, we share a mother and father. We come from the same gene pool. As a genetic engineer, I understand how important that is." He runs his hands through his light hair again. "You won't leave Potentia without Mother. We need to get her as well. Follow me and do not stop for anything. Even if the Territory Leader himself yells at you to stop, you need to keep moving. Do not lose me. Do you understand?"

Not able to sense any other option, I simply nod. He exhales deeply and opens the door. There is no one in the hallway. It won't be long until

Educator Haven notices I'm missing. Hopefully, the confusion from the words of alarm given in the auditorium will last long enough to prevent me from getting in trouble for missing class.

As soon as we clear the school, Dominic picks up his pace and runs. His increased height and physical stamina make it impossible for me to keep up with him. To my surprise, he stops to wait for me to catch up.

"Like it or not, you need to keep up." He starts off again and I pant my way back to our house. When we get there, I collapse on the couch in exhaustion. The only evidence of his running the three miles from the school to our house is a thin line of sweat above his brows.

The education system removed me from our physical fitness classes two years ago because it was deemed no longer beneficial for me. It sure would've helped today.

While I focus on my breathing to recover, a part of me is annoyed with Dominic. I only have a finite number of lessons left and he's taking me from them for this new game of his. Whatever that may be.

Once I'm able to sit up again, I focus on Dominic. He's rummaging through the cabinets. He pulls something out and before I can make out exactly what it is, he throws it in his backpack.

I walk over to join him. "What are you doing?"

"Keep putting the food packets into the bags until I return." And with that, Dominic is out of the room.

I may not know what his intentions are, but I do what I always do. I follow orders and pack up the food. As soon as I finish, Dominic is back.

"Okay," Dominic says. "We need to leave the territory. The request for our vehicle went through and our mileage has been approved. The employees at the registration building do not know what is going on yet. I just saw our vehicle is in our parking garage ready to go."

He finishes rummaging through his bag and says, "You go get Mother out of work. It would cause attention if you show up with the vehicle. Come up with some excuse to get her out of there. No one can know we are fleeing and it would draw more attention if we both go to her. She is more likely to listen to you. Meet outside the walls by the hill. Do you remember where it is?"

"How could I forget?" Before I can go too deep in my thoughts, Dominic runs out of the house carrying his backpack. I grab mine and go the opposite direction to find my mother.

CHAPTER SIX

The receptionist gives me a curious look as I walk inside the food distribution center. I worry she's going to stop me. She opens her mouth and my chest tightens in apprehension as I mentally prepare my story. I need my mother for an independent research assignment for class. No one will question that I need help. Before the receptionist is able to speak, however, a man I don't recognize runs up and starts speaking with her.

Thankful for my good fortune, I quickly walk past her through the sea of cubicles. Everyone is too busy to give me a second look. I keep my head down and find my mother examining some data. At fifty-eight, she has a little bit of grey, though her blonde hair easily covers it. New wrinkles I haven't noticed before line her eyes.

She finally glances up and her eyes widen at the sight of me. "Shouldn't you be in school? Is everything okay?"

"Everything's fine. Educator Haven instructed us to study independently today. I thought I would come here to go on a walk before lunch. Can you take a quick break?"

I can't make eye contact with her. I don't make a habit out of lying, especially with my mother.

"I really appreciate the thought, but we're swamped here at work. We're trying to figure something out and the numbers just aren't coming together. Is it possible we could postpone this?" Her focus drifts back down to her work.

"Please," I say. Her eyes dart back to my face, piercing me, and we finally make eye contact.

After a moment, she stands up, puts her things in her bag, and grabs my hand with her free side. I squeeze in reassurance and we venture out of her office.

"Oh, Annalise. I was just coming in to see you," a middle-aged man says while rummaging through his papers. "I have some new data I need you to run through for me to see if it sheds any light on this mess. If I could just find it…Ah, here it is." He pulls a sheet out of a large group of papers.

My mother takes the page. "Thank you. I'll look into it soon. I'm just going on a quick walk with my son."

"Soon? Wouldn't now be better than later? I don't want to have to pull rank on you, Annalise, but it's important that we all put forth our best effort in order to figure out…" His eyes widen when he notices me. "The solution to our problem."

Squaring her shoulders, my mother says, "I understand that, Paul, and that's why I've been working tirelessly. If you check my hours, you will find I've stayed late every day this week. Are employees no longer allowed breaks?"

"Of course they are. Given the situation, however…" He tapers off and stares meaningfully at me, then back at her.

"Given the situation, it's more important than ever for everyone to be working at their best. Now, excuse me, I'm taking my break," my mother says to her increasingly startled-looking boss.

His mouth opens a little in shock. "When will you get to it then?"

"Soon." She stares at him in a challenge. When he doesn't say anything else, my mother pushes us past him. As the door opens so we can leave, I can hear Paul yelling at someone.

"Probably trying to compensate for what just happened," my mother says. "I do feel sorry for whoever is taking the brunt of his temper, but there was nothing else to be done. Paul can be, for lack of a better word, quite an ass."

She breathes heavily from her exchange. Years of experience have taught me that silence is the best course of action when she's upset. Better her fuming at the ground than me. I say nothing and lead us to our meeting point. Everyone is so busy that no one takes notice of us leaving.

Not entirely sure how to explain why we're leaving, I don't say anything. Seemingly able to sense my mood, my mother doesn't prompt a conversation. The two of us focus on our journey to the hill where we're meeting Dominic. My thighs ache with the quick pace.

My brother is already there by the time we arrive. He still looks frightened but has regained some of his composure. I'm not sure if it's because he's had time to calm down or because of his refusal to show weakness in front of me again. Probably a combination between the two.

"I'm assuming both of you have brought me out here for a reason? I could get in a lot of trouble for skipping out of work, and you shouldn't be leaving school early." My mother looks expectantly at both of us.

Before I can answer, Dominic speaks. "I promised I would explain once we were all together." He takes a deep breath and continues. "There is something spreading throughout the territories. The government's claim that this illness is not dangerous is a complete lie. I do not know exactly what is going on, but I do know it is causing people to change."

"What do you mean by 'change'?" Mother's eyes narrow in confusion.

"I saw some footage that I was not supposed to see. They seem to lose everything they once were. The video showed a woman, about my age. She just was not right." He glances at each of us, pleading with us to believe him. "Her color was not normal and she did not look well. Something was off about her. She attacked someone with nothing more than her hands and actually bit him."

He takes a deep breath, runs his hands through his hair, and looks straight at my mother. "You taught me family was the most important thing. You may not see it, but I am trying. You always wanted me to look out for my younger, average brother and for once, I am. We need to get out of here before they shut everything down. They said it was spreading too fast to contain and they had no cure. The territory will be quarantined tonight. As soon as they said that, I left. I am not going to let this illness change everything we are."

I glance over at my mother. Her mouth is slightly open in shock. While she may not be the most outspoken individual, she's never had a problem articulating her thoughts.

Very quietly, my mother says, "At work they're having us track foods. They suspect that it's causing this sickness. We're following them to try and figure out what portion of the food is infected, but nothing is adding up. We haven't been able to discover a correlation between the outbreaks of this new illness and the supply. Maybe Dominic is right. Maybe we should leave." By the time she finishes, her voice is no more than a whisper.

"If both of you think we should leave, then I'll follow," I say.

My brother turns around to get one last look at the territory, faces my mother again, and then settles on me. "I need both of you to listen to me. When I say do something, you need to do it without question. I am the strong one. I am the one who will know what to do. I was made to lead."

Dominic stares me down to make sure I understand his message. I nod. He appears satisfied. Without another word, he takes the driver's seat and inputs our destination into the system.

"You can have the passenger seat," I say to my mother.

"No, you should take it. Your legs are longer." She seems to be in a daze.

I shake my head and open the door for her to get into the front seat. She gets in and surveys the distant walls of Potentia. I follow suit. Fear overwhelms me. I can't believe just a couple of hours ago I was excited about this drive. Now I'm full of apprehension and panic.

When the gate to get out of the territory is open, Dominic visibly relaxes and the vehicle takes us away from Potentia without any hesitation. I take one last glance at the tall buildings behind the walls. If everything Dominic said is true, what's going to happen to everyone left inside once they quarantine? Surely, they're just being overprotective right now.

Dominic's fingers tap anxiously on his legs. As much as I would like to believe this is some elaborate joke, he would have never left his training and risked his reputation unless something drastic happened. I take a few deep breaths to steady myself and dispel the anxiety in my chest. My mother looks back, concerned, but I shake my head. I don't want to voice my concerns with Dominic in the vehicle.

Soon, the only evidence to the passage of time is the sun rising higher into the sky. I'm startled when I glance at the clock to see that two hours have already passed. I glance at my mother and worry; she hasn't spoken since we left. "I think she's in shock," I say to my brother to break the silence.

"I do not know what you want me to do," he says. "You have always been her favorite."

I scoff in disagreement.

He ignores me and continues, "Make her talk and if you cannot, stop whining about it. I am trying to put all of the pieces together."

One look at my mother and I know she needs more time to come to terms with the situation. "Why did you have us meet at the hill? Out of all places?"

His eyes soften slightly when he meets my gaze through the passenger mirror. "I knew you would not forget that place. I had to ensure we all arrived at the same location."

"You're right. I could never forget. That was the day that I knew I would never fit in or belong anywhere. You made sure of it."

My brother breaks eye contact and returns his gaze to the front window. "I should not have done that. You may deserve a lot of things, but that was not one of them." He pauses and when he continues to talk, all the softness from his voice is gone. "We have our differences. Now is not the time to fix things. We need to get farther away from the territory."

"Where are we going?"

"As far away as we can get from people," Dominic says. "The car is programmed to get us to the lake and that is the best place I can think to go right now. As Accidia is less populated than the territories, the illness should spread at a lower rate."

"What does this mean?" I can't wrap my mind around the situation.

He sighs in frustration. "I told you everything I saw. I do not know any more than you do. Stop talking to me. I am trying to think," he says.

"Sorry." I apologize automatically and return to the relative comfort of silence.

CHAPTER SEVEN

Our vehicle drives east toward my grandparents' cabin. The sun is setting and it's getting harder to see the surroundings. This makes me nervous. If everything is happening like Dominic claims it is, why aren't there more people on the road? I have a slight suspicion this is going to turn into one of his cruel jokes, but then I remember everything he risked to get us out of Potentia. Even he wouldn't go this far.

"Dominic, what's the plan?" I press again. We're all hungry and my mother won't let us eat the food packets for fear that they could contain whatever is spreading across the territories.

My words break his concentration and he turns to glare at me for doing so. "We are still going to Grandmother and Grandfather's down by the lake. I have not altered the plan since you asked me an hour ago."

"It will be nice to go back home for a little bit," my mother cheers up at this thought.

"This is not a social visit, Mother," Dominic reminds her.

My mother stiffens and looks close to tears. I quickly lean forward and whisper in her ear, "It will be nice to see them again, too."

She smiles appreciatively and squares her shoulders as she regains her strength.

The miles pass by in a slow blur. Despite all the bad things Dominic has said, I can't help but feel excited over seeing my grandparents and childhood friends. I choose to focus on them instead of the panic that my brother spread through us.

My mother's voice penetrates through my daydreams when she addresses my brother. "Stop the vehicle. There are people up ahead and they might need help."

I jerk my head up to look out of the front window. Up ahead, two large men are walking down the road with their hands raised to get our attention.

My brother grits his teeth. "We're not stopping."

"Pull the car over and see what they need," she demands.

Dominic lets out an angry breath and surprises me by following her command and putting the codes in the vehicle to make it pull over.

He addresses us and says, "Stay in the vehicle unless I motion otherwise. Do both of you understand?"

We both nod. He gets out of the vehicle and closes the door behind him. He engages in a conversation with the two strangers. They're too far away for us to hear what's being said. Without preamble, one of the strangers points a gun at Dominic. My mother gasps and reaches for the car door.

"Stay in here. You heard what Dominic said," I say. Even though he's in danger, the thought of disobeying him is paralyzing.

Dominic places his hands in the air and one of the men motions for him to walk to the car. When my brother doesn't move quickly enough, he hits him in the stomach and knocks him down.

"I don't care what he said," my mother says. She opens the door.

My brother reacts to the sound of the door opening and yells at her, "Get back in. I have this under control."

It doesn't look like he's in control, but Mother obeys. My eyes follow my brother. He very slowly gets back on his feet and stares down the two men. Even though he is outnumbered, I still have confidence he won't get hurt.

He jerks his arms forward to push the man with the gun down. The man falls back and hits his head on the road. His hand holding the weapon goes slack.

The other man rushes to pick it up and point it at Dominic. Muffled shouting reaches the car, but I can't make out any words. Dominic glares at the man pointing the gun and knocks it away easily. When the gun hits the ground, it fires and hits our vehicle with a small pang. My mother and I jump in alarm.

Ruthlessly, Dominic pummels into the second man. His fists drip red as he picks up the gun. Without a moment's pause, he directs the gun to the men and shoots them each in the head.

Mother exhales and her hand jumps to her mouth. My eyes widen at my brother's murders and I rub my chest automatically. I've always been aware of his capability for violence, but I never guessed he would do this. He didn't even hesitate before taking the lives of those two strangers.

"Oh my," my mother whispers.

He bends down and uses one of their shirts to wipe the blood off of his hands. The sight sickens me and I have to look away. The surrounding trees offer me no relief from the image of Dominic's calm face as he took the lives of two people. How did he get this way?

Dominic opens the door. My mother looks blankly at him. "It had to be done," he says. He sets the gun down in his lap and takes a deep breath.

"What have you done?" My mother cries. Her mouth still hangs open in disbelief.

Dominic steadies himself. "They were going to steal our vehicle and leave us stranded. There's a strong possibility they would've killed us as well. I couldn't take that risk. I did what had to be done. I protected us." Dominic inputs the codes in the vehicle and waits. Nothing happens.

He tries again. When he gets the same results, he cusses angrily and reopens his door.

Before he can go back outside to examine the outside of the vehicle, my mother's voice interrupts him. "I didn't raise you to be a murderer."

My eyes shift between my mother and brother while I wait for his response.

After a deep breath, he whispers, "It was us or them and I chose us. I'm not going to apologize for protecting our family." Without another word, he exits the vehicle and walks toward the hood. His hand finds the bullet mark. He bends down for a closer look.

"Should we go help?" I ask my mother. I want to help Dominic, but I'm even more afraid of him now than I've ever been. I've always assumed there was some limit to his aggression, but now I'm not sure what he's capable of. Who were those two men?

"No," she says. "We need to leave him alone." I follow her gaze and focus in on the growing red pool of blood from the strangers.

Dominic opens the door and interrupts my thoughts. "The errant shot damaged the battery. I can fix it. It's going to take some time. Joe, get out of the vehicle and help me push it off the road into the trees. I don't want anyone to discover us here."

With a slight hesitation, I do as he requests and step outside to help. I avoid looking at the two men he killed—pretending they aren't there. The two of us push the vehicle while our mother steers. It's hard work and my muscles are thankful when we get it off the road.

"This will make it less likely for someone to spot us. Now we need to move the bodies."

I look at him in panic.

He sighs at my expression and says, "I'll do it myself. Just get in the vehicle and stay there."

Before I can respond, he walks back toward the bodies to hide them from any passing vehicles.

I keep the door open and sit back. I sigh in relief when the breeze hits and dries the sweat on my brows.

"Do you think he can fix it?" I ask.

"Your brother can do anything he decides he wants to," my mother says. I look at her in confusion to try and understand her detached tone, but her face is blank in contemplation.

I nod in agreement. From the time he discovered how prestigious it was to be a genetic engineer, he set his mind to it and got it accomplished.

I turn my head away from the evidence of the strangers' quick deaths to try to ignore what just happened. I lie down and before I know it, I somehow fall into an uneasy doze.

I wake up sometime later to the sound of Dominic yelling in frustration. The daylight has faded since my eyes were last open. The trees hiding us off the road are protecting us from the sun. My mother looks worried, so I distract her.

"What was it like to grow up at the lake?" Even though I've heard this story before, I love hearing her talk of her childhood. Her attitude toward Accidia is the opposite of the disdain the typical society members hold for the outside region.

She smiles at the memories. "It was amazing. As you know, my parents moved out to Accidia when I was about three to be more secluded.

I never had any relationship with my grandparents after that. They didn't support my parents' moving, even though my father continued to work remotely for the territory engineers." She laughs and continues, "It's ironic that he helped design and plan for the growth of the territories even though he left to get away from all of it."

"If you loved it in Accidia so much, why did you go back to the territories?" I don't understand why she would leave a place that I associate with happiness for the one where I feel the opposite.

"There just wasn't much opportunity for me at the lake. I had to start my own life, so I moved to Potentia for my job training and met your father," she says.

"What did you see in him?"

"I know you don't have a lot of kind memories with him, but he was a good man when we met. He was so confident and sure of himself. It was attractive." She shrugs and a smile plays at her lips as she remembers their early days—before I came along and ruined everything.

I drop my eyes in shame. "If it weren't for me, would he still be here?"

She looks away from Dominic and waits for me to meet her gaze. Once I do, she says, "Your father left because of his own problems. It wasn't a result of you."

"But he left because I'm Unplanned," I respond.

She studies me for a moment before answering.

"Elliot, you may not have been Planned like Dominic was, but you were a result of a conscious decision."

I look at her in confusion. She's never shared this information with me before. "What do you mean?"

"I wanted a child that was left up to fate. You were still planned, just not in the way that society considers," she says and smiles warmly at me.

My mind races back to the day on the public transportation when the two cruel ladies suggested that I should have been aborted. "Why?"

"Just as Andrew and Chris are Unplanned, all of my childhood friends were as well. There was nothing different about them. They were still all great people with the potential to do well. I guess I figured if I had a child that wasn't genetically planned, people would see how amazing you are and change their minds. That's why we stayed in Potentia and I wouldn't let you move out to Accidia with my parents. I wanted you to have that visibility within the territories and prove everyone wrong." Her eyes scan my face. "Maybe it was selfish of me," she finishes at a lower volume.

My voice cracks in emotion. All my life, I was told I was a mistake and I believed it. Now, she's telling me otherwise.

"I haven't proved anyone wrong, though."

She grabs my hand before answering.

"You will," she says and gently lets go of my hand.

"I…" I take a deep breath and admit what has been haunting me for the last week. "I'm not going to even be able to finish my schooling. Educator Haven told me I'm to start my career path in the janitorial field by the end of the month." I drop my head in shame.

She lets out a big breath. "I know. Educator Haven informed me."

I rub my hands together, still unable to make eye contact. "You already knew?"

"I was waiting for you to tell me. I didn't want to push you until you were ready." Out of the corner of my eye, I see her hands run through her hair. "This weekend, I was planning on sitting down with my parents to discuss your moving out to Accidia with them. You'll be happier there."

Even though I have always fantasized about growing up in Accidia, I can't help but feel hurt by the implications.

"You're finally giving up on me?" I ask.

"Look at me, son." She waits until I can bring myself to meet her gaze. "I'm not giving up on you. I'm giving up on them. Understand?"

The distinction makes me feel a lot better and I nod in agreement. In my own way, I was planned. I hold this information close to my heart.

"Then why did Father leave?" I ask.

She looks uncomfortable and this time, she's the one who drops her gaze. "Well, I may have planned to have you, but I kept your father in the dark about that. That's why we fought. He was mad at me, not you," she says.

I repeat my question. "But why did he leave?"

"He viewed you as my act of betrayal and defiance. I'm the reason he left," she says.

I furrow my eyebrows as I take in this new information. Her entire life trajectory changed because of me.

"Do you regret it?"

"Not for one second," my mother states. She squeezes my hand again and I can't help but smile.

Dominic interrupts the moment by leaning in my open window and saying, "I found the problem and will have it fixed this evening. We are going to stay here overnight so the solar battery can recharge in the morning with the sun."

"Thank you for working on it," Mother says. Dominic ignores her praise and heads back to the hood to keep working.

A few more hours pass with a tense awareness. Once Dominic finishes fixing the vehicle, he stays alert and watchful of the scenery. We've been completely and utterly alone, waiting for the sun to come back up for the battery to charge.

None of us has eaten anything since breakfast. We're bored, tired, and everything we do seems to upset Dominic.

"All right," Dominic says as he opens the car door. "I need to get out of this space and walk around to make sure we are alone. You and Mother stay here in the car and get some sleep." He walks away before we can say anything.

My mother leans back in her seat. "Oh, Elliot. I wish we had a nice bed to sleep in tonight. At least we'll be able to sleep in a real bed tomorrow at my parents' house. We should get some rest." She gestures for me to lie my head down on the seat behind her.

I spread out and lie down. Her hand reaches over to rest on my shoulder. We don't speak, but rather take comfort in each other's presence. I'm dozing when the door opens and startles me back to full consciousness. Dominic comes back into the vehicle. He stares at us for a couple of moments, analyzing our position.

Finally, he opens his mouth. "I walked around and did not find anyone. We should be safe for the night. If a car passes by, their headlights will wake us up and we can go from there. I suspect that they would not see us and drive right past."

"Thank you for looking, Dominic. Let's all get some rest. I'll take over and drive tomorrow," my mother says.

She's right. This isn't the most comfortable place to sleep. I struggle to get comfortable and eventually find my way into a light slumber.

* * *

Before I know it, the sun shines through the windows and the vehicle comes to life. I shoot up in alarm as we start moving again. I must have been more tired than I thought and slept through the rest of the night. I eye the bag with the food packets in it enviously once my hunger pains return.

None of us says anything and soon, my mind drifts again to the men Dominic killed. So quick—their potential was obliterated. How can he justify their murder so easily?

An endless sea of trees passes by to accompany my bleak thoughts. My stomach rumbles as a constant reminder of our situation. We've been in the car for hours and I've been daydreaming for the majority of it. My mother took over the driving to let Dominic stretch out on the passenger side.

"When are you going to want to talk about those two men?" My mother asks after miles of silence.

Dominic stiffens in the passenger seat and responds, "There is nothing to talk about. I did what had to be done."

Without looking at him, she replies, "Even if this is something you feel is justified, you have to be feeling other sentiments as well."

He takes another deep breath and repeats, "It had to be done."

My mother nods her head. "I understand that's what you think. When you're ready to talk about it, I'll be here to listen."

"There is nothing to discuss," he says to end the conversation.

To avoid the tension radiating from Dominic, I focus on a shadow moving in the distance. At first I think I'm imagining it, so I blink to try and wake up fully. It's still there.

"Stop the vehicle," I say to my mother.

She startles. "What's wrong?" Her hands stumble on the commands to stop the vehicle's course.

"We are not stopping again. Do I need to remind you what happened last time?" Dominic says, clearly unhappy at the direction of the last conversation.

"And it isn't going to happen again," my mother says. "No matter what you think you saw, we're still all people. We all deserve kindness and respect. We're stopping."

The vehicle slowly comes to a stop about forty yards behind the stranger. When she hears us approach, she visibly tenses and looks over her shoulder. After a couple moments' pause, she walks toward us and stops once she's about ten yards away.

"We have a little time to say 'hello'…" Dominic trails off while he opens his door. My mother and I follow him out.

When we're close enough to talk, the brown in her eyes meets my blue. I mentally place her age at about twenty-five, but her haggard appearance makes it just a rough guess. Her long, dark hair is tangled with small leaves in it. A smudge of dirt outlines her strong jawline. Clearly, she's been without the essential comforts of society for a significant period of time, though she's still in the basic white outfit of leisure time.

After scanning us, she addresses my brother. "My name is Jess. You're the first people who have stopped."

"Well, I am glad I could be your rescuer," my brother says.

Dominic is used to getting everything he wants and that includes women. Luckily for him, they've always fallen under his charm. He stays with them until he gets bored and then moves on to his next conquest.

Jess tucks her curly hair behind her ears and stands up straighter. I note, with embarrassment, that she's almost as tall as I am.

To my surprise, she says, "If I needed to be rescued I wouldn't be coming to you, now would I?"

I laugh before I can help myself. One look from my brother and I'm silenced. I'm going to pay for that later. I hope being able to witness his rejection will make it worth it.

The new girl analyzes this exchange and pauses in thought. She gives off such an impression of genuine strength.

When she talks next, she directs her question to me. "How did you all get out in time?"

"First of all, I'm Elliot. This is my brother, Dominic, and our mother, Annalise," I say as I gesture to each of them.

Jess gives my mother a quick nod when I introduce her, ignores my brother, and looks back at me. I meet her gaze a little nervously.

"But to answer your question, my brother works with the genetic engineers and saw some footage he wasn't supposed to and got us all out of Potentia."

"Of course he works with the genetic engineers." Her disdain is shocking. I've never met someone who didn't revere them. "What did you see?" Jess reluctantly addresses Dominic.

"I have seen many things but none as beautiful as what I expect you could be…with a proper shower. I can help you with that," Dominic says, clearly trying to win her over still.

"Dominic," My mother hisses in warning.

Jess clenches her jaw. "I asked you a question, not an invitation to disgust me." She pauses to let her words sink in. "Now tell me—what did you see?"

My mother smiles at Jess, even though she just put one of her sons in his place.

"A video of someone with a peculiar appearance who spent her energy attacking another person. I do not really know anything else. I just knew something was wrong and they were about to close down the territory, and I did not want to be trapped. I left and we have been on the road since yesterday afternoon." His tone is hard—as if he's trying to compensate for the blow to his ego.

"So you guys haven't actually seen anything firsthand? You don't know. . ." Without warning, Jess laughs. Her straight teeth gleam in the sunlight. "You guys don't know anything. You just happened to get out of the territory with basically no reason to? I can't believe it."

"What don't we know, dear?" My mother looks nervously at Jess.

"People are changing into creatures, for lack of a better word. Once they turn, nothing is left that shows any resemblance to what they used to be. All they do is try and…and eat other people."

"Eat other people? What are you talking about?" My mother's pitch rises piercingly.

"I mean they try to bite and consume our flesh. I know it sounds ridiculous, but you have to believe me." She pauses and looks past us. "I didn't and learned my lesson the hard way."

I put my arm around my mother to offer some consolation.

"Listen," I say. "At least you acknowledge how ridiculous you sound. Are you suggesting this illness is making people revert to cannibalism?"

"In a way, but that doesn't completely explain it. They just change into something and there's no reasoning with them—no stopping them unless you kill them." When she says the last part, her eyes drop in pain.

We all take her words in, trying to decide her level of sanity. After a considerable amount of silence, I ask her, "What's your story? Why are you here walking alone?"

She shrugs. "I got out by myself and have been on my own since then. Nothing to talk about."

I look over to my brother to see his reaction to her response. He seems to still be focusing on nursing his pride. My mother has all of her attention on Dominic with a worried look on her face. Jess, on the other hand, looks unhappy, yet determined.

Not sure if it's my place or not, I nonetheless say, "You can come with us. No one should have to go through this alone. We have a vehicle that's taking us to our grandparents' house on the lake. Maybe they won't be impacted by whatever is going on and everything will be okay there."

She deliberates and casts a few glares my brother's way, so I add, "Please come with us."

A few long moments go by while she decides what risk she wants to make: going at this alone or with a group of strangers she just met.

"I'll go with you for now. Don't think I need you all for my safety. I don't need protecting and I won't put up with any nonsense."

She intends the last part for my brother. A familiar look has spread across his face. It may not be recognizable to other people, but I know my brother enough to know what he's thinking. He sees a new challenge. I'm going to have to keep an eye out for Jess. She says she doesn't need protecting, but I'm not sure if I would be protecting her or my brother.

"It'll be nice to have you join us," my mother says. "My parents live just off the lake. I'll admit, we'll be a little tight on space, but I'm really glad we ran into you." She smiles at Jess. Jess considers her before returning the gesture.

"Now that we are all friends, let's get back in the vehicle," Dominic says as he motions impatiently for us to start moving.

I'm the first one to reach the door. "My brother and mother are already up front. Is it okay if you sit in the back with me?" I ask Jess.

"Oh, I can easily move and sit in the back," my mother exclaims.

Jess eyes Dominic and says, "I can sit in the back. I don't mind it at all." Her tone is nice, yet stern. She doesn't leave it up to discussion. Dominic raises an eyebrow but keeps his mouth shut.

"Right," I say, opening the door for her.

She climbs in our vehicle and I follow her. She exhales in relief. "To be honest, I haven't been able to really sit down and relax in days." Her voice is quiet enough that I doubt if anyone else could hear her.

I reply at the same volume. "You can relax. We're still a couple hours away."

She nods in acknowledgment and surprises me by listening. She immediately rests her head back and closes her eyes. After a few moments, her breathing slows and her mouth opens a little. She must have been really exhausted to fall asleep so quickly.

I take the chance to study her. Sleeping, her sharp features soften. The freckles on her nose hide within the dirt smudges on her face. I wonder what her story is. She intrigues me.

"Does Elliot have a crush?" Dominic says to interrupt my musings.

My cheeks go red and I quickly divert my attention to my hands.

"Dominic, don't say that," my mother says.

Dominic ignores her. "She would never be interested in someone like you. By the looks of her, she is Planned. You could never deserve someone like that."

"I'm serious, Dominic. Not another word." My mother's voice rises in pitch as her anger increases.

"I do not want him to get his hopes up and end up hurt. I saw the way he was just looking at her," he says, full of innocence.

"I don't know how many times I have to say this. You two are brothers and it's about time that you act like it."

I sneak another peek at Jess. Her breathing is quicker and her eyebrows are furrowed. She probably heard the whole exchange, at least the ending. I'm embarrassed, but know Dominic is right. She has the overall look of someone who is Planned. Her type always ends up with his.

I look outside the window opposite Jess and watch all of the nature pass by. It's easy to imagine everything is back to normal and we're just on another family trip to visit my grandparents. Everything looks exactly the same as it always has. Spring causes everything to come to life. Green fills the landscape. I take in the atmosphere and take a deep breath. Everything is so full of life and growing.

Except Dominic killed two men yesterday. Life isn't as full of promise as it would appear. I'm sure this won't be the last time I wonder what's happening to the people who are still in the territory—to the people who were left behind.

CHAPTER EIGHT

My grandparents' log cabin is finally visible through the woods. The sight of the lake and my grandfather's boathouse instantly calms all of my nerves. About another mile or so and we'll be there. It seems like it has been such a long time since we left Potentia. It's startling it's been less than twenty-four hours.

Jess laughed at us when she learned we weren't eating our food packets, so since then, we've been snacking on what we brought from our living quarters. We're only allowed to keep a finite supply of food so it's a good thing we'll be at Grandmother and Grandfather's soon.

I examine our group. Sleeping in the car and the stress of the unknown has left its mark on us. Even Dominic can't hide the bags under his eyes. However, the sight of the cabin makes everybody smile.

"It's beautiful, just like always. I somehow forget how nice it is up here. It really was a wonderful place to grow up," my mother says.

"I imagine it was a very peaceful childhood," Jess says. She eyes the calm setting nervously.

Even though I now know why my mother never let me live here, I can't help but feel like I missed out. Every detail of this place makes me feel at home. The large, thick trees that I grew up climbing surround our trail—trees that have been alive and thriving for longer than I can imagine, without any genetic manipulation.

The vehicle parks itself in the small clearing next to the boathouse and the four of us get out of the close quarters. Besides the waves tranquilly breaking in the distance, everything is very quiet. After all of the uncertainty and exhaustion recently, this place looks like a piece of heaven. Untouched by the development of our society, the cabin has always had a serene atmosphere.

Just to the right of the boathouse is a pile of firewood where my grandfather and I used to chop wood. I clench my fist in memory of bringing the ax down on the stump with my grandfather standing stoically next to me.

I exchange a glance with my mother. The amount of joy in her expression almost breaks my heart. Just as I need her, she needs her mother right now. It's going to be much better here. We make eye contact and her contagious joy spreads easily.

I look over to Jess so we can share in this moment. Her eyes won't stop darting around the cabin. I go to the other side of the vehicle. "What's wrong?"

I don't think she's going to answer me, so I'm surprised when she finally does. "It just seems too perfect. We haven't crossed paths with anyone. I know it's only been a couple of hours, but I would've expected to at least pass someone." She shrugs and looks toward the lake. "It's odd, that's all."

"Jess, we've just been lucky. We got out in time. You're going to love my grandparents. My grandfather seems to be getting more and more chatty every time I see him, but he means well. And my grandmother... well, honestly, she can be a bit overbearing. You'll get used to it. Hopefully, they have food cooking." I can hear the enthusiasm in my own voice. It must be very obvious to Jess.

She offers me a small smile and walks up the hill toward the cabin. I stare after her, wondering again about her history. I shake my head to clear it and follow her. My thighs burn slightly from all of the recent physical activity as I push my way to my grandparents.

Out of anticipation, my mother moves faster than any of us. The sun is setting behind the cabin and she walks in its shadow. She enters the house just as the rest of us step onto the patio. The door swings shut behind her. I smile in excitement as I pass their matching rocking chairs. I'm about to see my grandparents again. I really miss them.

As soon as I open the door, the smell assaults me. It's so strong the air almost feels thicker. This must be what death smells like.

I quickly scan the cabin for my mother. She approaches a small figure in the kitchen. My grandmother has her back turned toward us, her posture unnaturally hunched.

My brother looks at me and I see my own confusion mirrored in his face. Jess utters a small exhalation of air. My heart stills instantly in my chest. The entire energy of the cabin hints at something terrible, but I can't put my finger on it. Something is wrong.

My mother's hand reaches out to my grandmother, but what turns around isn't my grandmother. Dominic was right, their color changes and they just look wrong.

"Mom?" My mother articulates her last word before the thing that used to be my grandmother rips into her throat. Blood sprays all over the living room walls. Mother's head falls back and we make eye contact one last time as the life leaves her. Horrible moaning noises echo from my grandmother as it claws through my mother's weak flesh, the grey tinge smothering the healthy glow from her body.

My heart starts up again with a vengeance, beating out of control. Frozen in shock, I'm unable to move. I try to breathe, but it feels like I can't get enough oxygen. I close my eyes in an attempt to escape this horror—to escape the unthinkable. This has to be some terrible nightmare. I can't survive in a world without my mother. How could I? Something pushes past me and I reopen my eyes.

Jess knocks down a chair as she rushes forward toward my dead mother. I'm motionless, refusing to accept what just happened. This can't be.

My eyes follow Jess's movements. She approaches my grandmother and takes out a long knife. Numb, I absentmindedly wonder where she's kept the knife.

Jess closes the gap and stabs my grandmother in the head. The gruesome figure falls lifelessly to the ground and the groaning finally stops. Losing the support, my mother falls beside her. The two of them lie in a shared pool of blood in a last embrace.

Jess exhales a large breath and kneels down to stab my mother's head as well.

How can I exist in a world where my mother doesn't? The one constant, good thing in my life was just brutally destroyed by another person I love. This can't be happening. I blink hard, trying to wake myself up from this terrible nightmare. This doesn't make sense.

A noise echoes to my left and something moves toward me. When it comes into the light from the window, I notice it used to be my grandfather. It used to be the man who taught me how to fish, the man who would read me to sleep, the man who showed me how important it is to always be kind. This was the man who was my true father figure. Now, there is nothing in its dimmed, yellowed eyes. Where life and laughter used to flourish, an absolute void exists.

Jess races over. Before she gets to us, Dominic steps in and pushes it to the ground. It falls awkwardly and struggles to get back on its feet. Before it can, Dominic picks up the fireplace poker next to us and slams it down on my grandfather's head. Fresh blood sprays on the impact and it collapses to the ground. Seconds later, I follow suit.

My head drops in despair as tears flow down my face. The pain is overwhelming. The image of my mother dying is on an endless loop in my brain—her eyes fading from consciousness as her own mother tears her throat out. I can't stop crying. Her not being with me is unimaginable. I need her.

Losing parents at a young age due to death isn't supposed to happen in today's society, especially in this manner. This sort of tragedy just doesn't happen to me. It only occurred in the past before our society advanced to the point it has. I can't comprehend what just happened—or why.

I'm vaguely aware that Dominic mutters, "We need to dig graves now," and leaves the room to head back outside.

I'm not sure how long my grief consumes me before Jess walks over. I turn my head in an attempt to hide my face. She sits down next to me and tentatively strokes my hair. At her touch, I weep even harder. Still not saying anything, she delicately holds me against her.

Even though we don't know each other very well, the physical touch has a calming effect and I'm thankful for her presence. Gradually, my breathing evens out and I regain some composure.

"I'm sorry," I say. I hastily wipe tears off of my face.

"What are you sorry for? There's no reason to apologize for anything."

"I shouldn't be this weak. I should be better than this. How pathetic am I?" I laugh humorlessly and stare at the wall in front of me rather than look at Jess. I'm afraid if I make eye contact with her, the emotion will flood my system. The pain of the loss is just too powerful.

"Elliot. Look at me." She waits until I timidly look her way. The strength in her eyes is surprising. "You're anything but weak. It's one thing to hear about this, but a whole different thing to actually witness it." She pauses and considers for a moment. "And to your family no less."

"But I can't stop crying," I respond when another tear falls down my face. "No man should do that. Dominic would never do this." I pause for a moment. "Where is Dominic? Is he okay?"

She gently lets go but remains next to me. "He's fine. He went outside." I try to look away, but she grabs my face and forces me to meet her gaze. "You're not Dominic and you should be proud of that. There's nothing wrong with showing emotion when something horrible happens. Your mother was just killed in front of you and you no longer have your grandparents," she says.

"You don't understand, Jess. I'm not...I'm not normal. I'm not Planned. That's why I'm so weak—why I'm never good enough. Look at Dominic. He's so strong. Everything has always been handed to him. He's always had everything," I say.

"How you came to be doesn't say anything about who you're going to be. In my book, you can't even compare the two of you. And besides, he doesn't have everything," she says in a defiant tone. "He doesn't have me."

Jess stands up and holds out her hands for me. I grab hold and she helps lift me back to my feet. She offers me a slight nod and walks away.

Because of the strength behind her words, I leave the room. I refuse to acknowledge the dead bodies of my closest family members and stare pointedly away from the recent destruction, breathing in through my mouth.

I don't see where Jess went so I go outside to find my brother. He's digging in the garden behind the cabin. The calm lake is the complete opposite of the emotional turmoil I'm feeling. I walk up to Dominic. When he notices I'm watching him, he glares at me.

"Nice to see you are functional again, Joe. Cry enough?" Dominic laughs at his joke. "Come make yourself useful and dig for me. At least try to be helpful. I have been doing this since you had your breakdown. Hopefully, you can manage a few minutes."

I crawl down into the sizable hole and after a couple minutes of silence, I ask him, "How are you doing?"

"I am not as weak as you. I can handle myself," Dominic says. He's lying down on the ground enjoying the sun on his face. "In the long run, this will be good for me. Think about it, now I do not have to worry about Mother anymore. She just was not meant for this life, kind of like you. And she will not be sticking up for you anymore. Our whole lives she has been protecting her poor, average son and spending her energy celebrating mediocrity. She never got to appreciate the excellence of the son she already had."

I pause digging in disbelief. "How can you say that right now? Our grandparents and mother are…" I exhale air as the pain punches me in the gut. "They're dead." Tears threaten again at this admission.

"There is nothing we can do to change what happened, Joe. We need to look forward and understand what is going on." He looks around hopelessly at all of the nature that surrounds us. "I wish I had a laboratory to run some tests on their bodies."

The disgust at this enthusiasm temporarily overshadows my haunting pain. "For once, don't let your logic overrule your emotion," I beg.

His eyebrows furrow in confusion. "I am being rational and not letting emotion cloud my judgment, unlike you." I shake my head and continue digging the mass grave. Dominic takes a long gulp of water and continues. "Plus, Jess saw how truly pathetic you are. Her attention will cease to focus on you and will find its way to the genetically pure. How could she not be drawn to me? I am the complete opposite of the pathetic excuse for a man that you are. You are weak, unintelligent, just pitiful… "

I've never laid a hand on my brother. I've always taken every blow, both physical and verbal, my brother has ever given me. I always thought that was my fate—that it was my punishment for simply existing and causing my family to suffer and put up with an Unplanned.

I don't know if it's the death of my mother, Jess's confidence in me, or some combination of everything. No matter the reasons, I don't have anything left to lose. I no longer accept this as my reality.

Before I can talk myself out of it, I drop the shovel and crawl out of the hole. I interrupt his seemingly infinite list of all my faults.

"Well, you're a little shit," I say. I punch my brother in the nose and hear a satisfying crunch as it breaks. "I'd be better off without you. I'm so much more than you think I am." I stand up to get my full height.

His hands fumble at his nose in an attempt to stop the bleeding. His eyes widen in disbelief. I stand up and spot Jess in the trees, expressionless.

I walk back toward the house and when I glance back over at my brother, there is complete hatred in his eyes. This is far from being over, but there's nothing I can do about it now. I opened Pandora's Box and I need to accept the consequences of it. For the first time in my life, I stood up for myself.

I go back inside to the kitchen and exhale in disgust at the smell. It looks as if someone has tried to clean up but hasn't been completely successful. The bodies have been moved, but there are still signs of death with blood smeared across the walls.

Fresh pain threatens to break me again. I turn and walk out the front door. I take a deep breath of the fresher air and try to calm my emotions. With nothing else to do, I walk over to our vehicle and grab our remaining packets of food. I sit down and lean back against one of the tires. My head drops and I stare at my hands. What am I supposed to do now?

Footsteps gradually get louder and closer to me. I reluctantly raise my head and am surprised to see Jess instead of Dominic. She looks at me with an expression that I don't understand. Wordlessly, she takes one of the smaller packets of food from the bag and sits down next to me.

We eat our meals in a comfortable silence. The sun continues to lower and with it, the slight chill of the spring breeze reaches us.

Once she's done eating, Jess says, "I moved the bodies outside. We should bury them in the morning. It will help provide some closure."

"I was helping Dominic dig the hole before. . ." I trail off. I'm still in slight shock that I actually hit my brother.

She interrupts my thoughts by saying, "Last I saw of him, he was still digging. You might want to give him a little time to cool off. He looked pretty upset."

"I was thinking about looking through the basement. My grandparents have a lot of old pictures and various items from our childhood. I'd like to look at them again," I say.

"That'll be good for you," she says, "I'm going to go explore before it gets too dark."

I nod, even though she isn't looking at me. "Be careful."

"Of course," she replies. Despite the recent horrors, being with her gives me a little hope and makes me think that maybe, just maybe, things will be okay.

She walks out, away from the boathouse and lake. I slowly make my way to the front door. The vision of our last entrance into the cabin echoes through my mind and I'm almost surprised when I step inside and my mother isn't ahead of us. The smell has diminished but still hints at the recent death that the cabin held witness to.

I walk through the living room to the stairs for their basement. I turn on the light switch. Dust covers almost every surface down here. I scan the room and walk toward the boxes in the back corner.

I open the first one and look through all of the items. Some are more interesting than others. I quickly lose track of time, entranced by the memorabilia of my youth. Down here with all of our memories, my mother and grandparents are still alive. I fiercely hold onto that belief. They can still be with me.

I find an old picture of my mother holding me when I was probably a year old. I'm asleep in her arms and she looks at me with a small smile on her mouth. I carefully place a finger on the picture in a desperate attempt to connect.

A sneeze erupts from the other side of the room and I jump. I look up to find Jess watching me from the bottom of the stairs. She's recently showered and changed into clean clothes. She must have found my mother's old room. Her wet hair is darkening her pale shirt.

"How long have you been there?" I'm a little self-conscious.

Instead of answering, she walks up and holds out her hand. I give her the photograph. While she examines the photograph, I sneak a glance at her. With the water weighing it down, her hair is longer, cascading down her back. Clean of the dirt smudges, her freckles stand out a lot more. Her sharp features furrow as she looks at the image.

She very quietly says, "This is a precious picture. You're very lucky to have it." She hands it back to me and her fingers linger. "I came down to talk about our plans, but you looked so peaceful I couldn't disrupt you."

"I still can't believe everything that has happened." I shake my head at all that has changed in the last day.

She laughs humorously but I can tell something is troubling her.

Before I can question her, she walks out of the room. She's back at the bottom of the basement stairs and pauses for a moment, looks back at me, then goes up the stairs.

After she leaves, I continue to go through the boxes in search of anything meaningful. It comforts me that the memories are at least still alive with me.

I start looking through another box when there's a sharp pain in my head and everything goes black. As I fade into unconsciousness, I hear my brother's voice declaring, "If you do not need me anymore, then I am gone."

CHAPTER NINE

"Elliot...Elliot...wake up..." I can't tell who the voice belongs to. It seems so far away and my eyelids are unbelievably heavy. I just want to escape back to the darkness.

"Elliot, it's time. Focus. It's me, Jess." Of course. How could I forget her voice? Very slowly, I creak open my eyes. Concern sketches across her face. Quickly, relief flashes through and she smiles faintly.

"What happened?" I frown in confusion as my head pounds.

"After I left earlier, I went outside for a walk. When I got back, I came down here and found you like this. It looks like Dominic came down and got some revenge for the little stunt you pulled earlier."

I blink to try and see clearer. Her face blurs in and out of focus. I close my eyes again. "Where is he?" I ask.

"He must have left. His backpack is gone, along with most of the food and the vehicle." She pauses briefly. "He also buried the bodies."

There's a fresh stab of pain at the mention of their deaths. I take a deep breath and lick my lips.

"He went back," I say, opening my eyes again. "After all of the trouble he took to get us out of there, he went back to Potentia." I shake my head in disbelief. The motion causes physical pain in my head.

"The vehicle is only programmed for that journey?" Jess asks in understanding. I confirm her speculation and she raises her eyebrows in thought.

I try to sit up but get very dizzy the moment I move. She places her hands on my chest to keep me down and I let her. I reach behind my head and discover that the hair is crusty with blood. It surrounds a large bump. I touch it to test if it hurts. It does.

I moan and Jess takes my hand away from my injury and holds it in her lap. She lets me drift back into sleep.

I wake up with a severe headache. I've been moved back to a bed. There is no sunlight coming through the windows so it must be the middle of the night. Very quiet, light snoring comes from next to me. With a jolt, I turn to see Jess is in the bed with me. Careful not to wake her, I shift.

When she's sleeping, her defenses are down and she looks younger. She can't be much older than I am. She looks so much more relaxed. Watching her now, it's very easy to forget all that has recently happened.

I lay there for a while wondering about her life and how she came to be the way she is. Where is she from? She mentioned she had a brother, but what happened to him? Why was she wandering the streets alone? With questions about her past on my mind, I fall back into an uneasy sleep full of worry for the future.

I wake up again before Jess. I have vague memories of her waking me up a couple times in the night, but they're unclear. I manage to crawl my way out of the bed without disrupting her sleep. I find some medicine in the bathroom for my headache. After I take it, I go into the kitchen and worry about the diminishing amount of food. Dominic took a good deal of supplies when he left. The food that's left won't last us more than a couple days.

When I turn around from the pantry, my mother stands in the corner. I gasp, then realize it's just a coat stand. I take a deep breath to let my heart slow down. The next person I see isn't of my imagination, but Jess. She sits down at the table. We eat our breakfast without talking.

Once we both finish our meal, I rub my hands together and tentatively ask, "So…How did you sleep last night?"

She gives me a sharp look and answers the question I was really asking. "I didn't want to leave you alone. You're not supposed to let someone who has a concussion sleep for too long. I didn't want to have to change rooms constantly so I just stayed in there," she says and shrugs. She makes it seem like it's no big deal.

"I thought you were waking me up throughout the night," I say.

Jess smiles a little. "You were a bit groggy, that's for sure."

My hand travels back to my head to carefully examine it. There is still a bump, but it's smaller than it was the day before. It's still very tender.

I look out the large windows surrounding the table to enjoy the landscape. My best times growing up were always here in the cabin with my grandparents and Chris and Andrew across the small lake. Whether it be the quiet, relaxing fishing or even the silly games we used to all play, the lake has always been a source of happiness for me.

Now those memories are no longer a possible future. My mother and both of my grandparents are gone. As much as I want to deny it happened, they're dead. I need to face it. I push down a fresh pulse of worry as I don't know the fate of my two best friends.

"I'm ready to talk about what happened, Jess," I say. She looks confused. "I want to know what's going on. What exactly happened with my mother and grandparents?"

She nods. "I'm not sure exactly what's going on. I'll share what I know." She pauses to collect her thoughts. "I have no idea what started it or why, but there is some affliction that appears to eliminate entirely who the person was and replace it with something that's violent and only focused on attacking people. It seems to spread through biting. I don't know what about the bite is the actual factor in the next person changing, but I would assume it has something to do with the bodily fluids."

"That's disgusting," I say.

"Like I said, I'm not entirely sure, but these are just my guesses," Jess says again. "Think about what I did right after your mother was attacked."

It isn't something I want to dwell on, but I concentrate because I understand the importance of learning more about these things. This might be our new world.

I respond, "You stabbed my grandmother in the head." I pause for a moment. "But then you did it to my mother, too. Why did you do that?"

"I don't know if it's through the blood, saliva, or something else, but when a person is bitten by someone that's infected they turn into one of them. The only way I know how to stop them is by stabbing them in the head. I learned the hard way about how to kill them."

I can tell she's lost in thought, but I need answers. "If that's true, how come my grandparents weren't my grandparents? We haven't seen anybody else around. How did the infection find its way here? This place is pretty isolated."

She grabs onto one of my hands and says, "While you were helping Dominic with the graves, I examined their bodies. I think your grandfather had been gone longer, based on the look of him."

"The look of him? What do you mean?"

She shifts uncomfortably. "His skin was greyer and more saggy if that makes any sense. You remember how bad it smelled when we walked in here, right?"

I crinkle my nose at the memory. It was awful.

I nod and she continues, "My guess would be that when someone is bitten and transforms, their body starts to decay. That's why he looked worse off and it smelled so bad. But your grandfather did have a bite mark on his lower left leg. Your grandmother had a bite mark on her right arm. I can't give you answers to how they got bitten, but I know they were. I'm really sorry, Elliot. That's really all I know. Or think I know." She gives my hand a reassuring squeeze and stands to clean up after both of us.

I follow her back into the kitchen and she continues. "We've been locking up the house, but I don't know how secure that can be. I've been basing our safety off of an assumption we would wake up if they tried to get inside."

At this thought, I consider how safe the house is and how much I'm willing to risk on this theory. My eyes drift to the large, vulnerable window by the table. Beyond it, the sight of the lake sparks an idea.

"Jess, would you like to go fishing with me?"

Clearly startled, she looks up at me with frightened eyes. "Fishing? As in going on a boat in the middle of the water?"

I suppress my amusement. "Fish can actually taste pretty good and the water is relaxing. It'll be fun." When she continues to stare at me in reluctance, I say, "My grandfather taught me how to do it."

"Don't you think we should focus on more important things?"

"Having food is important. Plus, we don't need to decide right now if the house is secure," I say. What I don't tell her is how much I want to escape from the cabin and my thoughts. The idea of mindlessly fishing is very attractive.

Jess looks out the window and contemplates the lake. "I'll go just to make sure if you fall in, I get to see it," she says.

"Besides, maybe my friends and their younger sister will still be here. Andrew and Chris are about my age. Whenever we would come to visit I would spend a lot of time with them."

"What if they've changed into those things, too? You should prepare yourself for that possibility." She analyzes my expression.

"What if they haven't?" I say after a moment's pause.

I move our dishes over to the sink. I motion for her to follow me as I make my way toward the garage. Fishing was my special bond with my grandfather. It was one of the few things I was better at than Dominic.

The warm rays of the sun hit my skin when we step outside. It's such a beautiful day. The spring was always my mother's favorite time of the year. This is the type of day she would have really enjoyed. She'll never again get to enjoy such a day. I shake my head to dispel the thought.

I pause in confusion when we walk into the garage. My grandfather's small boat is missing, along with some of his supplies. I turn a baffled expression to Jess.

"He was always pretty picky about his stuff. Sometimes it almost seemed a little OCD the way he cared for it. I don't know why it isn't all in its proper place," I say.

"That's strange," Jess says and scans the rest of the garage.

I grab some of the supplies that were left in the garage. Luckily, my fishing gear is still in its place and appears to be in good condition. The two of us exit and walk toward the sound of the waves.

"I wonder if something happened when he was on one of his fishing trips. It's very unlike him to leave his stuff lying around..." I fade off when I see the boat clumsily put onto shore with his rod and tackle box still in it.

"Is that your grandfather's boat?"

"Yes, I wonder why he didn't put it up. He always would. Even if we had been out all day and were tired and hungry, he made sure everything was organized. And look," I say as I point to a bag of apples in the boat, "he must have gone across the lake to pick these for my grandmother. She loved it when he did that."

I walk closer to the boat and see his footprints. It looks like he stumbled and got on his hands and knees before getting back on his feet and walking toward the house. There is a discolored section in the dirt that looks like it could have been vomit.

I glance up at Jess in horror and she displays a look of understanding. When she notices my attention is on her, a mask of neutrality takes hold of her face.

Before I can react to her expression, she distracts me by speaking. "At least we found your grandfather's supplies. Let's go fishing. It'll be fun." She finishes by repeating my earlier words.

"Jess," I begin, unsure exactly how to phrase my questions. "Do you think he got attacked in the water? Can these things swim?"

She looks out toward the water. "I doubt it. From the way they move and react, I can't imagine them having the coordination to manage it. I suspect your grandfather got infected when he was picking the apples." Jess lets out a deep breath. "We still need to keep an eye out, but we should hear or see them with enough warning."

I turn my attention back to the boat. I circle it to check for any visible signs of damage. I don't notice anything so I put all of the fishing gear in and push it into the water. Once it's out a little ways, I motion for Jess to get in and soon follow her.

My grandfather believed that the best fishing came from as quiet an atmosphere as possible. Because of this, he didn't have a motor on his boat. I grab the oars and take us out to the deeper water.

The cove we share with Andrew and Chris's family secludes us from the deeper waves of the lake. If I look far enough across the water, I can make out the small outline of their cabin. The farther I get away from the beach, the more alarm shows through Jess's mask.

A strange thought crosses my mind. "Can you swim, Jess?"

Instead of answering, Jess just slowly shakes her head. Her eyes remain focused on the water. No wonder she wasn't excited about the prospect of fishing.

"Don't worry, you're not going to fall in. And even if you do, I'll come get you. I promise." I try to reassure her.

Her eyes leave the water to look at me and gauge my sincerity. She still looks doubtful so I decide to break one of my grandfather's rules. I take my shoes and shirt off so I'm just in my shorts.

"What…"

I don't hear the rest of her statement. I hold my breath and jump into the water. I make, at least according to my grandfather, an unacceptable amount of noise with my splash.

The cool water feels amazing on my skin. I stay under for a little bit just to enjoy it. I forget about all the horrors. For those few seconds, I simply appreciate the water. It could be any other visit. For those few precious moments, my grandparents are alive. My mother is alive. The world isn't broken.

I imagine my grandfather—not the man I grew up with, but the infected thing he turned into—under me, reaching for me, wanting to pull me down and take me with him.

I break the surface and take a deep breath. As the air enters my body, I quickly look around to assure myself I'm not in danger. Jess's panicked expression bores into me. It would have been smarter to not stay under the water so long.

"See, I'm fine. My grandfather taught me to swim when I was really little," I say.

I swim around the boat to prove my point. Her eyes never leave mine as she rotates in the boat to maintain eye contact. "I'm going to get back in now. It might be a little wobbly when I do. Just stay calm."

I put my hands on the boat and hoist myself in. Jess quickly compensates for my weight and leans back against the other side. She visibly relaxes once I sit down.

"Will you teach me?" she asks.

I nod and lean back against one of the seats. After the cold water, the sun feels warm and soothing on my skin and quickly starts to dry me off. I take a deep breath and reassuringly smile at Jess. She stares at my chest. I grab my shirt to put it back on and hide myself.

She carefully moves closer and pushes my hands away. After a couple of seconds, she moves her right hand to my scar and traces it down my chest. The feeling of her hand on my body creates goose bumps. I stay motionless and hold my breath at her touch. The scar starts in the middle of my chest and curves down my left side. About eight inches long, the red, angry line stands out against my pale skin.

"Tell me," Jess says once she's traced it a couple of times.

"It happened right after my father left us. Dominic blamed me. Not much of a story."

"What did he use?" Her voice barely conceals her anger.

"It was a knife from the kitchen." I shift uncomfortably. Besides the doctor that treated me, the only other people who knew about this were my mother and Dominic. Though, I don't actually mind telling Jess.

"He blamed me for Father leaving because of…well, just because of who I am." I pause to examine her expression. I don't see any evidence of pity so I continue my story. "He just came at me and lunged. I jumped back out of the way so it didn't get as deep as it could have. My mother heard the noise and ran in before he could have another attempt and took me to the doctor. Dominic claimed he was just playing around and didn't actually mean to hurt me."

"And everyone believed that?" she asks, shocked.

"I don't think my mother did. But he was always so good and perfect at everything else so they wanted to believe him. Plus, because my father walked out, the doctor felt bad for him because he was being punished for me. I'm quite the scandal, you know," I add playfully in an attempt to lighten the mood.

"Quite infamous, from what I understand."

A twinkle in her eyes shines through. I'm completely captivated by her. I inch my hand closer to hers when I hear a loud whooping sound.

"Get some, Elliot," a familiar voice screams, quickly followed by a catcall and splashes. I jerk my head up. While we were focused on my scar, Andrew and Chris had quietly rowed their boat out to greet us and jumped in the lake.

I blush and put on my shirt. A guarded expression replaces Jess's playful mood and a pang hits me, longing for her to remain unguarded. However, my two childhood friends—similar enough in appearance and age to pass as twins—demand my attention as they swim closer and closer to the boat.

Years of experience with them lead me to a pretty good guess as to what they're planning to do. I quickly strap all of the supplies in the boat and lock in the fishing gear.

I turn to Jess and say in a rush, "It looks like you're about to get your first lesson in swimming. Do you trust me?"

Her eyes widen almost comically at my words and her lips form a small circle when understanding hits her.

"Do I have a choice?"

"Not really," I say and grab her hand just as Andrew and Chris get to the boat.

"So who's this nice lady you tricked into comin' out here, Elliot?" Andrew asks. He sounds innocent enough, but his smirk gives away his intention.

"Yeah, some'd consider it rude if you don't introduce her to your friends, very rude in fact," Chris continues, his large mouth curved in amusement.

"Guys, this is Jess. Calm down. No need to do anything rash." I put my one hand up in defeat, keeping ahold of Jess with my other arm, as I speak to them because I know there is little chance of their not following through.

"Whoa. You have a temper now?" Andrew asks as they continue to tread water.

"We better help him cool off."

"She can't even swim," I say in a last attempt.

"Nice try," Chris responds.

Jess squeezes my hand tighter and her breathing rate increases. I tighten my grip.

The two of them take a deep breath and dive under the water. The boat starts rocking. I quickly lose my balance and fall out of the boat. Because we're holding hands, Jess enters the water with me. Unlike my last plunge, this time I quickly rise to the surface and pull Jess with me. We break the surface and tread water. Well, I tread water and keep Jess's head above the surface. I pull her back to the boat and help her back in before I get in myself.

"I didn't drown," Jess says only loud enough for my ears. She sounds surprised.

Before I can respond, Andrew and Chris climb into the boat and rush forward to hug me. Their sudden movement almost causes the boat to tip again. I quickly steady them. They look over at Jess.

"This here fine gentleman is Andrew," Chris points toward Andrew in his introduction.

Andrew bows slightly and points at Chris. His long, dark hair falls across his face. "And this impressive guy is Chris."

I laugh in appreciation. They've always fed off of each other so well.

Jess seems a little taken aback by their behavior but allows each of them a small smile.

"I'm Jess," she says.

"I'm so glad you guys are okay," I exclaim with joy once the pleasantries are over with. I look them over and they look very healthy. Their hair has grown out since I last saw them and it flows past their eyebrows.

"Why wouldn't we be?" Andrew asks as he shakes his hair out of his eyes.

My heart drops at their obliviousness. "Where have you two been these last few days?"

"Been here," Chris answers and gestures around the lake.

"Just, you know, livin' the dream," Andrew says. He tilts his head toward Jess. "Carly told us that you were comin', but she didn't say you were bringin' anyone. You been holdin' out on us?"

For a moment, I allow myself to pretend that their interpretation of the situation is accurate. I take a deep breath and steady myself.

"We need to talk," I say and sit back.

I inform them of all of the terrible things that have been going on since I last saw them. At first, I can tell they think I'm hosting an elaborate joke. When I describe how my mother died, they start to take me seriously. They know I would never joke about anything bad happening to her.

"That's all I know," I conclude. "I can't believe the two of you didn't know anything."

"Well, since our parents' accident, it's just been us three," Andrew says, clearly taken aback by the state of things.

"We hadn't seen your grandparents in a couple of weeks, but out here, that isn't that surprising. We stick to ourselves," Chris says.

I always envied their seclusion from the rest of the world and it clearly seems to have protected them from whatever disease is spreading throughout society. I wish that protection had extended to my grandparents.

"You know, we haven't seen you since our parents' funeral, Elliot," Andrew says.

"I should have come and seen you sooner, but I'm just so thankful you're all safe. Although, I don't understand how my grandparents got infected," I say.

"Your grandfather must have gotten bitten on his last fishing trip." Jess makes her first verbal contribution to the conversation since the introductions. She answers all of our confounded expressions. "You said it yourself, he always put his gear up. He didn't do that the last time. Plus, it looked like he was sick after he landed."

It all adds up and it makes me want to cry again. My grandfather loved my grandmother from the moment he met her and the idea of him attacking and killing her is unthinkable. He would have done anything for her and my only hope is that he had no idea what was going on when he hurt her.

"Whoa, man. That's unreal," Andrew says.

Not knowing what else to say, I look around. There is no other sign of life around us. Once again, I'm struck by how peaceful it is here versus what must be going on in the territories by now.

"If you think about it one way," Chris says to continue the conversation, "did we or did we not always say the world would come to an end before our little Elliot would show up with a girl?"

I sneak a glance over at Jess as I answer, "Nothing like that's going on. We found each other on the road back when my mother and brother were still with me. We've been together since then."

Jess looks at me with a smirk, lighting my face on fire.

"Okay, we believe you," Chris says.

"Yeah, sure we do." Andrew snickers.

"Now that that's settled," Jess says, "how much space do the two of you have at your house?"

"We've space for ya'll if that's what you're askin'. Easy peasy. Of course, you'll have to deal with our younger sister. She can be a lil' annoying." Chris nods along as Andrew speaks. "But it might get a lil' cramped for you two…friends."

"Great, we'll be over before the sun sets. We just have a couple things to do."

"We do?" I ask Jess. This is news to me. She simply nods while I stare back in confusion at her.

"We'll let ya'll have some time alone." They both chuckle as they jump into the water and swim back to their boat. I grab the oars from the bottom of the boat and paddle us back to my grandparents' house.

Jess and I make eye contact for several heartbeats before she finally breaks it. She stares out into the distance without saying anything.

When we get closer to the dock, I finally break the silence. "Can I ask you a question?"

Jess visibly tenses and answers after a pause. "It depends on what the question is."

"Why are we going over to their house? What's wrong with staying here?"

Just as quickly as she tensed up, she relaxes. "It isn't good for you to stay there. One, you need to get out of the house with all of the memories. Two, if Dominic comes back looking for you, your grandparents' cabin is the first place he'll go. And finally, it will be safer for everyone if we're all together."

"I guess that's true. What if one of the infected comes after them and they don't know what to do? I mean, I told them, but what if they panic?"

"Exactly. Trust me on this one, you don't want to be wondering 'what if,'" Jess concludes and I can tell by her tone that she means to end the conversation. So I let the conversation die out and continue rowing us back to the place my grandparents lived and died.

CHAPTER TEN

"Jess?" I rummage through the kitchen cabinets. We're going to bring all of the food over to Andrew and Chris's to have it all in one place.

"Mmmm?" Jess mumbles back, clearly distracted. She squints at an old can. "Do you think if it says it's expired it's actually expired? Or is that just a suggestion?"

"I'll let you be the test subject for that," I say.

She considers the can of food and says, "I might give it to your friends as punishment for forcing us into the lake." A smirk crosses her face while she places the can into her bag.

I should check the expiration dates of everything I eat going forward. Just in case. She has so many different sides to her. One minute, she's playful and the next, she closes up.

"What really happened to you?"

She freezes. "What?"

I barely hear her reply and hope that she will open up to me rather than closing up. "How did you end up alone?"

"It's not a good story." She turns slowly away from the pantry and sits by the kitchen table. We make eye contact. Her head falls and she stares at her crossed hands. "It's not something I'm proud of."

I'm not sure exactly what to say, so I sit down next to her. She briefly looks up in reaction to my movement but places her head back down as soon as I sit. What could have happened to make her feel ashamed?

"I didn't have the best relationship with my parents. When I was younger, everything was all right, but then my father started to drink heavily. All of our money went to support his addiction and it caused more stress, so he drank even more. It was a terrible, endless cycle." She takes a deep breath. "My father was a tolerable man sober, but when he was drinking…" Jess shakes her head and continues, "He would get angry, and then my lessons would start." Jess laughs bitterly.

No wonder she is so guarded—she grew up in an abusive household.

Her entire body language shifts and she sits up straighter to make eye contact with me. "Before my little brother was born, I was so mad at him. My mother was in labor for such a long time, and I was upset that my father would put her through even more pain. By this point, we could hardly afford to stay in our apartment, let alone pay to plan for a new child. In my mind, childbirth was just another tool he utilized to put my mother through more torment. I resented my unborn sibling. But when my brother was born and I first laid eyes on him…he was so innocent. Here I was, fifteen years old, and I knew what love at first sight was."

I close my eyes and try to picture the image of her accepting an Unplanned sibling instantly. Why couldn't Dominic do that?

She continues her story. "My father stopped drinking for a little bit and everything seemed to be better. And then one day when my brother was around six months old, I came home and found him with a red mark on his back and there were empty bottles on the floor. I'd never felt such strong hatred for anyone before." She takes another deep breath. "I stood up to my father. Luckily, he had been drinking so his reflexes were slow and I didn't get hurt myself.

"Seeing me stand up to my father gave my mother the courage she finally needed to leave. The next day, the three of us left and I didn't see him again until about a week ago."

Her tone changes and becomes even darker. Her gaze returns to her hands. "My mother may have left physically with us, but my father took a part of her away that my brother and I could never get back. I raised him as best as I could.

"When everyone was getting sick, my father showed up at our house. Almost a decade later and the sight of him still caused bile to rise in my stomach. He was already bitten and infected. My mother relented and let him stay with us because she couldn't stand the thought of him being by himself during his illness. It only took him three hours being back in our lives to destroy everything."

I can't believe how much she's sharing and don't want to risk her shutting down. Unable to resist any longer, I reach over and grab her hand. "At least you don't have to worry about him anymore. He's gone," I say in my attempt to comfort her. I want to be the strength for her that she was for her brother growing up.

"You don't understand. This was before I discovered how to truly kill them. He bit my mother and…" She sobs harder and I jump out of my chair to get closer to her—a reaction to her being in pain. I place my arm around her and pull her in close so I can hold her.

She pushes back against me and looks up at me with unfiltered grief as the tears run down her face. "The worthless piece of shit got to my brother, too. The asshole who abused me and my mother gave me one good thing in my life. All I ever wanted to do was protect my little brother and what happened? My father came in and took him from me as well."

I reach out and pull her in again. This time, she lets me hold her and she sobs into my chest. "Vis was in such a state of confusion that I was able to escape that night. I've been alone ever since."

"You're not alone anymore," I say. I gently rub her back in a motion I hope is comforting. "You're not alone."

I'm not sure how long the two of us stay in that position. I try my best to be as reassuring as possible. I may be uncertain how comforting my presence actually is for her, but I'm thankful she let me in. Until this point, I've felt that she was the one who knew everything about me. I've been an open book for her and she finally let me read one of her chapters, although a disturbing one.

Over time, she gathers control and pulls away. A quick swipe of her hands brushes her tears away. She straightens her shoulders and looks at me with renewed determination. Her eyes are red and blotchy from crying, but rather than seeing it as a weakness, as my brother would, I view it as more of a testament to her strength. She's lost her family, yet she's still here, fighting.

"Do you have any other family? Cousins?" I ask, hoping she still has some family left.

She shakes her head. "None worth mentioning. You?"

"My mother was an only child. It's just me and Dominic left on that side." There's no doubt that he's okay and will survive this epidemic. He was right, he's made for this. I shrug and continue, "My father had a younger sister. I imagine she would've had kids by now, but we lost contact with his family after he left."

Jess lets out a deep breath and says, "I would appreciate it if you didn't share that story with anyone. I'm not proud that I let him kill my family. I don't want anyone else to know my worst moment," she says.

A single tear escapes her eye and runs down her face. I gather my courage and step a little closer to her. I raise my hand and gently brush the tear away with my finger. I cup her face to maintain our eye contact. It's a similar motion to what she did to me yesterday. I hope it helps her as much as it did me. "There's nothing to be ashamed of."

"Just promise me you won't share the story," Jess says. She grabs my hand away from her face but holds on.

"Of course I won't tell," I say. I'm slightly offended she feels like she has to make me promise, but at the same time, I understand where she's coming from. She prides herself on the high level of strength that she possesses. "I'm glad you told me, Jess," I say.

She squeezes my hand and lets go. "We should keep looking for supplies. I'm starting to wonder about those damn expiration dates again."

I accept the change in the direction of the conversation. "I don't think I'll be eating those cans. Maybe one of them will be brave enough."

My grandparents' kitchen looks so bare after our scavenging. It's hard to imagine how empty the cabin will be once we leave. I'm so alone. The people I cared most about are dead.

"I want to talk about something before we go over there," Jess says as she carries a box of our supplies out the door. "I want to make sure we're on the same page," Jess says.

"Okay, we can sit on the porch before we go back to the boat. It's a nice day," I say. I don't like the sound of this conversation. Does she think I'm getting too familiar with her? Maybe I shouldn't have held her. I know we've only recently met, but it felt like the right thing to do.

I grab the other box and follow her out the front door. I take a seat in the rocking chair that my grandfather loved to sit in. Jess takes the other one.

Jess begins, "Tell me about them."

"Andrew and Chris?" She nods so I continue, "There isn't really that much to tell. Every time I came for a visit I always ended up spending time with them. Andrew is about six months older than me, and Chris a year younger. We always got along really well." I shift to get more comfortable. "They didn't like Dominic, so we bonded over that in the beginning."

"They have a sister?" She looks at me in a way that makes me feel exposed. It feels like she can read my thoughts.

"Yeah, she's a bit of a handful. Her name is Carly. She would always try to tag along when we would go out. She's thirteen. They pretend to dislike her, but especially since their parents died, they've become very protective of her." An image of her clinging to both of her brothers at their parents' funeral pops up in my mind. I shake my head to get rid of the image.

"How did their parents die?"

"Their father really liked to tinker. He found an old vehicle—the ones where you had to manually drive—and managed to put it back together. They were driving it one day when it was icy and lost control. They got into a bad accident. No one knew exactly where either of them were. The car didn't have a tracking system in place and it took hours to find them. By the time they were taken to the hospital, it was too late," I tell her.

It was an awful phone call to receive. They were always so kind to me. They didn't look at me with the pity or disgust that I grew up with, but rather accepted me.

"That's awful," Jess says, horrified. "When did this happen?"

I count back the months. "Not too long ago. It must have been around four months ago."

"All three of them are Unplanned?" she asks. I raise an eyebrow at her question. I thought she didn't care about this sort of stuff.

"Their parents didn't have the means." The only reason they were able to have three children was because of how much less regulated everything is out here. "Does it matter?" I admit, I'm touchy about this.

"Elliot, I was just asking a question. I'm glad none of them are Planned," Jess says.

"Oh." I've never really heard anyone iterate such a strong sentiment toward not going through the genetic engineering. I examine her closer. "Why?"

She considers her response before answering. "The wrong emphasis is placed on certain traits. A lot of things that society has deemed unimportant still make a difference in who a person is. It leads to discrimination against those who aren't Planned. I don't agree with mass prejudice against a significant segment of society just because of the way they were born," Jess says.

I tilt my head a little and examine her. She isn't like anyone I've ever met before. Having a younger, Unplanned sibling seems to have shaped Jess's viewpoint. Why didn't that click with Dominic?

"Are you Planned? What specialization were you given?" I ask, unable to help myself. I'm so curious about everything to do with her.

This time, it's she who appears to be a little affronted.

"Does it matter?" she repeats my earlier question back at me.

I chuckle at her response. I'm almost positive she's Planned. Her height and quick wit give it away. Plus, an Unplanned doesn't get through life in the territories with Jess's confidence and self-assurance. What makes her different than the other Planned, though, is that she manages to present herself in a way that isn't cruel or mean. She has many similarities to everyone in society, yet the end product is so refreshingly different.

"No, I suppose it doesn't make a difference. You're Jess," I say.

She smiles lightly and focuses her attention beyond the trees. "As you're Elliot."

Is that really how she views me? As a person who's unrelated to any science experiment but rather who I've become? I dig deeper into her beliefs. "Do you think when someone is born, they are who they are?"

"Our society wants us to believe that we're predestined and all of this genetic engineering makes everyone perfect. They think that the hard work is done once the genetic planning phase is complete. But look at you and your brother as examples. He has all the traits that everyone thought would make the best possible person, but do you really think he is?"

The last time my brother and I were compared like this, he used me as a way to fully demonstrate his superiority. But now, Jess is doing it the other way around. She truly thinks I am a better person than he is. I can't wrap my head around it. "I've spent my whole life wishing I was more like him. I've spent my whole life wishing I was him."

Jess redirects her attention to me. Her gaze has the odd effect of making me nervous and comforted at the same time. "Do you still want to be him?"

I look down at my hands, envisioning the limp bodies of the strangers Dominic killed. "I want not to," I finally say.

She nods as if she was expecting that answer. "It's a start."

CHAPTER ELEVEN

I kneel next to my family's mass grave and place my hands in the dirt, trying to get one last connection with them. So quickly, I was orphaned and then abandoned by my only other relative. How did it come to this?

I rub the dirt through my fingers, trying to memorize the feeling. With my clean hand, I hold the photo of my mother cradling me as a baby. So many of her features are echoed through my face. Seeing her young makes it even more apparent. This comparison makes the devastation of her loss slightly easier to bear. She's still with me, as long as I remember.

I carefully put the picture back in my bag and examine their final resting place again. The garden is so beautiful with sunflowers naturally growing around their grave. By next year, the mound of dirt will shrink down and be covered by the flowers. They would've liked it.

At least they have each other.

"Ready?" Jess's tender voice asks.

I nod my head and stand back up. It's time to move forward and focus on what's to come. Without speaking, we make our way to the lake. Just as we did earlier, I help her into the canoe. She seems to sense my desire to stay with my thoughts and doesn't try to make conversation.

Slower than necessary, I row across the cove to delay having to hold a conversation a little bit longer. The farther away I get from my grandparents' cabin, the deeper I push the emotional turmoil inside. It's too painful to deal with. I'm not strong enough.

I hope one day I'm able to revisit my grandparents' cabin, but for now, I'm thankful Jess had the good sense to get me out.

Another catcall greets us when we get within sight of Chris and Andrew's house.

"Are they always like this?" Jess looks unsure as to how to react to them.

With one last shove to the pain, I laugh quietly at her reaction. "They're just giving me a hard time right now. I'm sure the jokes will die down. It's just that I've never really, well, brought a girl back."

Jess chuckles.

I keep babbling, "Not that anything is going on or anything like that, but you know, they're just making fun of me. I know it's not like that or anything. I mean, there's a disaster going on."

I have to resist the urge to jump in the water and swim away.

"Elliot?" Jess interrupts.

I'm so grateful she ended my embarrassment. "Yes?"

"Stop talking," Jess says, amused.

Heat flows to my ears. The water has never looked so tempting.

"About time ya'll showed up," Chris calls out when we get closer.

"I never would've guessed our Elliot would've needed so much time," Andrew says.

Both of them wade out into the lake to pull our boat to the shore. Jess jumps out the moment she can. She's not going to feel comfortable in the water anytime soon.

"I'll teach you how to swim when you're ready," I whisper to Jess. She nods slightly in recognition of my promise.

"They ain't lyin'? You actually brought a girl over?" Carly's young voice rings out and interrupts us. She walks down the steps from their back door. Just like her brothers, her dark hair has grown since the last time I saw her. Her awkward years seem to be leaving her. She's going to be really pretty when she gets older.

"Hi, Carly. This is Jess," I introduce the two of them.

"It's been so long since I've seen another girl in the house. It's just been me and these boys." She squeals in excitement and her hazel eyes are still wide in shock. "I really thought they was lyin'."

"That hurts our feelin's. We're a lot of fun," Chris says.

Carly gives him a look that forces me to bite my tongue so I don't laugh.

"Yeah," Carly says. "So much fun."

"It's nice to meet you, too," Jess says with a chuckle.

Andrew rolls his eyes at his sister's enthusiasm. I can't help but smile. This all feels so normal and far away from the pain that occurred across the cove.

"The boys'll get everythin' inside." Carly closes the gap between her and Jess. "I'll give you a tour of our house. It ain't much," Carly admits. After a couple steps toward the house, she motions for Jess to follow her.

"I guess I'm going inside," Jess says, clearly entertained. She follows Carly's excited strut.

When she reaches Andrew, he whispers something to her that I don't catch. Jess nods slightly and goes inside. Andrew shakes his head in response to my wordless question.

When the front door closes and both of them are inside, Andrew says, "We haven't told her yet."

"What? How could you not tell her what's going on?" I look at both of them in disbelief.

"We don't wanna scare her," Chris says. "It's been rough since our parents died and she's finally smilin' again. I don't wanna take away her happiness if we don't have to."

"Why does she think we're staying here?" I don't know how we're going to keep this lie up.

"We told her you've come for a visit to introduce Jess to us," Chris says.

"What's she going to say when she sees all the food we brought?" I question the two of them.

"You're just being a real good houseguest?" Chris says in an attempt to lighten the mood.

"Listen, Elliot," Andrew says. "I know this ain't a long-term strategy, but we'll tell her when the time is right. Besides, it ain't really you or Jess's place to tell her about everythin'. Go along with it. Make sure Jess understands the next time you speak with her."

"I'll let her know, but I don't agree with the two of you. Carly has a right to know," I say.

"I know, just not yet. Let her enjoy life a lil' longer," Chris says.

I shrug. "Okay. Let's bring everything inside and pull the boat out a little more. I don't want it to drift off."

"Always so demanding."

I roll my eyes at Chris. There shouldn't have been so much time since I last saw them.

"I'm sorry I haven't been back since the funeral," I say with some emotion behind my words. "I should've been here more. I know it has been a rough time and I haven't been a really good friend."

"It's been hard on all of us," Andrew says. "There's really no need to apologize, though. You have your own life to worry about. I'm glad we're together now."

On this rare occasion, he's serious. The three of us pick up the boat and move it farther up the beach. With all of us lifting it, it's easy to transport.

"Let's move it over into our garage. We've room for it," Chris says.

I have a bad hold on the boat so I switch my grip. We journey to the garage in silence. Thankfully, the door is already open so we simply place the boat down in the corner. I grab a couple of the bags of food and Andrew and Chris take the rest. We have a short hike up to the front door from the detached garage.

"You really think we need all of this? I mean, how bad can it really be?" Chris asks.

"This might be the end of society as we know it. From what I understand, everything is going to change," I say.

"Well, good riddance is what I've got to say," Andrew says. "It didn't seem to care much about me anyway."

Chris nods in agreement.

"You're happy about this?" I ask. It seems like a bizarre thing to say. It's all we've ever known.

"I wouldn't say I'm 'happy' about it really, but it's just what it is. Sometimes, life falls apart and all we can do is try our best to pick up the pieces," Andrew says.

I don't think either of them really understands what's going on out there. I don't even truly comprehend what's happening. It's one thing to hear about it and a whole different thing to actually witness your grandmother kill your mother.

We reach their house, farther from the beach than my grandparents' cabin. I'm about to walk in the door when Chris places a hand on my shoulder to hold me back. "Remember, don't tell her what you told us." He stares at me intently.

I nod and open the door. Even though I know their parents are dead, I still expect to see them here. It's weird not seeing their mother offer us food or their father reading by the fireplace. If it's like this for me, it must have been really hard for them to stay here. I'm grateful Jess had us leave my grandparents' cabin. If they had the chance, I wonder if they would've moved.

"Come on, let's put all of this in the closet by the kitchen. It'll be fine there for now," Andrew says.

We walk into the kitchen and start packing the food away. We were fortunate that my grandparents had a lot of canned fruit.

Between the three of us, it's cramped in the kitchen. However, the familiarity we have with each other keeps it from being awkward.

After so long in Potentia with the society members I can't relate to, it's refreshing to be around people who understand me. "I'm glad to be with the two of you right now."

Andrew clasps my shoulder and looks me in the eye. "I'm so sorry about your mom and grandparents, Elliot. They was incredibly kind people and I wish you would've had more time with 'em."

"It just feels like…" My voice cracks. I cough and try again. "It feels like my life has shattered."

Chris nods and says, "I know it does. It may seem unthinkable now, but it'll get better. The pain never fully leaves. It's always with you. However, you'll start to focus on all of the good memories and realize how lucky you was to have 'em in your life in the first place."

I fight back the emotion from the loss. I look up at the ceiling to avoid eye contact.

"I wish I could talk to my mother one last time. I can't even remember what the last thing I said to her was. I want one last memory with her so I don't see my grandmother ripping into her throat anymore."

I close my eyes as the image of her blood spraying on the walls replays in my mind.

"It's gonna be very hard," Chris admits. "You gotta be strong enough to get through this, though."

Only because I've known them for my whole life, I'm able to admit my biggest fear. "What if I'm not?"

Andrew shrugs and replies, "You're gonna have to be."

I take a closer look at the two of them and am so thankful they're with me right now. Jess expresses who I can be and Andrew and Chris are my anchors to remind me where I come from. We're the orphans of society.

We move out of the cramped closet and sit down at the small kitchen table. Similar to my grandparents' cabin, there is a large window that allows us to look out to the water.

Chris looks curiously at me and changes the topic. "I know we've messed around with you, but are you and Jess gonna wanna share a room? I don't know how we'd explain that to Carly."

"We're just friends," I say. "We only just met."

My cheeks betray me once again and I blush. Both of them laugh openly at my embarrassment.

"Right, well you can put your stuff in our parents' old room," Andrew says. I shoot him a startled look. "I know, it's a lil' weird, but it's the only other room we have. Chris and I share our room. We'll have Jess bunk in with Carly. I'm sure our sister will love it."

"Are you sure?" He's right. It's a little weird for me to sleep in their parents' old bed. There's a reason why Andrew and Chris still share a room even after all this time.

"Absolutely," Chris says. "It's not gettin' much use anyway. Go ahead and move your stuff in there. We'll go make sure Carly hasn't bored Jess to death yet."

"Speaking of Jess"—I haven't heard so much as a noise from either of them—"where are they?"

"I would bet in the basement," Andrew says. "Probably in Carly's room."

I set my bag down and walk down the stairs to the basement. I've never known Carly to be quiet.

Behind me, Andrew says, "They're fine. Why you so worked up about it?"

I ignore him and take the steps two at a time. I can't answer his question. I don't know why I'm this worried.

I reach the floor to find Carly's door closed. I knock and let out a sigh of relief when Jess says, "Come in."

I open the door. Carly looks at Jess with slight annoyance. "Why'd you tell him to come in? This a girl zone."

"Oh, Elliot is fine, isn't he? He isn't one of your stinky brothers," Jess teases. I raise an eyebrow at Jess. This is yet another side to her.

"I guess not," Carly says. "What you want?" She directs her attention to me.

I'm a little taken aback. "I guess nothing really. I was just checking in to make sure the two of you were okay."

"We're okay. I was just showin' her all of my things. We was talkin' about girl stuff," Carly says.

"Talk about anything good?" I ask.

A smile plays on Jess's lips when she says, "You know—girl stuff."

"Right, well I'll leave you two to your girl time." I give both of them a small smile and head back upstairs. Andrew and Chris wait for me on the main level.

"I take it they're okay?" Andrew asks. I nod sheepishly. Their response is open laughter.

"What a shockin' turn of events," Chris exclaims.

"According to Carly, they're talking about 'girl stuff.'"

"I've no idea what that means and honestly, I don't think I even wanna know," Chris says.

"Why so curious, Elliot? Do you think they're talkin' about you?" Andrew asks.

I don't mind their teasing. It may embarrass me sometimes, but I've always felt this is how real brothers were supposed to act. They poke fun at each other, but at the end of the day, support one another.

"I'm going to go put my stuff in…" I pause. I don't know what to call the room. "Where I'm going to sleep."

They exchange a glance, drawing attention to my insensitivity for almost bringing up their parents again.

I walk down the hallway to the master bedroom. I've never actually been in their room before. It always felt like it would be an invasion of privacy if I went in here when they were alive. Even though they're dead, it still feels the same way.

I grit my teeth and pull the door open. It's obvious no one has been here in awhile. It feels like I'm intruding upon their space. A film of dust covers all the furniture in the room.

I set my stuff down by the bed and pull out the photo of my mother holding me. I gather strength from the image. Fresh grief compels me to take a seat on the bed as I reexamine every detail. Once I'm confident I could draw the photo if I had to, I put it back and grab my belongings.

When I place my bag on the bed, some dust floats up in the air. Slightly disgusted, I carefully remove the blanket from the bed and walk out of the room. I run into Jess.

"Oh," she exclaims in surprise. I drop the comforter to steady her.

"Sorry about that. Are you all right?" My arms remain on her shoulders for a little bit longer than necessary.

"I'm fine," Jess says.

She looks a little dazed and embarrassed. I'm not used to her being the one displaying those emotions.

"Well, good," I say. I stand there awkwardly for a moment. "I'm just going outside to shake out the blanket a little bit. Do you want to go into this room?"

"No, I was looking for you. I'll follow you outside," Jess says.

I pick the blanket back up as Jess motions for me to lead the way. I walk more slowly down the hall than I did the first time. Pictures of the five of them fill the walls. I've never been a big fan of staged family photos. They always seem to be a lie. For a long time, my own family portrait decorated our living room. The picture showed the four of us smiling. We were seemingly happy. The month after it was taken, my father left us and our family was broken.

I close my eyes for a moment to visualize the photo of my mother I just safely put back. I take comfort in the revelation that she planned for me and reopen my eyes to reality.

I open the front door and step outside. I hit the blanket a few times so the dust falls.

"That's gross," Jess says.

I can't help but laugh. "I know. Hopefully this gets most of the dust off," I say while I continue to shake it out. I stop once the dust finishes filling the air.

"Come with me down to the water. I want to put my feet in," Jess says. I place the blanket on top of one of the benches on the porch.

"Lead the way." I'm surprised she wants to go in the water.

We reach the shore and she takes her shoes off to step in. I follow her lead.

"They were thinking about having you share a room with Carly," I say. Her face becomes expressionless. Her mask is in complete control.

I get nervous and continue, "I know she can be a little much. She's still so young. But if you don't want to share a room with her, you can have the master bedroom and I'll sleep on the couch in the living room."

"I'll share a room with Carly," Jess says. She turns her body away from me and stares out at the sunset.

"Are you sure? I don't mind the couch. I don't want you to be bothered by her," I say.

"She isn't going to bother me."

I've always viewed Carly as a minor annoyance and I assumed she would as well. I admire the sunset with her. It seems so peaceful. It's unsettling that everything has fallen apart when it all appears so perfect here.

"They don't want to tell Carly what's going on. That's ridiculous." She turns to me suddenly in anger.

I sigh and look away from the sunset, focusing on Jess's true reason for wanting to speak with me. "They think they're protecting her."

"Protecting her?" Jess repeats in disbelief. "If she doesn't understand the danger she's in, how can she be protected?"

"I agree with you, but I also understand their side," I say. "They've been through a lot lately and they don't want to put her through another ordeal."

"Reality doesn't care what people want," Jess says. The bitterness in her tone is the same as when she told me about her history.

"She has four people to protect her. We're in a safe place. It's a different situation than the one with your brother."

Jess shrugs. I don't push her and instead change the subject.

"Where do you think everyone is?"

"What do you mean?" she asks.

"We can't be the only people left. How come we haven't seen more people? Infected or not," I say. At moments like this, when there are no other people in sight, it's easy to imagine us being some of the last people in the world.

"I've been thinking about it as well. I know we're secluded, but I would've thought we'd have run into other life," Jess says.

"Do you think everyone is dead?" Maybe if I say it quietly enough, it won't be a possibility.

"There have to be other people. They just aren't around us," she says. "Don't worry, we'll find more people. One way or the other."

"No matter what, I'm glad you're here with me," I say.

She turns her head toward me and offers a half smile. "Me, too."

The sun falls farther down. The light fades rapidly so the two of us make our way back to the front door. I grab my blanket and we enter our new home.

CHAPTER TWELVE

I yawn at the breakfast table from not having slept well this last week. It feels like I spend hours worrying about the future before I'm finally able to drift off into an uneasy sleep. Dominic always enters my dreams and twists them into nightmares. It's only during the day with Jess that I'm finally able to relax.

"I can't wait for school to start back up. I can't believe it keeps gettin' pushed back. I miss my friends," Carly says.

Jess shoots Andrew a nasty look when he says, "Don't worry, lil' sister, they'll reopen in no time. It's just takin' 'em longer to fix the plumbin' issue than they thought. You don't wanna go to a school that smells like poop, do you?"

She makes a disgusted face.

They still haven't told her what's going on. The timing was fortunate because in Accidia, their education takes second priority to maintaining the produce requests from the different territories. Because of the season, the education system was suspended when the infection spread.

Jess expresses her disapproval over this every chance she gets, but so far, the two of us have kept our mouths shut, as promised. I don't know how much longer Jess will be able to do this. Besides, Carly is a smart kid, and deep down she knows something is going on.

"I'm not worried," she says. "I just miss my friends from school. I don't understand why I can't go and see 'em."

"Because we've guests over, that's why," Chris says. "It'd be rude if you left while they're visitin'."

"But Jess don't mind. Do you, Jess?"

She puts her hands up in retreat. "I'm not getting involved."

Carly gives her an annoyed look and turns her attention to me. "Do you care, Elliot?"

"This is up to your brothers, not me," I reply along the same lines as Jess. I'm not as passionate about this as Jess is, but I still am getting more and more annoyed that they haven't told her yet.

Carly throws up her arms in anger. "Ya'll are unreasonable. I'm old enough to visit my friends when I wanna. Besides, Jess and Elliot been here for a week. They don't actually care if I'm gone for an hour."

"I'll tell you what. When you grow up, you can make those decisions. Until then, you have to listen to us," Andrew says. His voice rises in anger.

"You think that just because Mom and Dad died, you have all this power, but you don't. You're not them. You're not my parents," she says.

Carly stands up abruptly from the table and storms out of the room.

"Ya'll should've backed us up there," Chris says when her door slams in the basement. He looks dejected.

"You two should have told her what's going on," Jess snaps back. "She needs to know."

"I know we need to tell her eventually. Honestly, we haven't seen any of 'em. The longer the time goes on, the more it seems like it's all make believe," Chris admits as he drops eye contact.

"You need to tell her," Jess repeats.

The two brothers exchange a glance full of conflicting emotions. I understand where they're coming from, but I can't unsee the things I've witnessed. They have to prepare her.

"If you don't tell her tonight, I will," Jess says. I nod in agreement and both of them look at me in betrayal.

Andrew and Chris make eye contact for a long time before Andrew finally nods. "We'll tell her tomorrow when she wakes up, I promise. I wanna let her have at least a one more day to think everything is okay."

"Tomorrow," Chris says.

I look over at Jess. She appears to be pleased with the outcome of the conversation. I can't blame her. It has become more difficult each day to lie to Carly and pretend we're just here for a visit. The hardest part was when she asked where my mother was. Chris came to my rescue and told

Carly she was busy at work, but I was able to come due to a quick break before a major project at school.

"Today is going to be the day I learn how to swim," Jess says, changing the subject. "Elliot, will you teach me as soon as we're done with breakfast?"

"Of course," I say. "Why today?"

Jess shrugs. "Why not?"

I don't have an argument for that. "As soon as we're done with breakfast," I say.

"Well, don't mind us," Chris says.

"Yeah, I guess we'll just hang out by ourselves," Andrew says.

Jess rolls her eyes. "You two are obviously more than welcome to join us."

"I thought you'd never ask," Chris says.

This time, I'm the one who rolls my eyes at them. I chuckle and finish my meal. It's nothing special, but it's at least something to eat. The food packets are long gone, so we've been eating the spare produce. This morning, we had canned dried fruit. I stand up and grab everyone's plates and place them in the sink.

"I'll meet you all down by the water in ten minutes," I say.

Jess nods and stands up from the table. "Okay, I'll go get ready." Her hands shake and she takes a deep breath to steady herself.

"No need to be scared, Jess," Chris says in an apparent attempt to help calm her.

"He's right. We'll go get some arm floaties for you," Andrew teases.

Andrew and Chris laugh loudly. Jess shoots me a look, warning me not to laugh, but it has the opposite effect. I can't help myself. I chuckle.

Her mouth twitches in amusement so I know she isn't actually mad. Sensing this is a good time to make my exit, I leave the kitchen and head toward my room.

I change into my bathing suit and carefully place my precious photograph of my mother into the top drawer. I want to keep it safe.

I hear a knock on the door. I automatically reach for a shirt to cover my chest. The memory of Jess seeing my scars crosses my mind. They're something I've always hidden in shame, but she accepted them. If she didn't care, surely Chris and Andrew wouldn't either. I'm tired of living my whole life hiding it. There's no need to be ashamed.

I release my grip on the shirt. It remains in the drawer.

Full of newfound confidence, I call out, "Come in."

The door swings open and Jess walks into my room. She appears to be calm, but her eyes betray her inner conflict.

I furrow my eyebrows at her demeanor.

"Why are you so anxious?" I suspect the answer.

"You know why." She purses her lips. "Just promise me you'll keep me safe."

"Of course I won't let anything bad happen to you," I say. I hope she understands that I'm implying more than just the swimming lesson. It's amazing how quickly she's become an important part of my life. Her presence is what I've always needed.

She lets out a deep breath and relaxes. The anxiety retreats deeper into her eyes. It's still present, though not as close to the surface as it just was.

"I have a problem," she says. I nod in encouragement so she continues. "I don't have a bathing suit."

I laugh at this apparent oversight. I took mine from my grandparents' cabin before we left, but obviously packing a bathing suit was never a priority for Jess when she escaped from Vis.

"Can you borrow one of Carly's?"

She gives me an incredulous look and I backtrack instantly.

"Okay, so maybe that isn't a good solution."

"First of all, I'm almost a foot taller than she is. There is no way it would fit. I would look ridiculous," she says. A smile finds my face at the image. Her eyes narrow and my smile quickly disappears. "Secondly, I don't want to see Carly right now. I don't trust myself not to tell her the truth."

I let out a deep breath and try to release some of the tension from the situation of having to keep this major secret from her. "At least they finally agreed to let her know in the morning. I wonder how she's going to react."

"Once the shock wears off, she's going to be upset that we've all been lying to her this whole time," Jess says. "Is it weird if I look to see if their mother's bathing suit is still here?"

If it felt like I was crossing a line going into their room, this is going to feel even worse. "It's a little weird."

I examine Jess's body in calculation.

"I don't see the harm in looking. She was shorter than you and slightly heavier, but definitely a closer fit than anything you would find in Carly's room," I say.

The two of us go to the dresser and search for a bathing suit. After about a minute of searching, I touch material that feels right. I wrap my fingers around it and pull out two pieces. I hand them over. "This is it," I say.

Jess takes the suit and examines it for a moment. "No matter what, don't laugh at me when I get it on."

"I can make no such promise," I say.

"Of course you can't," she says with slight amusement in her voice. "Turn around and face the wall. I'm just going to change here. I don't want to have to walk all the way to the bathroom."

"It's about twenty feet away," I protest.

"Just turn around," Jess repeats.

I follow her command and turn away from her. Her clothes hit the ground and I'm thankful she can't see my face because I'm blushing again.

"Why didn't you ever learn how to swim?" I attempt to distract myself from the sound of fabric gliding across her skin.

"I was never really exposed to swimming. It just wasn't something that was taught at school. My father was too busy drinking to teach me when I was younger, and my mother was too focused on keeping him happy. It just never happened," Jess says. I can almost see her shrug at the end.

"That's a shame."

"It's just what it is. Can you help me tie the top of this bathing suit? I can't reach it," Jess asks.

"Sure," I say. I shift my body and have her back in my sights. Her right hand holds up the top of the suit. I blink as I take in her level of exposure. Her body is lined with lean muscles. She must have excelled in all of her physical fitness courses.

I walk closer and she turns her body away from me. Her hair hides the strings so I carefully move her hair to the side. I tie the string into a knot and take a step back.

"Thanks, Elliot," Jess says.

I examine the suit. The bottom part is baggy and runs the risk of slipping down once we hit the water. The top is a similar story. It covers her stomach and chest but simply doesn't fit. I can't help myself. I lie.

"It looks good on you." I break out in a smile.

A grin plays at Jess's face before winning out and shining through. Her entire face lights up when she smiles.

"You're an ass, Elliot," she says. "Let's get in the water before Chris and Andrew see this. I'm counting on being deep enough where it isn't as obvious." She places her clothes on top of the drawer.

"We better hurry then. We don't want them to see you in all of your glory," I tease back.

I motion for her to lead the way out. She purses her lips and exits the room. When she gets in front of me, it takes all of my energy to keep from laughing again. The bathing suit was made for someone with a completely different body. Despite that, she really does look good.

"I can feel you looking at me. I know I look ridiculous." Jess laughs slightly. I cough in embarrassment.

When we pass the stairs to the basement, there are knocks against Carly's door.

Chris calls out, "We're gonna be down by the water. Join us when you're done poutin' and we can go fishin' later."

"I'm sure she'll complain all about this later when I'm trying to go to sleep," Jess says without breaking her stride.

"Does she annoy you? The offer still stands. You can take my room," I remind her. We reach the door and break free of the house. The sun instantly warms my skin.

Jess looks back at me with a serious expression. "She doesn't annoy me. She's just a typical younger sibling," she says. Her attention returns to the water.

The two of us walk in silence for the remaining distance. I wonder what it's like to have a younger sibling and to be responsible for protecting them. Admittedly, Dominic never cared much for me, but we never had the relationship that siblings should. Carly is probably the closest I had to a little sister growing up.

"Does Carly remind you of your brother?"

"No," she says. She looks deep in thought. "Personality wise, they're completely different. My brother was a lot more reserved and tentative.

He never had the chance to discover his confidence." Jess sighs and smiles ruefully. "She does remind me of what it's like to have that relationship, though."

"What's it like to have a younger sibling?" I'm fascinated to hear what she has to say, to understand how Dominic should have treated me in another life.

She considers her response. "Overall, it's absolutely amazing. There's this little person that's so connected to you and you're able to help them and ensure they have the best life possible. You do everything you can to make sure they don't make the same mistakes you did." She pauses. "Of course, they can get a little tiring at times." She smiles to herself.

"Interesting," I say. I don't have any other words. I try to imagine a world where Dominic cared that much about me. It's unfathomable.

A new glint of amusement shines through her eyes. "You know she has a crush on you, right?"

I stagger and stop walking. She laughs at my reaction.

"That's ridiculous. She's so young."

She grabs ahold of my arm and pulls me along. "She hasn't directly said it, but it's obvious in the way she talks about you. Why are you so surprised?" Before I can respond, she continues, "You're the most consistent male in her life that she isn't related to."

"But I'm Unplanned," I remind her.

The idea of someone, even as young and naïve as Carly, harboring any of those types of feelings—or at least thinking she does—seems ridiculous.

Now that I'm moving by myself, Jess stops pulling. Yet she keeps her arm tucked in mine, our skin touching.

"So is she, Elliot. Besides, you're from Potentia. She's really romanticized the idea of the territories."

While she's fantasized about living where I grew up, I have done the same with Accidia. Who was right?

"Do I need to say anything to her?" I ask. I'm not sure how to handle this.

Once again Jess laughs at my panic. "Don't act any differently. This is something she will grow out of." She tilts her head and winks. "Or not."

I jokingly nudge her with my shoulder. We laugh together for the rest of the short walk to the beach, Jess humming contently.

We stop right in front of the water and she takes a deep breath. "I'm going to get in now."

"I'm right here with you," I say in a voice I intend to be soothing.

Our feet break the surface. Jess determinedly walks forward, deeper and deeper into the lake. I'm a little surprised when the water hits her waist. I'm shocked when she lets it rise to her chest.

"This is deep enough," I say. I want her feet to still be able to touch the ground if she needs to.

"The boys will join us any second and I don't think I can suffer the humiliation of having them see me in this wretched suit," she says.

She might be slightly terrified of water, but she's more afraid of losing her pride.

"Good call," I say. "The jokes would never end."

Jess splashes water toward me while a smile overtakes her face. I love it when her mask disappears and she truly smiles. I lower completely and the water feels amazing on the top of my head. I stay under for a few seconds and make my way closer to where Jess is standing. I pop out and spit water at her.

Her laughter fills the air and mine easily joins in. It's my favorite kind of duet.

"What's so funny?" Andrew's voice interrupts the moment.

"Did our boy Elliot have a wardrobe mess up?"

"You shouldn't laugh at him. I imagine it'd be quite embarrassin'," Andrew says.

"Well, you would know," I counter back. Admittedly, it isn't my best comeback.

Andrew and Chris sprint into the water and reach us very quickly. Reluctantly, I look away from Jess. Both of them eye my chest and the angry red scar that stares back at them. I always hid it from them growing up, even going as far as to make sure I always swam with a shirt on.

"What happened there?" Chris asks.

"Just an old injury," I say, trying to make it seem like it's nothing important. They look expectantly at me hoping for more of a story. I gaze right back at them. It's not something that's worth talking about.

"The water feels amazin' today," Andrew says to change the subject. He dives under. When he breaks the surface, water droplets fall freely from his long nose.

Chris looks excitedly to Jess. "Time to teach you how to swim," he says.

"You two can show me by example," Jess says. Both of them look confused. "Let me watch the two of you swim off. I learn by watching."

I chuckle at their expressions when they realize what she's really asking.

"Well, if that's the way it is," Chris says.

"We don't wanna interrupt anythin'. We'll go 'swim off' then," Andrew says in good humor. They splash us when they swim away. I watch their figures get smaller and smaller before returning my attention to Jess.

"Now, where do we start?" she asks and stares intently at me.

"First off, I'm going to get you on your back," I say.

Andrew screams out, "I bet he's been wantin' to say that for awhile."

Chris and Andrew laugh loudly.

Jess raises one eyebrow and smirks at their joke. My cheeks flush.

"I mean," I stammer, "I want you to learn how to float and be comfortable in the water."

Her eyes narrow and the uneasiness returns. "Why do I have to start with that?"

I shrug. I'm not really sure. "It's how my grandfather taught me when I was younger. Just trust me."

"You'll hold me?" Anxiety creeps through her voice.

"Of course." I step closer to her.

Even though she clearly doesn't want to, she lets me take her legs out from under her to get her to float.

"Relax," I say.

Her body is so tense. I keep my hands under her bare back and apply slight pressure to keep her above water.

I don't say anything. I watch her body as she visibly unwinds, her sharp features relaxing. The tension appears to escape her body through the water. Her suit top is loose and floats in the water, revealing her stomach. She has a small freckle next to her belly button.

"If I ignore the panicky feeling in my chest," Jess says, snapping my attention back to her face, "the water actually feels pretty nice."

She closes her eyes. The sun on her face highlights her scattered freckles.

"It does."

I let her enjoy the water for a little bit longer and then say, "I'm going to slowly take my hands away. Just concentrate on staying above the water. I'll be right here."

She doesn't argue so I follow through on my words. Her body tenses up and she slightly sinks. I'm just about to replace my hands when she forces herself to relax and steadies herself.

"Good job," I say. "You're doing it by yourself."

A smile touches her lips. I can't help but return her happiness and smile down at her.

A scream pierces through the silence. Both of our smiles disappear instantly. I turn in reaction to the noise and she splashes right next to me. My attention returns to Jess in time for her to flail under the water. I bring her back to her feet.

"Where'd that come from?" Andrew's raised voice is absolutely panicked. Another scream reaches us.

Without another word, the four of us run to shore. My thighs burn with the effort of pushing through the water.

Ahead of all of us, Jess sprints fastest toward the sound of the last scream. I pound the ground and push through my endurance to keep up. We run past the house and into the congestion of forest. The trees block the sun and my eyes adjust to sudden darkness. A sharp rock pokes into my foot, but I ignore it. I need to find the person the screams are attached to.

I almost run into Jess when she stops suddenly.

"Oh, shit," she mutters.

My heart drops when the smell hits my nose. The overwhelming odor of death and the fresher, metallic scent of a recent injury fill the air. I fear what I'm about to see. I don't want to look at the scene in front of me.

One of the creatures is relentlessly digging its hand in someone's stomach. Its discolored hands return to its greedy mouth and grab intestines out of the small body. The fresh blood drips down its chin and arms to stain its torn, discolored territory outfit. My stomach turns. I follow the mangled torso to the head. Familiar dark hair is attached to the small, broken body.

Andrew and Chris run past us with expressions of pure horror on their faces.

"Don't get any closer. There isn't anything you can do," Jess says. Her voice cracks in pain. Jess grabs each of their arms and holds them back from interrupting its frenzied meal.

"Is that…" Chris trails off. He turns his head to me in shock. The same color hair flips across his face.

"NO!" Andrew's wail of torment infiltrates my daze and shock. Unfortunately, it also distracts the infected from its meal and it notices us. It lifts its head in blank perception, showing its missing bottom lip. The remaining skin-flaps move sickeningly in the effort. Carly's blood escapes its mouth and falls back into her violated body.

I quickly scan the ground and find a thick branch. I pick it up and walk toward the creature before it can move toward us. It has to be stopped.

While the bone structure of the creature would have once given promise to a healthy, strong male, this new disease has stolen almost all of its strength and reflexes. I knock it off of Carly's dead body and pummel its head with my branch. For all I know, it could have been a fellow classmate from Potentia. There is nothing distinguishable in its face now, and with every hit, any hope of recognition is obliterated further. I slam the branch into its head so many times I lose track. Blood sprays up and hits my face. The image of my best friends' little sister being eaten haunts me.

I've known her since she was a strange little baby that Andrew and Chris proudly showed off. She was completely innocent. She didn't deserve this. No one does.

My arms tire. I ignore the pain and keep swinging down into its now concave skull, its wispy hair coated in brown gore. Blood covers the ground and forms a slimy glaze on my body.

"Enough," Jess says. Her voice gently distracts me from my frenzied attack. "It's over."

I summon all my strength and slam down one more time. The branch breaks. My body falls with my weapon to my hands and knees. The tears flowing down my face surprise me. Where did they come from?

"What happened?" Andrew says between his sobs.

"One of those things we told you about got to her," Jess says. I can barely hear her. The pain is too deafening. "She left the house."

"How's she dead?"

No one answers Chris. I blankly stare at her lifeless body. Another tear drops down, but I refuse to acknowledge it. I'm afraid if I wipe it away and admit that I'm crying, I'll lose control completely. There's too much death now. It isn't supposed to be like this.

"This is our fault," Andrew says, voice full of pain and emotion. "We're her brothers. We should've told her."

"No," Jess says. "You were trying to protect her. She had two amazing brothers who were simply trying to preserve her innocent outlook on life for as long as possible. This isn't your fault."

Her statement breaks my attention away from the corpse of my first kill, done too late, and brings it to her. I'm surprised to see tears falling down her face as well while she holds on to the shocked brothers.

She looks at me and realizes my attention is on her. Without another word, she stands up and walks over to me. Chris and Andrew stare forward at the scene in disbelief once she leaves them. She grabs my hand and the two of us support each other, desperately trying to ignore the two mutilated bodies next to us.

CHAPTER THIRTEEN

My arms tire from the weight of Carly's body. I limp slightly from the cut in my foot, but I push through. The physical pain is a distraction from the emotional agony that I can't escape. I can't get away from the anguish.

I'm the one who volunteered to go get her body, although there really wasn't much of an option. Andrew and Chris are both in shock and I left Jess to watch after them. Truth is, though, I wanted to be alone.

With every step, the pain gets worse. I welcome it. I savor it. It's the only thing that keeps my sanity intact. I should have protected her, but instead she was brutally killed. The guilt threatens to devour me. Where is my breaking point? How much loss can I take before I don't care anymore? I worry I'm getting close to my threshold. First my mother and grandparents, and now Carly.

For some reason, Carly's death strikes a different cord. She was so young, so innocent. She hadn't even lived yet. Her life was so full of possibility and promise but instead, there is nothing for her anymore. Her life peaked without anyone knowing it. Her screams haunt me and push me deeper into the darkness. Why is this happening?

If I'm this disturbed by witnessing the aftermath of her death, I can't imagine how Andrew and Chris must feel right now. There's truly no coming back from that, especially so soon after they lost their parents. There are too many horrifying images that disturb my mind. It's overwhelming. My mother. My grandparents. Carly. How did we get here? Society is supposed to be so advanced to protect us from Death. Yet here he is, claiming the ones I care about.

Every other death I've known about, even Ian's younger sister—though that seems like a lifetime ago—was affecting someone else. It was sad to witness, but it wasn't my family. The sadness that I felt was almost secondhand. It was a terrible thing to happen, of course, but the people I cared about were still healthy. My world was still intact.

The view of the house gets closer and I can make out three shapes waiting for me. The sun sets behind them so I can't see their faces. I shift the weight in my arms to get temporary relief. The shadows move toward me, closing the gap between us.

Jess is the first one to break the silence. "We're going to bury her back in the gardens."

"Okay." My voice cracks from misuse. It's fitting that they would want to put her in the gardens. After all, just recently we buried my family in one.

"Let me carry my lil' sister," Chris mutters, his voice full of heartbreak.

I nod and hand her over to him. I don't think I've ever been so gentle with anything in my life. The last thing I want to do is cause any more harm to her.

Chris caresses some hair out of the empty eyes. There is so much love and tenderness in one simple motion. Tears fall on her face. Wordlessly, Chris holds her tighter as he walks behind the house. Andrew follows with his shoulders slumped, dejected.

Jess and I stay put. I'm not sure if I have the emotional fortitude to fully prepare myself for this funeral. I would much rather lie in bed and go to sleep. It would be a wonderful escape from all of this pain.

Jess turns her head and we make eye contact. Her guard is down. She shows me all of her pain and hurt from today's events. Buried beneath the surface, however, is a fire of strength. Careful not to get burned, I take a deep breath and reach out for her hand. One step at a time.

We turn the corner and find Andrew holding Carly's body. Chris has broken the ground and is digging with an almost maniacal motion. I drop my eyes. This moment feels so personal. A flash of color catches my attention. I'm covered in blood. Some of it's darker and sprayed on me so it must have come from her killer. My chest is soaked with the fresh blood of Carly.

The sight panics me. I let go of Jess's hand and uselessly try to wipe it all off. It's only smearing and every attempt I make gets more and more frantic. I forget all about reality and focus on this task. I need it to come off. It has to get off my body.

"Elliot, you're fine. I'll help you get it off later." I vaguely hear her voice, but it doesn't break my trance. She doesn't understand. I can't have it cover my body for one more second.

A pressure begins on my back and reaches around to my chest. Jess's hands interlock on my chest and her face rests against my back. She's holding me together.

"Elliot, listen to me. We'll get it off afterward. Right now, we're going to bury Carly." The combination of her touch and voice brings me back to reality. I drop my hands and let them fall to my side.

"I'm sorry." The desperation to get the blood off is still very strong and my hands twitch in need.

"Let's go help them," she says and motions for me to grab her hand again. I take hold and interlock my fingers with hers. I do my best to ignore the blood that has now spread to her arms and fresh white shirt she put on. My hand shakes and Jess tightens her grip in reaction.

We walk over to them. Chris has made a great deal of progress for such a short amount of time. Maybe it took us longer to join them than I thought.

"Take a break, Chris. I can finish up," I say. Sweat covers his body and his breathing is labored.

"No, I will," Andrew says. "The two of us oughtta be the ones to dig her grave."

Chris stops digging and puts the shovel down. "After all, we was the ones that put her there."

They switch places and Andrew takes over the digging while Chris holds her body.

The beauty of the setting sun contrasts with the situation. It seems like it could be such a peaceful, wonderful moment. I stare out at the sunset. There's so much that could have been in Carly's life—that should have been.

The sound of the shovel thrown on the ground snaps me out of my daze. The hole is ready.

"Let me see her one more time. Elliot, will you hold her for me?" Jess asks. I nod and Chris sets her in my arms.

Jess keeps her back to them and pulls out a small knife. "Just in case," she whispers and stabs her in the head. I cringe but do nothing else to betray what has just happened. She swipes Carly's hair to cover her new wound and stashes the knife back away.

I study Carly's face for the last time. She was going to turn into a beautiful woman. Her youthful weight was starting to leave and in its place, the promise of a healthy teenager remained. She could have done so much with her life and it frustrates me that she no longer has the option. I let the anger over this injustice smolder inside of me. There's no one to blame but us.

Jess leans down and finds a small bloodless spot on her forehead to kiss.

"You will be missed," she whispers. It's a short, accurate statement.

Her death makes an impact on all of us. It may not reach a large number of people but to the four of us, she was important and it matters that she's no longer with us.

I want to say something meaningful and heartfelt but instead, all I do is agree. "You will."

I carry her body over to the grave. Andrew and Chris have already gotten inside of the hole. I carefully kneel down. Together, we place her into her final resting place.

The grieving brothers crawl out of their sister's grave and push the dirt over her body. The last thing that pokes out of the dirt is her feet. They finish filling the hole and the four of us stare down at the mound of dirt. It's surreal.

Chris clears his throat. "I'm so sorry, Carly. I wish more than anything that we could've protected you. I'm never gonna be able to live with myself for what happened to you." At this, his voice breaks and sobs take over.

Andrew continues for him. "We're your older brothers and we was supposed to keep you safe. That was our one job. We failed you. You couldn't have been more loved." His voice fails and the two brothers comfort each other.

This is such a private moment between the two of them. Jess motions for me to leave with her. We make our way through the back door and enter the house through the kitchen. The last time I was in here was when Carly stormed out in anger.

"Let's go clean you off," Jess says, interrupting my thoughts. She reminds me of the blood that covers my body. My skin crawls. I fight the desire to rub it off.

"Please," I beg.

She leads me into the bathroom and turns the faucet on, followed by the showerhead. After a couple moments, I test the water and make sure it has heated up.

I look back at Jess. She hasn't left yet. I give her a questioning glance.

"Keep your bathing suit on. You're going to need help getting it all off," she says.

I step in the shower and am disgusted when I see the water turn red as the blood flows off of me. I can't help it anymore and rub my arms to get it off more quickly. Jess joins me in her unfitted bathing suit and wipes my back down with a washcloth.

"Turn around," she says.

I do so without thinking and her hands find my chest. The washcloth trails up and down. I keep my head lowered to watch the process. With every swipe, less blood remains. The red color of the water, falling gradually, turns more and more pink until finally, it's clear.

"Close your eyes," she says. She waits for me to comply and applies the steady pressure of the washcloth.

With my eyes closed, it's harder to keep my balance so I hold on to her waist. She feels so sturdy and healthy. It's reassuring to feel this evidence of life. It's a promise that everything isn't over yet.

"I'm going to get out while you finish up. I want to look at your foot when you're done," Jess says in my ear. I keep my eyes closed for a little bit longer and when I open them, she's out of the bathroom. Her wet footprints are the only evidence that she was here.

I untie my bathing suit shorts and let them drop. It feels refreshing to take them off and be clean. When I'm satisfied that all of the evidence of today's events are erased from my body, I turn off the water and grab a towel. I dry myself off and toss the bathing suit in the trash. I never want to wear it again.

With a clean towel wrapped around my waist, I make my way to the bedroom and am surprised to see Jess sitting on the bed. She looks exhausted. Her fire of strength from earlier has reduced to embers, still emitting heat, but not as bright.

"I'll look away while you put on some clothes," she says and turns to face the opposite wall. She's changed into one of my shirts.

I quickly find a pair of shorts and cover myself. I sit next to her on the bed and sigh.

She nods and says, "Let me look at your foot. You were limping earlier."

She gets off the bed and leans down to examine me. Her fingers probe and my foot jumps back in reaction.

"Do you remember what you did?" She tilts her head and looks at my foot.

"I vaguely remember stepping on a rock. I haven't really thought about it," I say.

"We need to clean it out and put a bandage over it. I don't want it to get infected."   The last word echoes throughout the room. "Do you think…"

I start.

She furrows her eyebrows in thought. "I believe you should be okay. I think it's transferred through saliva."

My heart races while I remember her previous explanation. "No, you said bodily fluids. That includes blood." I jerk my foot away and look around the room anxiously.

Her voice remains calm as she tells me, "Elliot, take a deep breath. There's no sense in worrying about something that may not happen." Her face doesn't betray any fear, and I relax at this.

I shake my head to dispel the thought of my being infected. I take a couple of deep breaths, as instructed, and start to feel better.

"We can clean it tomorrow," I say. "Honestly, I just want to go to bed and forget."

"First thing in the morning then. Let me know if you start to feel sick," she says.

I nod in agreement and her tone softens. "Can I stay in here tonight? I don't want to go down to her room."

"Of course. I can sleep on the couch," I say without hesitation.

She pauses before saying, "No, I want you to stay in here with me."

"Okay, you can have the bed. I'll take the floor."

"Dammit, Elliot. I want to share the bed tonight. I don't want to be alone," she says. She no longer sounds timid. Instead, she's annoyed.

"Oh," I say, "if that's what you want. Is that a good idea?" I gesture toward my foot.

Jess nods and gets under the covers. She gestures for me to join her.

Getting off my foot is a physical relief, but I can't escape what I saw today.

"Jess?" I ask, timid.

"Mmmm?" she mutters as she turns off the lamp.

"Did you look closely at it? It didn't have a lower lip anymore. Its bottom teeth were in a permanent grimace. It did that to itself, didn't it? When it was eating Carly?"

Exhaling a deep breath, Jess answers, "I would suspect that."

Every once in awhile, I'll accidentally bite the inside of my mouth when eating. It's always a sharp reminder to be more careful to prevent further pain. That creature was so far removed from its humanity, it lacked any sense of self-preservation and tore its own flesh away from its weapon—its teeth. How did we come to this?

Jess scoots close enough so her breath unevenly hits my cheek. "Hold me and tell me everything is going to be okay," she whispers.

I bring her to my chest. "Everything is going to be okay," I repeat to her even though I don't believe it.

There's no way it can be.

CHAPTER FOURTEEN

I wake up and unwillingly prepare myself to welcome the new day. I take stock in my health and am relieved I'm just as healthy as yesterday. Jess was right. I wasn't infected.

My arm aches from slamming the branch on the creature's head, over and over. I lie in bed and try to go back to sleep. I want to delay joining everyone for breakfast as long as possible. There's going to be such an obvious hole in our group. I roll over and stretch out. I don't hit anyone. My eyes open in alarm.

Rationally, I know she probably just got up before me, but I can't calm the storm of anxiety that has infiltrated my senses. I jump out of the bed. I come down hard on my right foot and cringe. Maybe I should have let Jess help me clean it last night.

I push that worry away and limp out of the room. Andrew and Chris sit in the living room. They look completely numb. Chris reacts slightly to my entrance but doesn't say anything.

"Have the two of you seen Jess?"

Slowly, Chris shakes his head and stares back into the void. My panic rises and I struggle to push it back down to a manageable level.

"I'm going to go look for her," I say as calmly as I can manage.

My shoes rest just outside the back door. I cram my feet into them quickly. Once again, there's a twinge of pain but I ignore it. My mind is too preoccupied with worry. I can't get rid of the overwhelming feeling that something is wrong. Images of Carly's mutilation won't stop passing through my head—her guts ripped from her body. That can't happen to Jess.

"Jess?" I call out. No one answers. I limp away from the lake and into the forest. I call out every thirty seconds or so. Every time silence answers me back, my dread grows and threatens to drown me.

Finally, I hear her voice. "Over here," she says.

Just like that, my unease disappears and relief takes its place. I make my way to her voice. She's kneeling, hair messily put up, and fumbling with something on the ground. A long strand of rope is behind her. Her body language is very tense.

"What are you doing?"

"I'm trying to make a snare. Although I'm not doing that great of a job," she says, dropping the rope in frustration. She looks up at me and I can see the torment in her eyes. She's barely holding on right now.

I lean down next to her and pick up the rope from the ground.

"What are you trying to catch?" I ask to focus the conversation on the snare. I haven't seen much game in the area since we got here.

"I don't know if 'catch' is the right word. I found some rope in their garage and I've been trying to set some traps so the creatures can't sneak up on us again. We were naïve to think we would be safe here," Jess says.

"It isn't going to stop them all." I play with the rope in my hands and test its strength.

"If we make enough, it can at least help," she says. "We're surrounded by water except for this section. We should make as many as we can." Her eyebrows are furrowed together as if she's fighting to keep her emotions in check. "Do you have any better ideas?"

I look around the forest and think. Ideally, we could build some sort of fence or wall, but that would take weeks. I shake my head. Sometimes, a weak plan is better than none at all.

"Let me show you how to make them," I tell her. She looks confused, so I answer her unspoken question. "My grandfather taught us when we were younger."

What would Dominic think about Carly's death? He probably wouldn't care.

"I thought I could figure it out on my own…" She trails off, taking my attention away from thoughts of my brother.

"It was a good start," I say. "Watch me do one. Okay?"

She nods.

In my head, I hear my grandfather's low, steady voice instructing me on all of the steps. I grab the rope and create a noose. I talk her through how to tie the knot and we gather rocks to weigh the trap down. Finally, I attach it to a small limb and step away from the finished product.

"This will hold as long as they don't put too much pressure on the rope. Once they walk through, they will set it off and become ensnared in the trap," I say.

I admit, I'm proud of myself. It's one of the better snares I've made.

"Let's make another one. This time, I'll watch you do it."

I stand up and unwillingly startle when I put more weight on my foot. Jess shoots me a concerned glance but doesn't say anything. She's too focused on the task at hand. The next trap goes a lot smoother than her earlier attempt. It falls apart once and the second time, she corrects her mistake.

Our morning passes with few words shared between us. As time goes on, I take her lead and focus solely on making as many snares as we can. It feels like if we can just make enough of them, we'll protect ourselves and bring Carly back. This irrational thought keeps me going. We just need to correct our mistake.

As we finish the last snare the rope allows us to make, my stomach grumbles loudly. I never ate breakfast this morning. The sun has fully risen and it's beating down on my neck. We've been out here for hours.

"We should head back," I say. "Andrew and Chris are probably wondering where we are. Besides, I'm pretty hungry."

I stand up and stretch. Jess does the same.

"Do you think…" she starts. Her voice is so quiet I can barely hear her. She clears her throat. "Do you think if we had done this before she wouldn't have been killed?"

I breathe deeply and consider my answer. "It's possible," I say.

Her eyes immediately fill with tears. I instinctively pull her in and hold her.

"At the end of the day, we can never know. She left the house in frustration for being cooped up so long. Even if we had had the snares up, she may have just walked beyond them and whatever limited protection they offer."

My stomach growls again and interrupts us.

"Let's go back and get some food," she says.

She steps back but takes hold of my hand. The two of us make our way back to the cabin. Our shadows walk companionably next to us.

"I was really worried about you," I say. An echo of the fear returns and I look down at her to gauge her reaction to my words.

Slight confusion passes through her face. "What? Why?"

"I woke up and you weren't there." I shrug to try and downplay the panic I felt. "Andrew and Chris didn't know where you were and I thought the worst."

"I can take care of myself," she says.

She's making me feel silly for worrying. Maybe I don't mean as much to her as she does to me.

"How would you feel if you were in my place?" I ask.

She studies me for a moment and says, "You're right. I would be upset if you did that to me. I should've let someone know where I was going. I won't do it again."

I exhale a little bit in relief. "Thank you."

She nods and changes the subject. "How badly does your foot hurt? You've been favoring it all morning."

I put all of my attention on walking normally so she won't be able to tell how much it's bothering me.

"I'll take you up on your offer to help me clean it," I admit.

"You don't really have a choice in that matter," she says. "It needs to be cleaned. Who knows what you exposed it to yesterday and if it gets infected, we'll have to go to a territory and try to find some medicine."

I swallow a fearful curiosity over what has happened with everyone in Potentia. I send a silent prayer that Ian and his family are safe. It's bizarre that something so easy to get such as basic antibiotics has become a dangerous and worrisome ordeal.

The two of us make our way into the house. The guys are in the same position they were when I left them hours ago. I want to do or say something that can take away their pain, but nothing comes to mind.

"Hi," Jess says to announce our return. "Have either of you eaten yet?"

"No," Andrew says. His voice is emotionless.

"We'll make something for all of us," I say.

I spot the expired food cans in the back of the pantry and smile involuntarily at the memory. I drop my smile when I spot my friends out of the corner of my eye. Pain is radiating off of them.

Jess and I go to the kitchen. Not wanting to make a big ordeal for lunch, we put sandwiches together with some of the jam we took from my grandparents' cabin. My mouth waters with the thought of food. I try to remember the last time I was this hungry. A small pang of pain hits me. It was at the start of everything when I was with my mother and Dominic. Things have changed so quickly.

"Come and eat with us in the kitchen," I say to my grieving friends.

They shuffle their way to the kitchen and sit at the table. I've always associated the two of them with laughter and happiness. Even after their parents died and I saw them at the funeral, I could still recognize them. Now, their pain overshadows everything else about them. It suppresses their entire being.

"Thanks for makin' lunch," Chris says.

"I appreciate it," Andrew says. They're just words, devoid of feeling.

"Of course," Jess says. Her worried eyes glance over at me.

I grab my sandwich and eat it in five bites. I'm still hungry and wish I had more. I know once it hits my stomach, I'll feel a lot better. Jess must have been pretty ravenous as well because she finishes right after me. On the other side of the spectrum, Andrew and Chris slowly make their way through the meal. They pick at it very disinterestedly.

"We're going to go to clean Elliot's foot. He cut it yesterday," Jess says.

"Okay," Andrew says to acknowledge her.

He picks up his sandwich to take a small bite. It's almost painful to watch. I'm grateful to get out of the room. Their agony is overpowering.

I shuffle my way to the bathroom while Jess follows. I open the door and turn on the light.

"Sit on the edge of the sink and put your foot in the water," she says.

I untie my shoe and feel instant relief to get my foot out of the confinement. A bloodstain stands out. I reopened the wound today while walking.

I hop up on the edge of the sink and do as I'm told. Jess turns on the faucet and places my foot under the stream. My foot twitches when the warm water hits my wound. The blood washes away while she reexamines my injury.

"This is really deep, Elliot. I'm surprised you didn't really feel it when it happened. I'm going to pour alcohol on it," she says and gently lets go of my foot. She reaches under the cabinet and takes out a bottle of clear liquid. "It's going to hurt."

I brace myself as she pours it on and curse at the sting.

"That should be good enough," she says. "I'm going to put a butterfly bandage on it to help it close and then wrap it."

"Aye, aye, doctor," I say through gritted teeth.

She turns off the water and dries my foot off. She's being as careful as she can, but it's still sensitive.

Her confident motions shed light on an aspect of what role she served in Vis. "You were training to be a doctor," I say with certainty. "How far into your training were you?"

Her eyes widen in surprise and she admits, "I had just received my assignment a few months ago, at the start of the year."

I nod as another piece of her clicks into place. Not wanting to overly pry, I ask, "What do we do now?"

"We do everything we can to make sure we don't lose anyone else," she says as she starts to place the bandage on my foot. "Is this too tight?"

"No," I respond. She finishes up and tapes it in place. I move my foot to test it. It'll work. "Thanks."

She offers me a slight smile in response and changes the topic. "The thing that Andrew and Chris need right now is time," Jess says.

"It's hard seeing them like this."

"We can't take away their pain and make this situation better. That being said, we can try to distract them and make time go by faster," she says.

I look at her curiously. "How?"

"We need to keep them busy. Long term, we need some sort of barrier to block any more of the infected from getting to us. Might as well start now. We can put them to work and have them cut down trees and work on getting all the materials for that ready."

"I like that. To be honest, I could use the distraction as well," I say. I welcome anything to escape the haunting and emergence of terrors in our lives.

"Me, too," she says. "Let's work on bringing our friends back."

CHAPTER FIFTEEN

A drop of sweat rolls slowly down my back. I set the ax down to wipe some away from my eyes and take a long swig of water. The sun has heated it up and I wish the water were colder.

To my right, Andrew and Chris saw at a tree to break it down. Behind me, Jess sharpens one of the sticks. We've been working from dawn to dusk for the last five days on a goal to get enough supplies ready to build our makeshift fence. By the time the sun goes down, we're so exhausted we go straight to sleep.

Grief has become our relentless, insatiable demon. There's no defeating it completely, but we can distract ourselves. The strong labor has been therapeutic for all of us. At times, we all forget the death and find ourselves making small jokes. It's a nice return to normalcy, but it never lasts. One of us always remembers and the demon reappears.

I instinctively reach for my back pocket to get strength from the picture of my mother. My hand comes up empty as I remember I left it inside to keep it safe from the physical labor of the day. I swing my ax back down at the tree in frustration. My arms ache with overuse. I ignore the discomfort and strike again.

Chris breaks our mindless physical labor. "What's that smell?"

"It's awful," Andrew exclaims.

The smell reminds me of the time when a possum died in my grandfather's boathouse and it took us a while to find it. Recognition for what this means to us now immediately follows. Jess stands up quickly when it reaches her.

"Where is it?" Jess's tone is demanding.

Chris and Andrew's expressions switch from mild amusement to one full of terror when they understand. I share in part of their fear. My only interactions with the creatures have been when they killed those I care about. At least this time we're prepared and together.

"Come to me. Get away from the trees," Jess says.

I don't want to expose myself to the horrors within the forest so I back up toward Jess. My foot aches slightly at the movement, but it's manageable. Andrew and Chris are less calm and run the twenty yards to Jess. The four of us anxiously await its appearance.

"What if there's more than one?" Chris looks around frantically.

"Then we'll kill more than one," Jess says. Her teeth clench with anticipation.

Andrew shares his brother's panic. "Should we run to the house?"

"No, we'll take care of them now," I say. I hope I sound bolder than I feel.

No one says anything. The four of us await our fate. The smell gets more nauseating with every passing moment. Finally, two break through the tree line.

"Should we shoot 'em?" Andrew asks. He pulls out his father's old gun and aims.

"Don't shoot," Jess states. "We don't want to waste any bullets. There's no need to be afraid. Watch how slowly they move." As she says this, one stumbles over one of the branches. "They're clumsy. As long as you're smart, they can't hurt you. Don't give them the chance to surprise you. Take it out in its head."

At her instruction, I follow their every movement. My imagination has created an image of them in my head much more intimidating than they actually are.

"I'm going to take care of one and then I want the two of you to kill the second," Jess says.

"Us?" Andrew and Chris say at the same time. In another situation, their reaction would be comical.

"You need to learn sometime. Now watch and learn," she says. She tightens her grip on her knife and slowly makes her way to one of the infected. Without any hesitation, she plunges the knife into its head and it falls instantly. She leans down and retrieves her weapon.

The other beast lunges at her. However, Jess is quick enough and easily evades it. She motions for them to step toward it.

"Use your head and don't miss," I urge them.

They nod and determination replaces the fear in their faces. Chris takes my ax from me. Without any comment, they walk up to Jess and she hands Andrew her knife.

It reaches the three of them and Chris swings his ax and plunges it into the creature's chest. It falls to the ground and Andrew finishes the deed by penetrating its head with the knife. He takes the knife out of its head and spits on it. Chris expresses his anger by kicking its side.

After a moment, Jess says, "As long as we play it smart and there aren't too many, we're going to be fine."

They nod in agreement.

"Can we get rid of it? It smells horrible." Andrew's voice has an emotional twinge to it.

"You two burn them. Jess and I will go check the snares and see if we've stopped any from getting through," I say.

I can't help but wonder if they trapped anything or if it was just a waste of time. We haven't checked them since we made them a few days ago. We've been so preoccupied with getting the fence supplies put together.

She directs her attention toward Chris and Andrew. "Good idea. Will the two of you be okay?"

"Yeah, we'll burn 'em," Andrew says.

"Be careful. Take the gun," Chris says. Andrew nods in agreement and hands me the weapon. I place it under my shirt, tucked into my shorts.

"Of course," I say.

Jess grabs her bag and we walk into the tree line. We get farther and farther away from the cabin. I was hopeful the smell would disappear, but it seems to stay with us.

"There's more," I say unnecessarily. "Where are they coming from?"

"I'm not sure. It's a little worrisome that they're showing up now. I wonder what changed..." She trails off, fully alert.

We come across the first snare and discover it's occupied. One of the beasts snarls hungrily at us. Luckily, the rope has held. I make a move toward it and Jess grabs my arm and stops me.

"We should let Andrew and Chris kill it. If it hasn't escaped yet, it's not going anywhere," she says.

It did seem to help them to kill the last one so I agree with her. We make our way through the line of snares that separate us from the outside world. A surprisingly high number of the snares have captured their targets. We leave them in plans to let Chris and Andrew help us kill them. It will be good training and help relieve them of some of their grief and anger.

Finally, the air begins to clear. It's a subtle difference at first because we've grown used to the smell, but it soon becomes obvious. It's easier to breathe. The snares on the west side are untouched.

"They must have come from the east," Jess says. "That's where Vis is."

I came from the west so this offers me a little hope. I smile to myself and take in the serene atmosphere. It has been a rough time, but we may have made it through the worst. Maybe I needed the world to fall apart so I could come together. Maybe this is how things are supposed to end up.

Interrupting my thoughts, Jess reaches out and grabs my hand. She smiles and looks up at me and I'm simply astounded. How could I have been so lucky to find someone who is as beautiful and strong as she is?

After a couple more yards, she lets go of my hand and sits down in front of a large rock. "Sit with me for a bit, Elliot. We can tell Chris and Andrew about the traps later. Let's enjoy the moment."

She couldn't have picked a nicer place. The view of the lake is so serene and peaceful. It's easy to forget about the recent horrors here.

"We'll know if one of them gets close to us by the smell," she says.

She scoots forward a little bit so I sit down behind her and lean against the rock. It feels good to get off my foot. I place my arms behind myself to prop me up. Jess leans into me in response. I push the pain of the last couple of weeks down and take in the surroundings. I try and focus on the positives. Too much time has been spent tallying our losses. At least the four of us are together and have a plan.

Also, it's nice to have a quiet moment alone with Jess. As much as I enjoy spending time with Andrew and Chris, it seems like one of them is always popping out and preventing Jess and me from really being alone.

Although I would never admit it, their mood has been contagious. It's a relief to get away from all of their pain and try to forget.

Jess shifts a little and her hair catches the breeze. Her hair gets into my mouth and I blow out in reaction. She leans away and looks at me. She says, "Whoops."

I smile back at her and without thinking, tuck her hair behind her ear. When I realize what I'm doing, I pause and make eye contact with her. A strange look crosses her face as she reaches up and holds my hand on her cheek. Nerves course through my body while I try and gain courage. I lean in close to her.

An obnoxious cough comes from behind me.

Jess immediately lets go of my hand. In annoyance at the distraction, I close my eyes. When I open them again, the shock in Jess's expression, combined with hearing his voice again, makes my heart drop.

"Now, Joe, that is no way to greet your brother's return, is it?"

I jump up and whip around to find myself staring at Dominic. It looks like he hasn't shaved since we last saw each other. It gives him a dangerous edge.

In disbelief, I mutter, "Dominic? What?"

Dominic barks a humorless laugh. "Glad to see you are still the same, intelligent individual. If I were one of the Letum, I could have killed both of you easily. I did not interrupt anything, did I?" Dominic looks at us knowingly with a smirk.

Surprise at seeing him again slows down my reaction time. A single word stands out and I ask for him to clarify. "What did you call them?"

"We have been calling them the Letum. It suited them," Dominic responds.

I nod in agreement. They're a symbol for death and ruin. It's fitting.

"What are you doing here?" Jess asks Dominic. She slowly stands up behind me.

He puts his arms out in front of him and appears to be affronted. "I have not seen my little brother in weeks and this is the type of greeting I get? Ever think I just missed little Joey?"

"What are you doing here?" Jess repeats without a change in tone. She steps closer and places a hand on my lower back, relaxing me.

Dominic's eyes narrow at her movement.

For a second, my brother's carefully constructed mask falls apart and reveals a tinge of jealousy. Just as quickly as it appeared on his face, it leaves and is replaced by an expression of bored neutrality.

"I came back to make sure you are alive, Joe. Frankly, I am pleasantly surprised that you are. Looks like you tricked another person into taking care of you."

"Well, as you can see, I'm alive. If you came here to insult me, you can go ahead and leave." I demand.

Just as she always does, Jess encourages my strength and nerve.

"Touchy, touchy." Dominic clicks his tongue. "We are family, remember?"

"And the last time you saw me, you knocked me unconscious."

My heart pounds and I focus all of my energy on hiding this from him. I need to be strong.

"And the time before that, you broke my nose. Water under the bridge, Joe." Dominic nonchalantly shrugs.

I pause and consider him. Dominic whistles a familiar tune.

At the break in the conversation, Jess steps forward again and grabs my hand. I know she's doing it to help steady me. Dominic wordlessly observes this moment, mouth clenching. I move my hand back to encourage her to step behind me again. She either ignores me or doesn't realize what I'm trying to get her to do. I assume the former.

He may be an ass, but he's right. He's my brother and we're family. If Dominic is willing to forgive and move forward, surely I can as well.

"Where have you been then?" I want to get some answers. It's what my mother would have wanted. And deep down, it's what I've always really wanted.

"I wandered around for awhile—honestly, pretty upset with you—but eventually found my way back home. I had to see, you know?" Dominic pauses for dramatic effect and I finally give in.

"Who all made it? Have you seen Ian?" I ask.

"Ian? I remember now. He was your classmate that had the audacity to blame the genetic engineers for his sister's death." Dominic smirks. "I saw him a week ago."

I let out the breath I had been holding in relief.

"What about everyone else?" Jess reminds him.

"There have been no survivors from our governing board. Our Territory Leader, along with the other upper politicians, is dead. There is only an exclusive group of us within genetic engineering. There are some exceptions, of course, but everyone must serve a purpose—now more than ever."

"What's it like there?" I ask, trying to picture how much everything must have changed.

"You are lucky I got you out in time. Potentia is completely overrun. I was close to desperation when a group of genetic engineers found me. They had secured the laboratory and were maintaining security. They are researching to try and turn this whole mess around."

Curiosity obviously gets the better of Jess and she momentarily forgets her hatred for my brother. "They're looking for a cure?"

Dominic nods, amused by her reaction. "I have been helping them, but we hit a dead end, so I decided to take a break and come check on you."

"What did you get stuck on?" I ask.

"Oh, Joe, why would I waste both of our times in an attempt to explain something that, in the end, is not going to make sense to you?" Color floods my cheeks when I take in his insult. "Since you are on this side of the lake, I assume you have synced up with your friends?"

I raise an eyebrow. "Yes. Why?"

Dominic quickly responds, "The only reason you're alive today is because I got you out of the territory. Stop treating me like the enemy."

His outer appearance looks like the opposite of what's going on inside me. Whereas he seems so sure of himself, I'm full of conflict and doubt.

"I'm sorry, Dominic. We've been staying over at their cabin for the last couple of weeks. Carly was with us until a few days ago. She didn't make it."

"So it is just the four of you?"

As soon as Dominic asks this question, Jess tightens her grip on my hand.

I nod and he continues. "I have not seen either of them in a long time. Let's go say hello."

"What are you doing here?" Jess asks one more time.

Dominic jumps down from the rock and stands directly in front of us. I look up at him.

He shrugs and says, "I will tell you on the way to the cabin."

He motions for us to lead.

Jess narrows her eyes at him.

"Okay, I will go first. I remember the way," Dominic says and chuckles at her.

He takes a big step forward and heads in the direction of the cabin. Jess and I follow behind him.

She leans in and whispers so quietly in my ear that I'm almost not sure she's actually speaking. "Don't trust him."

I nod slightly and address Dominic. "Are you going to tell us why you're here?"

Dominic glances back at me with a smug look on his face. "Are you really that curious?"

"Just answer the damn question," Jess says.

"Temper, temper. Someone needs to teach you some respect," he says, mask temporarily falling again. My stomach turns at that comment. "Like I said before, right after I left Grandmother and Grandfather's house, I was really upset. I didn't know what to do by myself so I drove the car back west. I regretted leaving the territory with you and Mother so I went back there."

Jess glances over as she notices my body tense and says, "Careful."

I'm not sure who she is warning.

"You asked for what I've been doing so that's what I'm telling you. Don't ask for the truth and then get upset when I give it to you," he says.

Dominic walks a few more paces before returning to his story. It bothers me how intrigued I am.

"I'm not saying this to be hurtful, but just to be honest. You and Mother were always weak. I should have stuck, from the beginning, with the people with proven track records for being successful."

"Are you saying you regret saving your mother and brother?" Jess asks.

Dominic gives her an annoyed look. "Listen, you're missing the point of the story."

"And what's the point then?" My patience is dwindling rapidly.

"If the two of you will stop interrupting me, I'll get to it."

Dominic takes a deep breath to steady himself and we pass one of our snares. He examines it for a moment and laughs. "What are you trying to catch? That's too big to catch any rabbits around here. You need to shrink the trap." He shakes his head in disbelief and keeps moving.

"Anyway, I made it back to Potentia. To be truthful, I was not very hopeful when I got back. There were so many of the Letum swarming the streets. I was lucky and got spotted. The other genetic engineers came in a vehicle and took me back to the laboratories."

He cringes. "The smell is horrible in the territory. They have installed heavy-duty air purifiers in the building, but outside of it…it's just the worst." He stops and looks back at us. "You know why they smell so bad, right?"

The two of us reluctantly shake our heads. Despite her clear disdain for Dominic, Jess is interested in his story and what he's learned.

Dominic's eyes light up with excitement. "The infection operates within the body's endocrine system and once it is introduced into the blood system, it turns the body against itself and it starts to consume itself. Their bodies are decomposing with every passing moment. That is why we think they attack us—for their own survival. It is actually quite interesting."

"Yes, fascinating," I say. I'm disturbed at the whole idea.

Dominic continues his monologue. "Obviously, everyone was ecstatic for me to show up and greeted me with open arms."

Of all the things that have changed, his arrogance has not.

"So since then, I have been working with the team to figure out what has caused this epidemic."

"But you said you're stuck. What are you doing here?" I ask.

"Is it really that hard to believe I wanted to check up on you?" Dominic looks slightly offended. "Despite everything, you are my brother. We share genetics. Not as much as I would like, but we still came from the same two people. That makes you extremely important to me."

I ignore the slight alarm in my head and hear what I want to. He cares and is acknowledging the bond we share. I look over at Jess with a small smile on my face. Her eyebrows furrow and a frown is etched on her mouth.

Before I can fully interpret her look, a familiar voice calls out, "Ya'll finally back? You're not very quiet walkers." Andrew's voice sounds slightly less pained than before. Killing the Letum must have helped.

Chris continues, "It took ya'll a really long time to check the snares."

"A very long time," Andrew says. "Ya'll can't make me an uncle this young."

Dominic raises an eyebrow. I break eye contact by looking at the ground.

Jess leans in and embraces me. It startles me, but I return her hug. I do my best to tune out Dominic's snort.

Jess breathes into my ear. "Be careful. He's up to something."

Just as stealthily, I whisper back, "He's my brother," and pull away from her.

Ever so slightly, she shakes her head. I turn to my brother and take a step forward.

We pass into the view of the cabin. Smoke rises in the distance from the Letum's last journey. Shock quickly takes over both Chris and Andrew's face when they spot Dominic. Dominic chuckles quietly in amusement.

"We ran into him in the woods," I say unnecessarily.

"I am very pleased to see the two of you still alive," Dominic says. He sounds so sincere. Why would he be happy to see them? He never seemed to even acknowledge their existence while growing up.

"Thanks?" Andrew says in response. He's just as surprised at Dominic's concern for his well-being.

Dominic smiles and whistles the same tune he did when he ran into us to begin with. I struggle to remember where it came from. After the second time through the tune, a tree branch snaps behind us.

Jess cusses.

"Do not be an idiot. Do not be a hero. Elliot and Jess, walk toward Andrew and Chris," Dominic says. "If you run, you will be shot."

I peek behind us. There's another tall figure with a weapon aimed at us. I look back to Dominic. He's pulled out a gun from his waistband. He uses it to motion us to get closer to Andrew and Chris. I can't think of another option, so I take a step toward them to follow into our own trap.

CHAPTER SIXTEEN

"Why?" I ask.

I'm an idiot. Why did I trust him and bring him back here? I shouldn't be so desperate for his approval that I let him take advantage of me over and over again. It's an endless cycle.

"I told you, you are my brother. Like I said, we share genetics. I need you," Dominic answers. His tone is very straightforward. "I need to be protected by this virus and you are the closest genetic match to me."

I don't understand the correlation between them. "Why does that matter?" I ask.

He shrugs his shoulders. "I need to run tests on you so I can understand how to protect myself."

My voice cracks as I take in his words. "What sort of tests?"

He answers with a smirk. "Some basic genetic testing. It is nothing too painful."

I take a deep breath in relief.

His smirk widens and he continues, "However, the tests will conclude with the virus being introduced to your system to force you to turn into one of the Letum."

I have no words. The shock of his actions overshadows the fear that follows with his words. I let myself believe we could be a team and he betrayed me in an instant. I have no value to him as a person. All I am is a body he can run experiments on.

"How could you do this to your own brother?" Jess hisses at him.

Dominic studies Jess before answering. "It's actually quite simple. Humanity needs me more than him. I have the opportunity to find a cure whereas my brother is simply lucky to still be alive at this point. This is his opportunity to serve society."

Jess shakes her head in disgust. I shift my gaze toward Chris and Andrew. Their expressions of fear are a perfect match. Both of their hands are in the air and they look between the different weapons in a frantic motion.

"Keep walking. That's it, Joe. Don't try anything," Dominic says to remind me to join them. "Although, Jess, you can come stand by me."

The other man holding a gun at us barks laughter and sneers. Using his free hand, he grabs his crotch and licks his lips. My stomach turns.

Jess and I make eye contact and I know what I have to do. I can't let Dominic get ahold of her.

I stop moving and Jess reacts and does the same. I do a slight motion with my hand to get her to keep moving. She looks at me in question. I repeat the motion. This time, she takes a step toward our friends.

"What are you doing?" The man shifts his gun to point at me.

"Joe…" Dominic says. "What did I say?"

I take a deep breath to steady myself. I turn around to face Dominic. He looks back at me with an amused expression. His smug look angers me more than I thought possible. I reach in my back pocket and pull out the gun Andrew gave me earlier. Dominic's expression changes to shock when my weapon points at him. Very quickly, his mask returns to hide his thoughts.

The man bellows, "Drop it."

"Stand down, Phillip," Dominic orders his companion. Phillip remains tense, yet moves his finger off the trigger. Slowly, he lowers his weapon and continues to glare at me.

Dominic redirects his attention to me once he's been obeyed. "If you shoot at me—notice I say if because I doubt you could actually hit me—we'll kill all of your friends, just like I did with Ian when he begged us for help. Did he really think I would forget his accusations so easily?" Dominic spits out, trying to unnerve me further.

Ian's green eyes pierce through my memories. How could Dominic be so petty to enact revenge over a differing mindset? Dominic doesn't deserve to be here when people like Ian and Carly aren't anymore.

I maintain my position, trying to remember everything my grandfather taught me about shooting guns.

Chris exclaims behind me, "What are you doing?"

I ignore Chris and keep my focus on Dominic.

Dominic tilts his head. "Yes, what are you doing? Being completely honest, I am surprised you had the bravery to threaten me. But what can you possibly gain from pointing a weapon at me?" He seems genuinely curious.

Adrenaline courses through my body. "If I shoot you, your friend is just going to retaliate and kill us."

"So drop your gun," Phillip demands. His eyes dart between my brother and me.

Dominic brings back all of my childhood memories. He brought all of the pain and misery of my life before and it greets me like an old enemy. Every time I was told I should have been aborted. Every laughter, every judgment, and every single time I felt worthless and pathetic. I take my gun off of Dominic and angle it toward my head.

Jess gasps and her footsteps speed back to me.

Phillip raises his gun and shifts his aim toward her.

I ignore Jess and address myself to my brother. "If I shoot you, I can't really win. But if I shoot myself at least you can't win."

"You really think I believe you would kill yourself?" He's trying very hard to appear unconcerned, yet a small stutter in his voice gives him away. Phillip looks to him nervously for instructions.

"You do believe me. You need me alive. You need someone to run your experiments on. With me dead, your survival chances diminish." My heart pounds in my chest. My hands are sweaty and I worry that I'm going to drop the gun. I tighten my grip and stare back. My body is full of resolve. There are some realities I refuse to accept.

Dominic clenches his jaw and squares his shoulders. "I'm not letting you go."

"Then let them go," I say. "If you let them go, I'll come. As soon as they're out of sight, I'll drop my weapon and let you take me back to Potentia."

My brother and I maintain eye contact. Each of us gauges the other's willpower.

There's a touch on my back and Jess whispers in my ear. "I'm not letting you go with him."

I don't want to go with him either, but if there is a chance I can spare Jess, I have to take it.

A big smile crosses Dominic's face and it's even more alarming than his weapon pointed at me. "Fine," he says, "I'll give you a choice. You can let one of them go. We're taking you and two others with us. You get to make the decision which one lives."

"No, all three or I shoot myself," I try again.

"You can choose one person to walk away. If you shoot yourself, you're right, that will not do me much good. But I'll be able to comfort myself with the fact that I can make three of your closest friends' lives miserable until I kill them," Dominic says. He's regained control.

I look back at Chris and Andrew in desperation, begging them to understand. They nod and give me permission to doom them.

"Jess leaves," I say and seal the fate of my childhood friends.

"Very well, Jess, you may leave. I would do it quickly before I change my mind." Dominic's smug look has reestablished itself.

Jess leans in to kiss me on the cheek. "Don't give up hope."

I nod slightly.

She addresses Dominic this time and says, "One day you're going to look back on your life and realize how truly small and pathetic you are."

He chuckles and says, "I will tell that to myself as I am injecting your little boyfriend and his two companions with the virus."

Jess spits in his direction and sprints away without another word. My chest tightens at the sight of her leaving. I wish we could have had a real good-bye. At least she's getting away. Dominic won't get the opportunity to touch her.

She fades into the trees and soon, I can't even pretend to hear her steps. I do as promised and drop the weapon. Dominic walks up to me and kicks the gun away. He punches me in the stomach and I fall to the ground, gasping for breath.

"She must be smarter than I gave her credit for," Dominic kneels and whispers in my ear. "She was all too willing to leave you, she didn't even look back. How does that make you feel, Joe?"

I don't want to think of those implications so I turn the conversation around and gasp, "What would Mother say to you right now?"

His face betrays nothing. No emotions shine through. "I don't care what you think she would say. She's dead."

His indifference somehow manages to upset me even more. I didn't think that was possible. "She's your mother. How do you not care?"

"She *was* my mother," he corrects. "And why would I care? From the moment you were born, all of her attention was on you. While I was succeeding in everything I attempted, she focused on you. When I got assigned the genetic engineer career path, she didn't even care. Not once did she ever truly support me. I never had a real mother or father. You made sure of that," Dominic says.

My mother was always there for me. She supported me in everything I did. She's the reason I had any amount of self-worth. Did we not grow up with the same mother?

For the first time, anger leaves my voice and I say, "She may have treated us differently, but that doesn't mean she loved you any less."

"Careful, Joe, your idiocy is showing. That's exactly what that means. She clearly chose you and a life of mediocrity over one of brilliance and success. What a waste of a life."

I instantly stop feeling bad for him. There's no point in talking with him. He isn't going to be reasoned with. I don't want to give him the satisfaction of beating me down. I return to my feet to join Andrew and Chris.

This is the first time I've been able to really focus on them. A small film of anxious sweat covers their faces.

"I'm sorry," I say only to them. "I couldn't let him get to her." I don't regret my decision, but I do wish I didn't have to make it.

"I'm not gonna lie, this sucks," Chris mutters. His voice breaks in emotion.

As always, Andrew continues. "But it had to be done."

"I'm not saying we're happy about it."

"But we understand why you sent her away. At least we'll stay together," Andrew finishes quietly.

All the times I felt sorry for myself and felt truly alone, I was so mistaken. Growing up, I had two great friends and I never truly appreciated it. Maybe I'm finally realizing this because our friendship is about to be torn from us.

No words come to mind that can appropriately convey the emotion I'm feeling. Rather than stumble through some words that won't do it justice, I reach toward them and the three of us hug. I try and put all of my appreciation for a lifetime of friendship into the contact.

Dominic says, "This is not good-bye for the three of you. You will still hear plenty of each other. In fact, Andrew, I will turn you first and let you bite Chris to infect him. Rather fitting, is it not?" Dominic and his friend laugh.

I look at my brother in disgust. How could I have ever envisioned him as someone I wanted to be? I'm grateful I'm not Dominic. It isn't just him that's wrong. When presented to my classmates, almost all of them agreed with him. Our society's values were completely shot. A small part of me is thankful for the infection. At least it destroyed a system that was already broken.

I square my shoulders and harden my tone. "I'd rather be dead than be you, Dominic," I say.

"There are things worse than death. You will discover that soon enough," Dominic says. His eyes narrow and his hatred for me has never been so evident. I return a portion of that hate to him but still a small part of me wants to believe that there is hope for us to become the brothers our mother always wished for us.

A smell hits my nose. My eyes widen in alarm and I look over to the forest opening and see a horde of Letum coming toward us. Dominic curses under his breath. He motions for Phillip to join him and they move toward the group and start shooting.

"This way," a voice whispers from behind me. I've never been so relieved to hear Jess. I look behind me. Jess motions for the three of us to join her. She must have released the traps and guided all of them to us.

I turn back around to grab my gun. Just as I pick it up, I step on a branch and it cracks. I hold my breath, hoping in all of the excitement, it will go unnoticed. But luck has never been on my side.

This time, it's Jess who curses. I look to Dominic just in time to see him turn his head. Understanding and hatred fill his face when he spots Jess. He raises his gun and aims right at her. I'm about fifteen feet away from them.

"Don't you even think about it!" I yell. I raise my gun and point it at my brother.

While Phillip is busy killing off some of the swarm, one of the Letum sneaks by and closes in on Dominic. Andrew and Chris focus their attention on Dominic, both of their faces alight with desperate determination. At the same time, they step in front of Jess to protect her.

"Behind you," I try to warn as it gets closer to him.

Dominic smiles at me, "I'm not unintelligent. I won't fall for that. Step aside, boys. She had her chance to get away."

The Letum is just feet away from him. "I'm serious."

"No, I'm serious. Step aside. Little brother, you're never going to shoot me," he grits through his teeth.

In my mind, my grandfather's calm voice reminds me to hold my breath before I pull the trigger. I take a deep breath and fire my gun. Dominic's eyes widen in disbelief and he fires back.

The Letum behind my brother falls forward onto him and pins Dominic down, weapon falling out of his hand at the impact. From the ground, he turns his head to bring his focus back to me, my gun still raised at him, shock covering all of his features.

"No!" A terrible scream full of pain and agony pierces through all the moaning of the Letum. I forget all about Dominic and face the scene behind me. Andrew supports the limp body of Chris. Dominic's aim was perfect. The bullet went through Chris's head. I stumble over to his lifeless body.

"Chris…" I look around in desperation for something to reverse what just happened. Andrew sobs and cradles his brother's limp body.

"We have to run now," Jess reminds us. I take my eyes off of Chris's fatal gunshot wound and put my attention on her. She's staring beyond me at Dominic.

He's pushed the Letum off of him and returned to his feet. His gun lies two feet away from him. His voice pierces through my shock as he rushes forward to pick it up.

"Don't make me kill another one of your friends, Elliot. Put down your weapon and come with us."

I look at the stream of blood running down Chris's dead body and feel the familiar numbness returning—my escape from the pain.

Slowly, I look back to my murderous brother and ask, "How did it come to this?"

Dominic raises an eyebrow at this statement and turns his eyes down to look at Chris. His gun moves down a fraction of an inch.

Just as we make eye contact, Phillip grumbles, "What are you doing, Dominic?" as he continues his struggle with the Letum.

Another one is getting closer to Dominic. He eyes the impending attack and fresh determination returns to his face and his gun aims again.

"Ya'll run. I'm not finished with him," Andrew says, shaking with hatred.

"No, run. Come with us," I beg.

"Take care of Elliot." Andrew addresses Jess as he gently sets Chris down. He turns to face Dominic. "Now, run."

He marches over to Dominic. Dominic looks at him, amused.

Jess pulls at my hand and we break into the forest. Dominic grunts in annoyance. There's a quick bang followed by a scream of pain. I freeze, mid-motion and Jess pulls harder at my hand to keep me moving.

My survival instincts kick in. I dig my heels in the ground and ignore the pain in my foot. I push off into the unknown.

CHAPTER SEVENTEEN

Pain shoots through my right foot with every step. The dampness in my sock lets me know I reopened my wound. Every once in a while, I'll step on a rock that will hit the exact same spot and press through my shoe, causing sharp pain.

We've been walking nonstop through the forest since we escaped Dominic, and it's midafternoon the next day. When we hit a paved road, we hid within the trees to avoid the sight of anyone driving by. With no real reason behind it, we choose north and have been walking in a daze.

We're wearing clothes suited for physical labor, as we were working on the fence that will never be. Unfortunately, they leave our legs and arms exposed and we've been bitten by mosquitos and cut from branches more times than I can count.

Every attempt I've made at starting a conversation with Jess has been shot down. Finally, I can't take the silence anymore.

"Jess, I'm sorry that Dominic is my brother. I wish more than anything he didn't come back. I need you to talk to me," I say. I duck to avoid a tree branch.

When a few minutes go by and she still hasn't given any indication that she heard me, I try again. "Please, Jess. Let me know what's going on inside your head. What are you thinking?"

She stops and turns to me. "What am I thinking? I'm furious." Her hands shake.

"I know, it's all my fault. I'm the reason he came back," I say. I drop my eyes to the ground. "It's my fault they're dead. He wanted me."

Her tone softens. "You think that's why I'm mad? You think I'm mad at you?"

I nod, dejected. "It's my fault."

"Elliot, how could I be mad at you?" She stares at me in confusion. "I'm infuriated because shitty people like Dominic exist. I'm upset because we had found a home. We finally had a system going and we were making it work. Yes, we lost Carly, but we were on the road to recovery. I'm mad because some people place such a higher value on themselves than others. It's ridiculous that people who are genetically planned view themselves as being on such a high pedestal." She grabs my hand and squeezes it. "I'm upset at the way society is, not at you." She squeezes again. "Never at you."

"I'm the reason he came back," I say. "He came looking for me."

"If you weren't there, he still would have come for them. You're not responsible or accountable for Dominic. You're not him."

I want to believe her, but my actions toward Chris and Andrew haunt me. "You don't think I'm a horrible person?"

"Of course not," she says. "Why would you ever think that? Especially now, after seeing that display of human nature."

"I'm just as bad as Dominic," I exclaim. "I was willing to let my friends die. I did end up getting them killed. It's my fault." Their loss has punched yet another hole through my heart. It's not fair that I'm still alive while everyone else is dead.

"Listen carefully, because I'm only going to say this once. We don't have time for you to feel sorry for yourself." She takes a deep breath and continues. "Your actions are nothing like Dominic's. You were given a horrible choice to make and Chris and Andrew agreed with you. When the time came, you tried to save all three of us and sacrifice yourself. Dominic would never do that."

Her tone softens again. "What happened to them is terrible and unthinkable. I'm genuinely going to miss their quirkiness and I can't imagine how hard the loss is on you. But not for one second can you think that it's your doing."

Her eyes lock in on mine. I take a deep breath and take in some of her strength. I try to believe her words. She raises her left eyebrow in question and I very slowly nod in acknowledgment.

"Please don't shut me out like that. I don't know how to interpret it when you do."

She lets go of my hand and continues walking. I've fallen back to a couple of paces behind her.

After several minutes, she surprises me by responding. "It's just what I'm used to. In my experience, every time I get close to someone, they leave."

"I'm not going anywhere, Jess," I say.

She watches her feet as she walks and says, "What people promise and what people actually do are two different things. That's what my father said and he would leave that night to go get drunk. That's what my mother would say and she would check out mentally and leave me to care for my brother." Her voice breaks. "And I never thought my little brother would leave but he was taken from me as well."

"I know you have had a lot of terrible things happen to you, but that has made you who you are today. We're both damaged." I motion to my foot for a literal example of what I just said. "At the end of the day, though, we're a team and in this together." I hope she picks up on the sincerity in my voice. "Please don't shut me out."

She shrugs. "Okay, I'll try."

A little bit of dread leaves my chest. At least we're in this together.

Jess holds a branch away and waits for me to walk through before letting it go. I speed up. She eyes my limp and looks questioningly at me. I ignore the pain and walk even faster to reassure her that I'm okay.

More time passes—the only evidence being the shifting of the sun. Despite Jess's trying to convince me otherwise, I can't erase the feeling that I caused Andrew and Chris's deaths. Everyone around me keeps dying and I'm the common factor.

I don't know how to function in such a world where death is a common occurrence. With the exception of the children deaths, everyone in my life was healthy. When someone would pass on, it was a result of a life that had run its course. I was never able to relate to the stories of the sufferings that used to exist before our society established itself. Was this truly how life used to be?

Jess's voice breaks through my train of thought. "You need to get out of your head."

I blink and my eyes refocus on the surroundings. Jess stares back at me, worry creasing her brow line.

"I just don't want you to get hurt. You're all I have left," I say.

Jess has a particular expression on her face that I don't know how to interpret. She stops walking. Unable to maintain her eye contact, I take a deep breath and push ahead.

Very quietly, she says, "Elliot…"

The sound of her footsteps catches up to me and her hand gently touches my back. I stop moving and freeze. Her arms wrap around me and her forehead leans on the back of my head, her steady breathing on the back of my neck.

I close my eyes and take another deep breath. I let her comfort me. I'm not sure how long we stand there in that position together. In the middle of the forest with the trees surrounding us, we find a temporary peace.

I come back to reality when the pressure of her head moves and she kisses the back of my neck. I take another deep breath and prepare to face her.

Before I can, her entire body tenses and she abruptly turns around. A familiar scent is in the air. I jerk around to face the danger. A group of about fifteen Letum are walking toward us. Despite being ripped and covered in aged blood, it's not enough to hide that they came from the territories. The one closest to us is in the green outfit of food distribution, like my mother.

My eyes dart between all of them. "Jess…there's too many. What do we do?" I ask.

"How many do you think you can take care of without being overwhelmed?" She questions, clearly calculating our chances. We both take a step away.

"I'm not exactly an expert killer. Maybe we should just run?" I say although I know it isn't a good option. We're already exhausted from walking through the night and all day. It's starting to get dark again, and my foot slows us down more with each step.

She deliberates for a second and nods. We take off. The fading light makes it harder to avoid all of the nature surrounding us and I'm afraid one of us is going to fall and hurt ourselves.

Okay, to be honest, I'm worried I might fall.

"Let's move to the street," I manage to say to Jess as I run onto the road. I would rather take my chances with Dominic and the rest of his crew than the Letum coming up behind us. Besides, breaking an ankle tripping over a fallen branch isn't exactly going to help our situation.

For a while, the only sounds are our feet hitting the pavement, our ragged breathing, and the sound of the Letum chasing us. While they seem to be maintaining a steady, albeit distressed, pace, the two of us are slowing down. The pain in my foot is getting progressively worse.

I stumble as my foot gives out. Jess grabs hold of me to help take some of the pressure off of my foot.

"You need to leave me," I say through clenched teeth. "I'm slowing you down."

Out of the corner of my eye, I see her shake her head.

"No, we're in this together, remember?"

I look back behind us. It's hopeless. "We're not going to make it together." I try to pull away, but she holds on and keeps pushing me.

She shakes her head again in stubbornness. "That's exactly how we're going to make it."

I don't believe her. We should have taken our stand before we got tired.

The distance between them and us shrinks rapidly due to our exhaustion. They're about fifty yards behind us. I push through and try to gain my speed to keep up our unsustainable pace. Thirty yards. Their moaning is getting louder. Twenty yards. It feels like my side is on fire. Fifteen yards. Jess and I make eye contact. The same dread I feel is echoed in her face. The sounds of their dead weight shuffling is directly behind us. This is it.

They say when you're about to die, your life flashes before your eyes. I don't completely agree with that. It's more like an explosion of memories that you have no control over.

I'm five years old. My parents are fighting. I don't know what about, but I know it isn't good. Dominic comes up and hits me. He tells me it's my fault they don't like each other anymore.

Two years later. Father tries to help me with homework. He storms out of the room screaming how dumb I am. I cry. Mother tells me not to listen to him and that she loves me no matter what.

It's the night my father left. Mother is in the kitchen making dinner, sobbing. Dominic walks toward me with his hand behind his back. Wordlessly, he shows me the knife and lunges. I turn my body and cry in shock. Mother runs into the room in a panic.

I'm about ten and at my grandparents' cabin. Grandfather is teaching us how to fish. When I catch a fish before Dominic, he throws me into the lake out of anger.

I just asked my first crush, Caroline, if she would like to go to the school dance with me even though she's a little older. She laughs and tells me she's already going with someone. Not able to find anyone to go to the dance with me, I sit at home and watch Dominic get ready. Right before he leaves, he tells me he's going with Caroline and taunts me.

I'm twenty and waiting on the hill. One of my only friends at school, Amber, is meeting me here. Ever since I got her message, I've been able to do nothing else but daydream about what's going to happen on the hill. There is familiar laughter coming from the other side. I run over to see my brother kissing Amber.

It's my twenty-second birthday and my brother is out. It's just me and my mother at home for dinner. There's no pressure to be anyone else.

The Letum are about ten yards behind us. I haven't even begun to live and I'm about to die. My side aches with every breath and it feels like I'm not getting enough oxygen. A light is approaching quickly. I guess people really do see a light before they die.

The rational part of my brain recognizes it as headlights from a vehicle. It keeps getting closer and I grow afraid it's simply going to hit us. At least it's a better way to die than being eaten by the Letum.

"Dominic," Jess breathlessly predicts.

The vehicle screeches to a stop right in front of us and at this point, we're barely ahead of the massive group. The headlights are blinding. Out of the car springs a tiny shadow that races out. Close behind is a much bigger figure holding a large stick-like object.

"Not him," I pant back.

At this point, Jess takes out her large knife. The four of us turn and face our attackers. I hit the one closest to me in the chest with the small blade I had with me. The force knocks it to the ground, its shirt coming up and revealing an emaciated chest where, even in the dark, I can easily make out each rib. Before it can get up, I jam my weapon in its head. I'm so exhausted that the next one coming at me takes three lunges before I finally connect with its head to kill it.

I scan the scene. The two strangers fending off the group look to be in control. Jess is fighting off three of the Letum. I run over to help her before she becomes overwhelmed. I stab one in the head through its eye. When I pull the knife out, its eye comes with it and pops out. I resist the urge to gag.

Jess holds the last one back. It drips its own blood as it gnaws on its lip. I stab it and it instantly stills.

I check up on our two saviors. There is one more left and it lunges at the smaller figure. Luckily, the Letum is much too slow. Before it can reattempt an attack, the larger person slams down a weapon and crushes its skull. It's over.

I stash my weapon back in my pocket and wipe my hands across my dirty pants to get some of the gore off of them.

Jess and I make eye contact, her expression numb, and I take her in my arms. We stand there for a few seconds just appreciating the fact that we're still alive.

A fake cough takes place about ten feet to the left, breaking our embrace. "Well, no big deal or anything, but we just saved your asses," the bigger figure says. He's taller than even Dominic and just as intimidating physically. However, his lopsided grin combined with his big ears makes it difficult for him to be truly frightening.

The smaller person quickly jabs him in the side with her elbow and says, "What he's trying to say is it's nice to meet you. I can't believe we got here in time." She speaks very quickly. "What are the chances? We were just driving back to our cabin when we saw you two. How long have you two even been running? Where did you come from? How did you get here?"

The tall man laughs down at her and says, "She gets pretty talkative when she's excited. You wouldn't know it from the size of her, but she's a noisy little thing." He then smiles down at her and there is such affection and tenderness in his expression that there is no doubt he would do anything for her.

I take another look at this talkative, tiny person. She can't be much taller than five feet and has fiery red hair put in a braid. Everything about her is small. Her ears, nose, even her hands look tiny. She turns to survey the scene and I notice she has a small, yet slightly noticeable, baby bump.

"Don't listen to him. He can't hear that well, you know, with his ears so high up." She places her left hand on her stomach.

"And she can't hear anything, being so damn low to the ground." He takes a moment to laugh at his joke and I find myself laughing with him. "By the way, my name is Matt and this little thing is Allison. We came from Robur. What about you two?"

"My name is Elliot and her name is Jess. We came from the lake where my grandparents used to live," I say, not wanting to fit into any predetermined notions from belonging to a territory.

"Used to live?" Allison asks.

"They aren't with us anymore." I pause to examine them closer. "Do you know what's going on?" I blurt out.

They exchange a look and Matt replies, "We have some ideas, but nothing for sure."

Should we share with them the information that Dominic told us? I don't want them to feel threatened by the idea of my brother.

Sensing my discomfort, Jess joins in on the conversation and asks, "How did you get your hands on one of these vehicles? They allow free travel?"

"Yes. I was lucky and managed to get it out of Robur in time. Listen, I would love to continue this little chitchat, but we shouldn't stay out in the open too long. Would you two care to join us for a double date?" Matt makes it seem like we're conspiring together.

"Do you know of a safe place?" Jess asks.

Instead, Allison answers. "Oh yeah, it's totally safe. We've been staying there since it all started."

She then looks between the two of us, obviously deep in thought. "Are the two of you together romantically?"

Jess and I share a look and things immediately get awkward.

Matt, clearly amused by the sudden change, laughs at the tension. "You'll have to excuse her. She may have a small nose, but that doesn't mean she doesn't just love sticking it in other people's business." He smiles down at her before continuing. "It isn't that far. It's my family's country home."

I look over questioningly at Jess and she nods.

"Sure," I say, "We'll come with you two. It'll be nice to take a break from all this running."

"You bet, brother," Matt says and we start making our way to the vehicle.

With no warning, Allison stumbles and almost falls. There appears to be nothing on the ground except, well, the ground.

When Matt sees this, he lets out another booming laugh. "Did I mention you would be traveling with a swan?"

I open the door for Jess as we get into the backseat of the car. Getting off my foot feels absolutely amazing. It throbs and aches, but at least sharp pain is gone.

"There's some water in the red bag," Allison says.

Jess and I bump hands as we reach for the bag at the same time. I open the bottle and close my eyes in appreciation as the cool water slides down my throat.

The moment we stop drinking, Jess says, "While I appreciate the two of you saving us, I have to ask—what's your story?"

Allison says, "We came here right after we got out of Robur. We barely beat the quarantine and this was the only place we could think of. We've been driving around finding supplies from the homes nearby."

"What exactly do you know about them?" Jess says.

Matt puffs out his chest and looks meaningfully in the distance. "I'm glad you recognize us as having superior knowledge and come to us for answers."

"Sometimes you just have to ignore him," Allison says. She playfully nudges Matt in the side, taking some of the severity out of the situation. "We don't know that much. That's probably not what you want to hear, but it's the truth." She takes a deep breath. "We learned pretty early on that you have to hit the head hard enough to kill them. I've seen a lot of them with bite marks so we're assuming that's how whatever this is transfers."

"That's exactly how this infection spreads," Jess says. She's so quiet that I almost don't hear her. She zones out and seemingly stares at nothing. The mood of the conversation drops dramatically and I'm at a loss as to what to do. I settle on grabbing her hand. My touch seems to startle her out of her thoughts and she blinks a couple of times before refocusing back in the present.

"My brother was a genetic engineer and spent some time researching this infection. He said it's some disease, but that's about all the information he shared with us," I say. I choose to omit the reason why they smell so bad.

"Where is your brother now?" Allison asks.

"He's not with us anymore," Jess says.

"I'm so sorry for your loss," Allison says. She leans back to pat my shoulder lightly in reassurance.

Jess gives me a warning look, so I follow her suggestion and let them think that my brother is dead.

Matt clears his throat and continues the conversation. "That's about it then. Wait. There is one more thing. Let me ask you something real quick." He looks questioningly at both of us and doesn't continue until I nod. "How many have you seen?"

"Jess has seen and dealt with more than I have," I say.

"Not that many more," Jess says. "It seems like for the most part there aren't that many out here. At least until recently."

"Exactly. That's what we've picked up on, too," Allison says. She looks excited that Jess caught on to their train of thought.

I still don't understand what they're talking about so I lean forward and raise an eyebrow in question.

Matt reenters the conversation with a quick, low voice. "Think about it, brother. How many people live in just one territory alone?"

I put my hands up to emphasize the high number. "Beyond count."

"Exactly. And that's just in one territory. Where is everyone?"

I let out a sigh of air when I finally understand his point. I make eye contact with Jess. She stares back with a guarded expression.

"Are you telling me," I say, "that you think everyone is locked up in the territories?"

"What if there is a territory that was locked down in time? There could be a whole territory that's completely untouched. If we could just make it there, everything would be okay. If the walls around each territory are good enough to keep them in, then surely they have the capability to keep the disease out.

"We're from Robur and we know that they fell. We went back there first and didn't have to get too close to know it had been taken. Who knew something could smell that bad." Allison shudders at the memory.

Matt continues their theory, "After we got over the disappointment, we planned on going to Vis. If they aren't infested they could help us.

They have to have the answers. They just have to." He finishes and looks up expectantly at Jess and me.

For the first time in a long time, there's a little seed of hope. Everything they say makes complete sense. Maybe everything can go back to normal again. Well, at least as close as possible. I smile over at Jess, expecting her to return my optimism. Instead, a small tear falls down her cheek.

"Vis has been overrun. I was there when it happened," she says. "There is nothing left in Vis except these Letum. You won't find any answers there."

"What? You didn't mention..." I begin. I knew she came from there, but I didn't know she stayed while the territory was being overrun.

Even though the hope of Allison and Matt's plan is new, it still hurts when it dies. Allison closes her eyes at Jess's announcement and Matt's shoulders drop.

After several moments, Jess finally says, "It wasn't relevant then. It's relevant now."

Once again, she leaves me speechless.

Rather than focus on this new information, I decide to move the conversation on. "The only other territory is where I am from, Potentia. My brother got my mother and me out right before they shut everything down. My brother said the genetic testing facility is secure but besides that, the whole area is overrun."

"Well, shit," Matt says. "There goes that idea. I guess we're going to get to know each other a little better while we try and figure something else out."

"Seems like as good a plan as any," I say through a large yawn.

Matt chuckles and says, "Get some rest, brother. You need it."

Without the adrenaline propelling my body forward, my eyes drop. The pressure of Jess's hand enclosed around mine lets the exhaustion take over.

CHAPTER EIGHTEEN

Not much time goes by before the vehicle jerks to a stop. Jess and I rub our eyes while Matt quickly gets out of the car.

"We're almost there," Allison whispers. "Matt is just opening the gate for us."

I sit up straighter and look out the windows. Darkness surrounds the scenery and I can't make anything out but basic shapes of a heavy congestion of trees. Matt reenters the vehicle and drives it through the gate. Before I can offer to close the fence for him, he hops back out and takes care of it.

Allison explains the house. "The doors and windows will all be locked, but it's still a good idea if we take turns keeping watch. There's a light fence around the property, but I'm not sure how much I trust it. The size of that last group was a bit alarming. Don't worry, though, Matt and I will take watch tonight so the two of you can rest a little bit."

At this point, Matt gets back inside and moves the vehicle forward to park next to their house. I eye the relative safety of the property and feel such a swell of gratefulness to be alive.

"Thanks for everything," I say. "I can take my turn of watch starting tonight. I owe the two of you for saving us."

"There's really no need. We can get it for the night," Matt says.

Jess inserts herself in the conversation and says, "I would feel bad if we didn't contribute to the watch."

Matt and Allison exchange a glance and Allison says, "If that's what the two of you want, I'm not going to complain about getting more sleep."

"It will be much easier to take turns with four people," Matt says. He looks excited at the idea of sharing the responsibility. He examines us a little closer. "I'll take the first watch, though."

I smile at his enthusiasm. "We're happy to help."

Matt nods and opens his door. I take the cue and step out onto the grass. I cringe at the sharp pain in my foot and quickly glance toward Jess to see if she noticed. Her attention is focused out on the road we came in.

"Why do you have a fence?" she asks.

Matt and Allison exchange another glance before he answers. "This was my family's vacation home. They strongly discouraged anyone from visiting."

Matt opens the front door and lets the three of us in. My eyes widen at the furnishings inside the house. They're a lot nicer than those in our apartment in Potentia. It must have cost a lot of money for them to transport it all out here. Despite the obvious wealth associated with the house, it has a small, cozy feel that makes me want to find a bed and fall asleep.

"I'll give you a quick tour," Allison says. She clearly has a higher energy level than I do right now. "Obviously, we just walked into the living room. The kitchen is connected to it. Out to the left is the backyard." She turns in the opposite direction and leads us down a hallway. "We'll all have to share a bathroom, but it's at the end of this hallway."

"The two of you have been living here for how long?" Jess asks.

"We came here right as everything started, hoping it would be safe. Plus, if either of our families is okay..." Allison pauses for a moment. Her hand falls on her growing stomach and finishes, "Well, this is one of the first places they would look."

Allison takes a step forward and continues the tour. "Matt and I have been in the room closest to the bathroom, but either of the other two rooms is fine for you to sleep in. Extra blankets and towels are in this closet," she says as she opens the door and reveals various supplies.

She looks both of us up and down. "Elliot, in the room to your right, there should be some of Matt's older clothes in the closet. They will be big for you, but at least you'll have something clean to wear. And Jess," she ticks her tongue in thought. "Matt has a sister that's close to your size. Her room is just down the hall by the bathroom. Feel free to look around and get whatever fits."

Jess looks down at her outfit with a frown. "A change of clothes would be very nice. Thank you."

"Of course. Just let me know if you need anything. I'll let the two of you get settled." With this, she walks back down the hallway toward the living room and patio.

I go into the closest room and glance enviously at the bed. I ignore the temptation and instead open the closet. Too exhausted to really care, I grab the first pair of shorts and shirt I see. When I turn back around, Jess is still standing in the doorway with a questioning look.

"Do you, um, want to stay in here with me?"

"I don't want to sleep alone," she replies.

She puts her battered bag down and turns to me. "I'm going to go grab some clean clothes and take a shower. I'll try and save some hot water for you, but no promises."

She winks and leaves the room.

If she's going to shower, then that means I have to as well. I don't enjoy being dirty, but I'm exhausted and want to lie down and recuperate from the day. My foot is absolutely throbbing. I decide to go check up on Matt and give him some company while I wait for the shower to open up. He's kissing Allison, so I turn my head out of respect and wait for her to pass by.

Once she does, I sit down in the enclosed porch with Matt. He opens a beer and hands it to me. "My father has always enjoyed brewing his own beer so we have some stockpiled."

I've only ever had alcohol at special occasions, such as when we celebrated Dominic's work assignment. Typically, consuming alcohol is frowned upon in the territories, as it doesn't produce anything beneficial for society. Matt's father must have had special privileges to be able to produce unregulated beer.

After a few minutes of companionable silence, Matt breaks it. "I have to ask. How did the two of you get in the position you were when we found you?"

I deliberate what I should tell him. "We were over around the lake staying with two of my friends I have known since childhood. A group of genetic engineers came to capture us for testing."

"Are you serious?" Matt's eyebrows are almost to his hairline.

I nod and take another sip. "Apparently they think they can figure out how to turn this whole thing around. They killed my friends. Jess and I were able to escape."

Matt closes his mouth and regains some of his composure. "Do you know where they went?"

"I would guess back to Potentia to get back to the lab," I say.

His face lights up. He quickly recovers his emotions and changes the subject. "I know I gave Allison a hard time for it earlier but are you two together? I mean you looked like it after we killed all the Hungry."

"What did you call them?" I ask.

"Oh, the Hungry. It's just what I call them because eating is all they care about." He playfully nudges me. "Nice try dodging the question."

I laugh. "I thought I got away with it." I take another sip and enjoy the feeling of it going down my throat. Water and a shower would probably be a better idea at this point, but I don't have the energy.

He taps his head and says, "You can't get anything past this bad boy. Many have tried, but none have prevailed."

I sigh before I respond. "You know, I honestly am not sure what's going on with Jess. Sometimes it seems like we're almost a couple, then other times, not as much."

"Hmmm, well do you want to be together?" he asks.

"She's wonderful. Any guy would be lucky to have her."

"Once again, nice try. Do you want to be with her?" He stares me down and I know I have to answer him.

"Of course I do. It isn't just her looks. She's beautiful, but it's more than that. She gives me strength and makes me better. She believed in me before I did myself."

"Here, have another beer, you're going to need it. You got it bad, brother." He laughs good-naturedly and hands me another drink.

I take it happily. "How about you and Allison? How long has she been pregnant?"

His face turns to shock. "She's not pregnant."

"I'm so sorry," I say, embarrassed. "I don't know what I was thinking."

To my surprise, he laughs loudly. "I'm just kidding. She's around five months pregnant. Maybe close to six." I join in and laugh with him. His laughter abruptly stops and he turns serious. "Listen up, this is really important. Do I have your full attention?"

"Yes, you have it," I say. I sit up in anticipation.

He rubs his hands together in excitement. "What's Mozart doing now that he's dead?"

"Mozart? The music composer? What does that have to do with anything? He's been dead for a really long time. How is this going to help?"

"Just answer it," Matt says.

When I come up with nothing, I shake my head in surrender.

"He's decomposing," Matt tells me and immediately laughs at his own joke. "Get it? Decomposing." His laughter is infectious and soon I laugh with him.

"If you're done with the life-changing advice, I'm going to go shower and go to bed," I tell him when our laughter quiets down and I finish my drink.

"Okay, sounds good. Peace with you. I'll wake you up for the watch when it's time."

I nod and walk away. I get to the front door and stop for a moment. "Hey, Matt?"

"Yeah?" he says.

"Thanks for saving our lives and bringing us here. I really appreciate it," I say. The simple statement seems inadequate. I hope my sincerity comes across.

He chuckles and says, "Still waiting on the letter of appreciation, brother."

"I'll get right on that."

I walk back toward our new room. I'm grateful that we ran into Matt and Allison. In a serious time with so much tragedy, having someone who can make you laugh is infinitely valuable. That's a lesson we learned from Andrew and Chris. It's also helpful they have a functioning vehicle as well.

I'm lost in these thoughts when I open the door and glimpse Jess changing into her cleaner clothes. I immediately look to the ground and utter an apology. I stumble out of the room. My cheeks burn and I curse myself for not knocking before I barged in.

To delay having to face her again, I go into the bathroom to take a shower. The bathroom is pretty small, yet functional. A pink, flowery pattern covers the wall. I laugh to myself at the idea of Matt living in a house filled with pink flowers.

Once I get under the hot water, my mind goes blank and I simply enjoy the feel of the dirt and scum coming off my body. I know I must have gotten horrendously dirty, but there was nothing I could do to avoid it. There is dried blood on my hands, reminding me of Carly's death.

I quickly wash it off and relax once the evidence of the battle goes down the drain. I let out several deep breaths while the water cascades down my body. Out of all the modern technologies, hot showers are my favorite. They're simply therapeutic.

Too soon, the water loses its heat so I hurry up and clean my body. I pay special attention to my tender foot. The soap and shampoo are some berry scent. Allison must have picked them out. I grab one of the soft pink towels as I get out and dry myself as best as I can.

I neglected to grab any clothes to change. The idea of putting back on my filthy clothes disgusts me, so I go out in my towel holding the clothes away from my body. Out of habit, my mind drifts to my scar. I take a deep breath and take a step forward. I have more important things to worry about.

I knock lightly. I don't want to make the same mistake twice. When I don't hear an answer, I very slowly open the door to find her sleeping on her stomach in the middle of the bed. Her shirt has rolled up, exposing her lower back.

I quietly grab Matt's old clothes and put a shirt and pair of shorts on. I carefully nudge her over so I have room to sleep. She moans unhappily but eventually allows me to move her slightly so I can get into bed.

I stare at Jess, taking comfort in the fact that we're both still alive and together. She must feel my attention on her because she opens her eyes a little to scowl playfully at me.

"You're creepy." Jess's words are slurred with sleep.

I chuckle under my breath and pull her in tight. She snuggles in and her breathing slows down once again. Her hair is still wet and feels cool through my shirt. I inhale deeply and recognize the same berry scent coming from her hair.

Finally getting a chance to relax is amazing. What's more, however, is the knowledge that we're safe. We're alive. This wasn't something I thought would be possible just hours ago. I'm grateful to be here. I close my eyes and moments later, I join her and fall asleep.

* * *

"Elliot, wake up. It's your turn," a deep voice informs me and I wake up. "You go for two hours and then wake up Jess for her turn. Have fun." Matt then leaves the room, presumably to go to bed himself.

Those two hours went by too fast. I force myself awake and maneuver out of the bed. Jess rolls over but remains sleeping. I cringe again when I place weight on my foot.

Even though I'm jealous she gets to keep sleeping, I'm glad I didn't wake her. I step out of the room to walk to the patio. There aren't any lights on in the house, so I stumble a little while I make my way. Eventually, I reach the front door. I pause for a moment and open it.

The night breeze is a little chilly and I wish I had a blanket or light jacket. Besides the crickets, the only other noise is the leaves lightly rustling in the wind. Overall, it's very relaxing. I take a seat in one of the rocking chairs and begin my watch.

The only source of light comes from the full moon. With all of the darkness, it's easy to imagine my brother storming through the trees. I know Dominic better than anyone else and there is no way he's finished with me. He isn't the type of person who gives up. If he thinks testing on me is his highest probability for his own well-being, he will go to any length to ensure his survival.

I can't let what happened with Andrew and Chris happen to anyone else. I need to somehow make sure that Dominic never finds us again.

At the same time, I can't help but feel guilty for not searching for Andrew. A small voice in my head wonders if he could still be alive. I know it would be a suicide mission to try and find out, but I can't help but think about it. At the end of the day, however, I can't put Jess's life in danger. I saw the looks Dominic gave her after he saw us together.

Yet, Dominic let us get away. He could have shot us. Instead, he lowered his gun. I know I saw the indecision in his eyes. Not only did he not shoot us when Jess and I ran away, there was also no evidence that they tried to catch us. It doesn't add up.

The house seems safe here. I don't want to jeopardize it and have Allison and Matt make us leave. Should I warn them about Dominic?

I make myself end that unsettling train of thought and decide I don't like keeping watch. While I understand it's necessary, I wish it wasn't. I'm still not used to the idea of the Letum and how quickly everything fell apart. How could a society that prides itself on its superior genetic planning destruct so easily?

Our generation is stronger and smarter than ever before, yet the moment this outbreak occurred, people stopped caring about each other. No matter how bleak a situation looks, I could never imagine capturing another person to run experiments on. Why is it so easy for Dominic? I can't fathom his ability to shut out emotion and focus solely on logic. With all of the recent loss, though, maybe it would be easier if I could be more like him.

Surely there is a place where it's safe and we can start over. Although I know it isn't entirely possible, I'm unable to put away that thin string of hope. There has to be a way for society to come back from this.

The time ticks by slowly. When I'm about to fall asleep, I glance at my watch and am relieved to find my two hours are up. Even though I don't want to wake Jess, the pull of sleep overrides my desire to be chivalrous and spare her this duty. I take one last look around the property and go inside to wake her.

She's the complete opposite as she was earlier. She rests in the fetal position and when I get closer, I can see her tears. I touch her gently. I want to end whatever nightmare is causing her pain as soon as I can.

She starts to wake up but before she does, she mutters out, "Why not me?"

"Shhh, Jess." I try and soothe her. "Everything is okay, wake up. The dream is just a dream."

She opens her eyes and once she understands what's going on, she wipes her tears away. Jess doesn't utter a word and leaves the room to take watch.

I fall asleep worrying about her.

CHAPTER NINETEEN

When the sun rises in the morning, Jess lies unresponsive in sleep. I get out of bed carefully so as not to wake her and leave the room.

Allison must hear me because she turns to me from the porch. With a beaming smile, she motions for me to join her. I sit down and try to fully wake up. Luckily for me, Allison starts talking, helping to speed up the process.

"So, how did you sleep last night?" She smiles warmly at me.

"Pretty well. Although, I still can't believe that I was able to sleep at all. I thought for sure we were going to die yesterday."

She nods. "That was a close call."

I change the subject, not wanting to let the sense of doom return. "How did you and Matt come to be here?"

"It's a long story, but I'll give you the highlights," she starts. "We've known each other since we started school. We quickly became best friends. It's probably pretty obvious, but Matt's parents planned him. Me, on the other hand, I'm just what popped out.

"He was in the middle of his training to be an educator whereas they were still trying to figure out what to do with me. I was hoping I could be an educator with Matt, but they would never let an Unplanned teach."

She breaks her story and asks, "By the way, what were the two of you studying for?"

Too ashamed to admit I had been assigned to the janitorial field, I say, "I'm Unplanned, too. Still waiting, just like you."

She nods. "And Jess?"

The image of her wrapping my foot in the bathroom plays through my mind. "She had been assigned the medical field."

Allison's eyes light up. She touches her stomach and says, "That'll be helpful in a few months."

I'm not sure how much Jess has already learned in her training, so I'm not familiar with her abilities. I make a noncommittal noise and eye Allison's stomach. Hopefully, the territories will be secure again by the time the baby comes.

She takes a deep breath. "Growing up, Matt's parents always discouraged us spending time together, but there wasn't anything they could do, due to us being in the same schooling year. We were always together and it was no big deal until we got older and went from loving each other to actually being in love with each other. His parents caught us together once and they were not happy."

She sighs sadly and looks like she's reliving the memory.

Once she composes herself she keeps speaking very quickly. "They met with my parents and while I wasn't part of the conversation, I got the general idea of it once I wasn't allowed to see him anymore. Of course, that didn't stop me." She then gestures at her stomach and laughs.

"We'd been seeing one another for awhile when this whole mess started. Everyone was at work when the sickness came into our territory. Fate was with us, though, because Matt and I were sneaking out to see each other to discuss this little blob. We hadn't told anyone yet."

I raise my eyebrow at this.

She laughs and says, "I wore a lot of baggy clothes. Once our parents got over the shock, I wonder what type of grandparents they would have been…"

Alison's eyes unfocus as she ponders what could have been. While children born out of wedlock aren't unheard of, with the two-kid limit, a lot of people elect out of the pregnancy, especially since it will be an Unplanned. I have new respect for the two of them given the amount of bravery they've displayed by sticking together.

My curiosity interrupts her thoughts. "I thought Robur was more progressive about everything. My mother used to say that there was a higher percentage of Unplanned there."

Allison continues her story. "That's true overall, but not for Matt's family. His father was on the city council and very conservative about genetic planning. He felt like if his son was with me, he would dilute his genetic superiority."

"I know the feeling," I say. I look at her in a new light. She was subjected to the same discrimination I was. There is nothing worse than being told you're worth less because of something you have no control over. We make eye contact and something passes between us, a bond and understanding of what we both went through.

Allison looks back toward the yard. "He wasn't a bad person overall. He was under a lot of pressure to maintain this perfect image and I was a threat to it."

I admire her for not wanting to talk badly about him even though it's clear he treated her unkindly.

"It's still hard," I say.

"It is what it is," she says. "But anyway, their vehicle didn't have any mileage restrictions on it. One of the perks of being a high-ranking official, I guess. But it always allowed them free travel, so we took advantage of it. We ran back to his place to grab some things and the vehicle."

"What about your parents?"

She looks over at me and drops her eyes.

"I'm not sure. You have to understand, there wasn't any time. We barely got out ourselves. I didn't want to leave them." She holds her stomach, deep in thought. "We had to give our child the best shot."

"I'm sure your parents would just be thankful the two—or three—of you are safe."

"Maybe one day we'll see them again," she says.

"If there is anything this whole thing has taught me, it's that anything is possible." Trying to cheer her up, I tease, "If that was the short version, I can't imagine the long version."

"Oh please, I left plenty of the good stuff out," she says and winks, making me thankful I got the edited version.

She laughs at my expression, but the laughter stops and she points out in front of the house. In the distance, there's a small group of the Letum walking toward us. It's hard to tell exactly how many there are, but it looks like either three or four.

"Should I go wake the others?" I say as soon as I see them.

"For only a few? I can take care of this myself. I'll save one for you if you're lucky."

"Should you be putting yourself at risk? I mean, in your...um... condition?" I ask while gesturing toward her stomach.

"Don't start. I hear enough of it from Matt. I'm not dying, I'm just pregnant. And that means I'm allowed to eat more, right? Well, I'm hungry for some Hungry."

With that, she grabs her weapon—it looks like an old baseball bat— and races off to meet them. Her stride isn't as fluid as I imagine it could be if she weren't pregnant. Before long, I doubt she will be able to run off like this.

I cuss under my breath and run inside to grab a machete by the front door. By the time I get back outside, she's about halfway to the group. I sprint to help her out. The pain in my foot has become an all too familiar companion.

Even for someone who's pregnant, she's still so damn quick. She opens the gate and attacks them without pause. She seems so tiny compared to all of the monsters, but they're much too slow to catch her.

By the time I get there, she's killed all of them but one.

"I guess it's your lucky day. I saved one for you."

She's breathing hard and her hands are shaking. Her body must be coursing with adrenaline right now.

Every time the creature tries to come at her, she simply hits it hard in the chest and it falls down, knobby knees collapsing. It would be pretty amusing if they weren't once people.

"I know you want it," she says as if she's trying to sell me something.

I need to get used to killing the Letum, so I grab my weapon and swing down hard to hit it in its expressionless head. It moves out of the way just before I can make contact and forces me to slam my hurt foot down on the ground to steady myself. The pain is shocking and I come down on my knee. I look up in a panic at the creature in time to see Allison swiftly move to kill the last one.

"Looks like I found someone just as clumsy as I am. Kind of a bad time to fall down, though," Allison says. She examines all of the bodies to ensure that they're all dead.

"I can't believe I fell," I say as my foot absolutely throbs in agony. I would have thought it would be getting better by now, not worse.

Seemingly satisfied, her focus shifts to me. Her eyes narrow at my hands clutching my foot and she says, "What's wrong?"

I release my foot and stand up. I do my best to hide it, but still I cringe slightly when I put pressure on my foot.

"Just a scratch," I say.

She looks at me expectantly for an elaboration.

Instead, I ask, "What do you want to do with the bodies?"

Her eyes narrow at the change of subject. "Matt has been piling them up just beyond the fence over in the small valley and burning them periodically." She points out to the west. "Don't worry about the bodies right now, though. Matt will move them later."

"Are you sure? I don't mind helping out." The last thing I want is for them to think I'm freeloading.

"Yes, I'm sure. Let's walk back," she says and gestures for me to head toward their house.

I frown at her change in attitude and walk silently back toward the patio. I concentrate on making my walking as effortless as possible. I don't want to appear weak.

Allison's voice stops me from going inside once we get back on the patio. "Sit down and show me your foot."

I let out a deep breath. "There's nothing to see."

Truth be told, I'm afraid that it has gotten worse and don't want to see it myself.

When she responds, her voice is stern, yet gentle. "Elliot, if you were bitten, I need to know. Let me see your foot."

I turn around in shock to face her. "I wasn't bitten. I just have a cut on my foot that's healing." At least, I hope it's healing.

Once again, her eyes narrow in skepticism. "Show me."

Now that I understand her fear, I want to eliminate it. I quickly sit down and remove my shoe and sock. I hold it out for her to see, but don't look at it myself.

She inhales sharply. "You're right, you weren't bitten." She looks closer and says, "Elliot, that's infected. What did you do?"

I force myself to look and my heart drops. Pus leaks from the angry red wound. No wonder it's so tender.

"I stepped on a rock when…" I hesitate as Carly's unwarranted autopsy flashes through my head. I clear my throat. "It's gotten worse," I say to acknowledge how bad it looks.

"Stay here," she says and goes back inside.

While I wait for her, I continue to examine my foot in disgust. I should have stayed off of it for a while to let it heal. Retrospective thought doesn't make the situation any better. It just allows you to regret the decisions you made.

Allison comes back to the patio with a syringe in her hand. Before I can ask where she got it, she says, "Matt's parents had a small supply of medicine that we took before we left. This should clear up the infection, but you'll need to take it easy for a few days to let it heal. You don't want it to get infected again."

I've never been a big fan of needles. I tense up as she gets closer to me, but remain still. She inserts it into my foot and releases the medicine through my body.

"Thank you," I say.

"Of course," Allison says. She smiles maternally at me. "Like I said, stay off of your foot as much as possible. If it stays infected, we'll have to go to a territory to get more medicine."

I raise my eyebrows in shock. "You wasted your only dose of antibiotics on me? Why?"

She pats my shoulder. "I wouldn't say it was a waste. I meant it when I said to make yourself at home here. You're part of our family now."

I don't have any words to express how grateful I am.

She must sense that because she changes the subject. "It's nice being able to have control and take them out. Better them than us, right?"

"How often do you run into these things?" I ask.

"Well, up until recently, it was really rare to get more than one every couple of days. Now, though, we normally get a group once or twice a day. The numbers keep getting larger. The group that was chasing you was by far the biggest we've seen. I guess that means things are going to get worse before better. I don't mind clearing out the infestation. The Hungry are too slow and stupid to be any real threat."

She smiles one more time and then focuses her attention back toward the horizon. The mounds of dead bodies are visible. Will I be able to adjust to a world focused around the necessity for violence?

"How did you learn to damage their head to truly kill them?" I ask.

She takes a seat and sighs as she rests her feet up. "I'm sure the same way you did. From trial and error."

Because they're still together and haven't mentioned losing anyone, their trial and error was probably a lot less costly than Jess's.

"I'm going to wash up as best I can. I got some mud on me when I fell." I notice she's even more covered than I am. "You can first. You probably need it more."

She looks down at herself and shrugs. "I'm fine. I still have a little time of my watch left. I'll just wait until after you're done. You should go wash your foot."

I walk inside. My foot still aches, but at least I know it's going to get better.

I meet Matt in the hallway and see the alarm in his eyes as he notices the dirt on my body. He quickly glances toward the patio and can see Allison.

"Did she go on one of her Hungry rampages again?"

I nod. He's quiet for a moment and then says, "Did she say she was 'hungry for some Hungry'?"

I nod again and he starts laughing.

"She decided that was her catchphrase. I told her she could do better, but I guess she's going to stick with that. Hungry for some Hungry." He shakes his head in amusement.

"What's yours? We've been calling them the Letum."

"I like that. It's fitting. I haven't come up with one yet, though. I have a couple of ideas going around in the old noodle, but I need something that's as awesome as I am."

He smiles mischievously at me. "I'm going to go scold her for running off. She always has a funny reaction when I do that." He jumps up and shakes his hands in excitement and bounds off to see Allison.

I'm right outside the bedroom door when it slams open. I jump in alarm at the sudden movement and noise.

"Whoops," Jess says when she realizes what happened.

"Why don't you open the door like a normal person?"

She looks defensive. "I heard some loud noise so I got out of bed to see what was going on."

"A loud noise? What loud noise?" I'm confused now. What could she be talking about?

"I don't know, it was just loud. Kind of like a bear mixed with a hyena?"

As she's telling me this, I can't help but crack a smile.

"What's so funny?"

"That loud sound you heard was actually Matt's laughter."

She simply stares at me for a moment and then asks, "Why is he laughing? What's there to laugh at?" I can tell she's slightly embarrassed. Seeing her like this is amusing.

"I don't know if you have noticed, but I'm a pretty funny person," I tell her and I brush imaginary dirt off my shoulder.

She gives me a glare that's supposed to be angry, but I can tell she's fighting laughter so it doesn't have much effect on me. She finally notices the mud on me and gives me a questioning look.

"Oh yeah," I say, straightening myself up. "While you were sleeping, a group of the Letum came, we took care of them, and Allison gave me some antibiotics for my foot."

I neglect to tell her that I fell. I don't want her to think I can't take care of myself.

"They have antibiotics?"

"They had antibiotics," I correct. "Allison gave me their only dosage."

A flicker of surprise crosses her face before she controls her expression again. "That was very kind of her. I was trying to figure out where the safest place would be to go get some for you. I'll examine it again this evening to make sure the antibiotics are working as they should."

"Aye, aye, doctor."

"You're too happy in the mornings," she says.

"You're too grumpy in the mornings," I say and quickly move to avoid another one of her playful jabs in the side.

CHAPTER TWENTY

"They're back," Allison calls out.

I breathe a sigh of relief at Matt and Jess's return. They've been gone since yesterday morning and we've spent our time anxiously awaiting their return. The idea of a supply run is necessary, yet I'm not a fan of Jess putting herself in extra danger. It's amazing how quickly she's become intertwined in my life.

I gingerly stand up from the couch I have been resting my foot on. It's accompanied by a slight pain, but it's vastly improved from two days ago when Allison gave me my antibiotics. Since then, Jess and I have spent our time recovering from our journey here and the physical exhaustion it took.

I step outside just as Jess steps out of their vehicle. I immediately scan every motion and am relieved she looks unharmed. She brushes her wavy hair out of her eyes and smiles when we make eye contact.

"You're never going to believe how lucky we were today," Jess exclaims and gestures toward the vehicle.

Now that I'm assured of her health, I examine the vehicle. The back seat is packed in familiar small boxes.

"Is that what I think it is?" I ask and open the door to the vehicle.

Matt breaks away from his embrace with Allison and says, "If you think it's enough boxes of food packets to last the four of us for months, then yes, it's what you think it is."

Allison's hands jerk to her mouth. Matt laughs at her reaction and picks her up to kiss her again.

Jess smirks and jokingly shakes her head. "We broke into a house and it was fully stocked with food packets. On the downside, our meals will be unbelievably bland these next few months."

"This is amazing," I say as I rummage through the top box. They were compiled by the food distributors in Vis. They must have had a cabin out in Accidia that they weren't able to escape to.

Jess nods. "We were very fortunate to come across it all. It's one less thing we need to worry about."

She waves at Matt to get his attention, then says, "Matt, let's go ahead and bring all the boxes inside to keep them safe. Allison, you're supposed to take it easy during pregnancy. Go sit back down."

Allison raises an eyebrow at this statement and surprisingly doesn't argue.

I grab the top box to help and Jess takes it out of my arms.

"I don't want you to stress your foot anymore while it heals. Go with Allison and sit down."

Matt laughs openly at this exchange and I open my mouth to disagree. Jess gives me a look that sends me turning around and walking up the patio. I know she's right. My ego just doesn't like it.

I sit next to Allison on the couch. The two of us make eye contact and start laughing. The idea of our being banished inside to sit is, for some reason, very humorous. My sides ache from the effort of laughing for so long.

We finally regain our composure and Allison says, "It's nice to have people who care about you, isn't it?"

Her question takes me by surprise and the mood changes instantly. All of the people who have cared about me my whole life are dead.

Although Allison is a very talkative person, she seems to sense this shift and doesn't say anything else. It's startling that Jess is probably the person who cares most about me, and I her.

Unable to remain sitting with my thoughts any longer, I grab the boxes from Jess. I'm not sure what exactly she sees in my facial expression, but whatever it is, she doesn't protest. Instead, she turns back around to go grab more from the vehicle.

Once all of the food packets are safely stored inside, we all go outside to eat dinner on the patio. Besides the scraping of our spoons against the bowls, the only other noise accompanying us is the sound of the evening nature. We eat on the patio so we can keep an eye on everything while still having each other's company.

"Okay, I got another one for you," Matt says between bites. "What do you call someone with no body and no nose?"

"Nobody knows," Allison says without hesitation. It's obvious she's heard this one before. Nonetheless, Matt's booming laughter, a mix between a bear and a hyena, as Jess described it, fills the patio.

When he stops laughing, his face gets serious again. "I have one that even Allison hasn't heard yet."

"Oh, I highly doubt that," Allison says.

"You need to believe in me, babe." Matt pretends to be wounded. Allison rolls her eyes. Satisfied with her reaction, Matt gets serious again. "Think about this one. What did the fish say when it ran into a wall?"

Jess and I look expectantly at Allison and she shrugs. We all try to think of the answer and the more time that goes on, the happier and more pleased Matt looks.

"You guys give up?" He looks smug.

"Dam. He says, 'Dam,'" I answer and laugh with Matt. I can't help but be amused at Matt's enthusiasm.

When we finish our meal, Jess says, "There is something Matt and I need to tell the two of you." I sit up straighter in my chair and Matt nods for her to continue. "We drove straight to Vis to see if we could get a clue as to how the territory has been going since I left."

Matt takes over her story and says, "The wall to Vis was opened and the surrounding area was crawling with the Hungry. We couldn't get as close as we would have liked because of them."

"All of those people…" Allison mutters.

Jess's mask protects her thoughts and hides whatever she's feeling with her home territory succumbing to the infection. Without any emotion, she continues, "We suspect that's why there have been a larger number of the Letum lately. They escaped the confine of Vis and have since then been roaming, looking to satisfy their needs."

I dart my eyes to look around the property to assure myself the Letum from Vis aren't upon us right now. I sigh and redirect my attention toward our conversation.

Matt and Allison exchange a glance and he nods his head.

Allison takes a deep breath and says, "Matt and I were wondering if the two of you would like to stay with us long term."

Jess furrows her eyebrows. "Why do you want us to stay? The food packets will last a lot longer if it's only the two of you eating them."

Matt looks affronted. "Jess, we found those packets together. If the two of you decide to leave, half of them are yours."

"Really?" I ask. I grew up with Dominic and his high level of self-importance that overshadowed everyone else around him. Where did Matt learn this selfless behavior? It wasn't in the territories.

"Of course, Elliot," Allison says. "And Jess, this place may be relatively safe, but there's strength in numbers."

"And both of you don't mind us staying here?" I ask, still unable to understand why they would be willing to split their supplies in half.

Matt says, "Brother, look at how we found you. You two were about to bite it." He stops for a moment and considers what he said. "Or rather, be bitten."

"Besides, as much as I enjoy Matt's company, it would be nice to have a little girl time every once in awhile. Right, Jess?"

The look of alarm that spreads across Jess's face at the thought of having to contribute in girl time brings the whole table to a new round of laughter.

Once Jess understands what's so funny, she allows a small chuckle and gives me a meaningful look. "I'm going to go through my bag and see exactly what I have. I want to know what we can contribute." She grabs her plate and heads inside.

I pause for a couple of seconds in indecisiveness and say, "I think I'm going to do the same."

Allison and Matt both smile.

Matt says, "It's okay, brother. We understand. Go talk things over. We'll stay out here and give you your privacy."

I nod gratefully. When I get to the room, Jess quickly closes the door behind me. We look at each other for a moment and then I say, "What do you want to talk about?"

"Isn't it obvious? How do we know we can trust these people? It's really nice that they saved us, but what do we know about them?"

I pause to consider my answer. We just meet them, yet I'm considering tying our safety with them. "I've had a good conversation with both of them and they seem like good, genuine people. I think we can trust them. Plus, Allison is going to need someone to deliver their baby."

Her eyebrows shoot up, almost comically. "I can't do that yet. I only just started my training."

"But you've studied it," I say.

Jess brushes her hair out of her face. "That's not the same as actually doing it."

"You're her best option right now." I smile halfheartedly.

Reluctant acceptance crosses her face. "We can stay at least until she has the baby. Then, I want to revisit this conversation."

Relieved, I eagerly nod. That will be plenty of time to convince Jess we should stay.

She continues speaking and says, "I'm worried about their plan. I don't think they're going to find anything in their search and if they do, it isn't going to be what they hoped." She looks sad at this thought.

"What else are we going to do? We'd be dead without them. Besides, what if we ran into another group of the Letum? What if it was even bigger? Matt and Allison are good fighters and we can all keep each other safe."

She nods. Jess knows I speak the truth, but issues a warning. "We don't want to be in a group that turns on each other. Your own brother attacked you. This situation has the potential to change people, and not all for the better."

I look at her more deeply and try to understand where this is all coming from. I agree with everything she said, yet it seems like there's something she isn't sharing with me.

"What are you really worried about?" I ask. "We clearly aren't in any shape to leave right now and they've been more than accommodating. Allison even gave me their only dose of antibiotics for my foot. What's actually going on?"

For a few seconds, she doesn't look like she's going to answer me. She surprises me and says, "I don't want to get close to more people just to watch them die." The only sign of the emotion she experiences is the slight twitching of her hands.

"Jess." My shoulders drop. "I know it has been really hard. We just need to learn from the past and make sure history doesn't repeat itself."

"Do you honestly think we can all be safe and stay protected from this epidemic?" she asks. Her eyes stare into mine.

I don't dare to lie. I choose my next words carefully. "We have to try. We need to do our best not to live in fear of what could happen." I hope the message sinks in with myself as well. "We can't let all the bad prevent us from finding happiness elsewhere."

"Why should we open up to people if we're just going to lose them? Does it really make a difference in the end?" she asks.

"It does," I say. I confidently pull her into an embrace and try to pass some of my strength on to her.

Normally, she's the one who gives me hope and passes on her fortitude to me. Now, I'm able to do that for her. I've known all along why I like her but have been unsure why she's appeared to return those affections. For the first time, I understand the value I can give to her. It seems as if there's something new between us as if some line was crossed.

CHAPTER TWENTY-ONE

And so, we settle into our new lives with a newfound sense of security. Besides pacing through the barrier and keeping watch, our lives, for the first time in a long time, feel normal.

The four of us mesh together and become a family.

The only evidence of the endless passage of time is Allison's expanding stomach. Nothing particularly exciting happens, but that's part of what makes it so wonderful. We heal from both our emotional and physical wounds.

One day, Jess and I are out on the patio partly to keep watch, but also to give Matt and Allison a little privacy. We share the bench and her legs lie nonchalantly across my lap. Spring has transformed to summer and a calm breeze blows toward us to keep it from getting too hot. Jess hums a little under her breath as she reads one of the books she borrowed from Allison while I keep an eye on the calm atmosphere.

Matt's booming laugh interrupts the moment, quickly followed by a little squeal. Jess and I make eye contact. I struggle to keep from laughing out loud. With the window directly behind our heads, any noise inside easily travels to us.

"Want to go on a walk?" I say. Another noise comes from inside. Jess's eyes widen in a mixture of shock and amusement.

"That sounds like a great idea. Let's go around the barricade and give them a little…" She pauses in an attempt to discover the right word and spreads her hands out. "Space."

She removes her legs from my lap and jumps off the bench. I follow suit and the two of us grab a weapon by the front door before leaving the patio and sound of the commotion inside.

I close my eyes and tilt my head up to let the sun warm my face. A crash of some sort reaches us still and we pick our pace up.

"Let's go across the barrier. I'm getting bored with the trail on this side," Jess suggests once we reach the fence.

It'll be safe enough. We'll smell them before they get the opportunity to sneak up on us. Lately, it seems like the smell is getting stronger.

"I don't see the harm in that."

"Good."

Jess hops over the fence in an easy motion. I smile and follow right behind her, although a little more awkwardly. She's in such a strong state of happiness. It's contagious.

"Why are you in such a good mood?" I ask as we turn to the right and begin our walk between the trees. They block most of the sunlight and only small breaks in protection allow it to reach us. "Not that I'm complaining or anything," I clarify after she gives me a sharp look.

"Are you saying I'm normally grumpy?" she asks. Her face is serious, but her eyes betray her to show she's in a joking mood.

I decide to follow along. "Yes, that's exactly what I'm saying."

Her mouth opens in shock and she playfully nudges me. My boot catches a rock and I almost lose my balance and fall into the ditch to my left. I exhale quickly at the close call.

Her laughter rings through the air. "If anything, you're the serious one."

"Don't project yourself on me," I say in good spirits, thankful to have recovered. That was almost embarrassing.

Before she can respond, the inevitable smell comes. Jess rolls her eyes and sighs in annoyance. Four of the Letum are approaching us from behind. I nudge Jess and we both turn around. Nothing we can't handle. They're more of an aggravation than anything. The sound of us laughing must have attracted them to us.

"I'll take the two on the left and you get the other two," she says.

"Done," I say and start calculating my next move. We've faced worse situations, so I'm hardly even nervous. This is just a normal part of life now. I grip my machete harder in preparation and ignore the annoying mosquito biting at my leg.

The Letum stumble their way toward us and we get into action. To my left, Jess is a flurry of motion as she takes out her two. I swing down hard and my weapon slices through one's head without any real hesitation. The other one reaches out to me so I kick it back. It falls on the ground and I slam my boot down on its face. It explodes. All four of the Letum lie on the ground motionless. I wipe some of the gore off my boot by using one of the rocks next to the ditch.

"Nicely done," Jess says while she kneels down to examine the smashed head in appreciation.

I turn toward Jess. "The head on the first one seemed weaker than normal. I wanted to test it out. Dominic was right. They truly are decomposing."

Jess gets back to her feet and looks at the other three Letum. "I wonder if they will ever just stop existing if they can't satisfy their hunger," Jess murmurs.

I shrug even though she can't see. The implications of that theory are overwhelming. That would mean this would all eventually end.

"It's possible, I guess."

She looks toward me and her eyes widen in fear. A pressure on my ankle starts. I look down at my foot to find one of the beasts gnawing on me. I shake my foot away in disgust and plunge my weapon into its head.

"Son of a bitch," I yell in frustration. I can't believe I was so stupid and let this happen.

"Elliot!" Jess's voice is full of anguish and fear.

I look around to make sure there aren't any others.

"Let's get over the barrier before we get snuck up on again," I say.

I slam my machete back down on the creature in frustration and walk back to the barrier. Jess doesn't say anything and follows me closely. We hop back over the fence to our safety. The sun beams down on us and instantly takes away the small chill from the shadows.

"We shouldn't have gone to the other side," Jess says.

I turn back around to her. A single tear falls slowly down her cheek. I take a step closer and wipe it off her face.

"Don't cry. Everything is all right."

She shakes her head and miserably says, "But you were bitten."

"I have boots on." I lift up my pants to show her. "He didn't break through the leather. All I felt was the pressure of his bite."

She stares at me in disbelief. I smile to try and reassure her.

"Show me," she finally demands.

I sit down and untie my laces and buckles. I take my foot out and hold it for her to examine. My sock is completely white with no evidence of blood. She grabs it and looks it over carefully.

"See, I'm fine," I reassure her again.

Seemingly unsatisfied, she takes my sock off and feels around my ankle looking for any sign of broken skin. Besides the scar on the bottom of my foot from the cut on the day Carly died, my foot and ankle are completely unscathed.

"I don't believe it," she says, still in doubt. "I thought I was going to lose you."

This time, I shake my head. "I'm not going anywhere," I say.

A strange look comes across Jess's face and she does what I haven't had the courage to do. She grabs my face and kisses me. I enthusiastically return her gesture. I let myself fall backward and her steady pressure on my body doesn't relent. I put one arm around her waist to hold her and my other hand rests in her hair.

The kiss ends and she places her head on my chest.

"I would have let myself almost get bitten a long time ago if I knew that this is how you would react," I say.

I expect her to playfully hit my chest but instead, she snuggles in tighter.

"I really thought you were going to die." Her voice is so quiet it's barely audible.

I let out a deep breath. "For a second there, so did I," I admit.

"It would have been all my fault," she says. "I'm getting careless and I took you out there with me."

"I went right along with you. We're getting so used to the Letum that they don't seem as dangerous anymore. Let's be more careful in the future. I don't want my boots to get dirty," I say to lighten the mood and swat away another bug.

She doesn't take the bait and remains serious. "I can't lose you. That's something I won't accept."

I pull her chin up and lightly press my lips on hers. "Just as I can't lose you, Jess."

We lie there and watch the sunset. Her humming vibrates lightly on my chest. I can't help but smile at this. She only does it when she's happy and content. I doubt she even realizes she's doing it now.

Too soon, we're interrupted by Matt's loud voice calling out, "Jess? Elliot? Come back. We made dinner."

I sigh and say, "We should probably go to the house."

Jess nods and the two of us stand up. I subconsciously grab her hand and we make our way back to the patio.

Matt and Allison stand right outside the front door waiting on us. He spots our hands.

"Hubba hubba."

"I wouldn't be making any jokes right now," Jess fires back. "At least not after what we heard earlier."

Allison, now in Matt's sister's wardrobe to support her increased size, blushes while Matt grins.

"Should we go eat?" Allison asks in a clear attempt to change the conversation. Her hands hold her stomach without conscious thought.

"That sounds good," I say. I allow the topic transition and we all move into the house to eat at the dining room table.

Our blended family shares the meal with an easy conversation flow. After dinner, we move out to the patio and play a board game. Matt and I team up against the girls. Much to the detriment of our pride, they crush us.

"We'll get you next time," Matt says.

"Oh, so the two of you took it easy on us?" Allison asks.

"It wouldn't be fair if we were perfect at everything, now would it?" Matt says. We all laugh at this statement.

"Maybe we can play a different game. The two of you seem to be able to communicate telepathically. We can't do that." I try to defend our loss. The game involved drawing out certain actions. Neither of us is very good at drawing. We didn't stand a chance.

"I'll let the two of you sit out here and nurse your pride. Allison, do you want to come inside with me?" Jess asks suddenly.

They make eye contact.

"That's a great idea. Losers should take first watch," Allison says with a giant smile on her face.

"It's settled then." Jess stands up and helps Allison to her feet. Allison is getting awkward in her movements. The two of them disappear into the house.

"Okay, what happened earlier?" Matt says the moment they leave earshot.

"What do you mean?"

"Jess clearly just went inside to talk to Allison about something," Matt says. Amusement echoes throughout his face.

"What?" My eyes widen in shock. "How do you know that?" I'm embarrassed now. What's she telling her?

"I've been around women enough to know their tricks. Allison has pulled that one on me before," Matt says.

"Oh." My mind races with the details she could be sharing right now.

Matt laughs at my expression and says, "Well? Spill it."

"We kissed," I admit.

Matt reaches out for a high five. I accept it.

"It's about time. What took so long?"

"What do you mean?"

"Well, it has been clear since we met the two of you that there was something going on. I'm surprised it took this long, that's all." He shrugs.

"I'm just glad it did," I say with a satisfied grin covering my face.

"Well done, brother," Matt says. "If you stay with me for the first hour, I'll take the rest of the watch. After they've had plenty of time to talk, go to Jess."

"It's my turn to take the first watch tonight. Are you sure?" I ask. His offer is very tempting.

"No worries, I'm sure you'll return the favor someday," Matt says.

"I suspect you'll be wanting more time once the baby comes," I say.

His eyes light up with excitement. "I can't wait for our baby to get here."

"You're going to be a great father," I say.

"I plan on it," Matt says. The sincerity in is voice assures me that the child is going to grow up with a phenomenal father who will be extremely supportive of his children.

I wonder how differently my life would have turned out if I had had someone like Matt as a father. A small part of me envies the unborn baby. He's always going to encourage his child and make sure they always feel valued.

But what kind of future do we all have in this new world?

CHAPTER TWENTY-TWO

Jess is still awake when I open the door. She looks away from her book and returns my smile automatically. I climb into our bed and we shift until she's between my legs, with her head resting on my chest and both of us facing the same direction. Jess leans into my body and continues to read. I play with her hair while she hums under her breath. I lose track of time.

Slowly, Jess sets her book down and looks up with her brow furrowed in concentration. She looks as if she's about to say something, but she pauses and closes her mouth again.

Finally, she breaks the silence by saying, "I'm happy."

I chuckle at her simple comment. "I'm happy as well." I kiss her on the neck. The heat on her skin feels warm on my lips.

This time, she's the one who giggles. "I'm trying to be serious, Elliot."

"In that case, I'm seriously happy," I say. I try to kiss her again, but her movement prevents me.

Jess turns around and stares at me intently. Her right hand holds the back of my head while her other finds my chin. She leans in and kisses me. Every thought in my mind is focused on how much I care about her. How much she means to me. How much I love her.

She gently pulls back and whispers in my ear, "After everything that has happened, I didn't think I could ever be this happy again."

I lean in, but she smirks and places a finger on my lips.

"Let me finish. I didn't think you were a possibility for me. I didn't think I would find someone who would make me so utterly content. Thank you."

She moves her finger and curls it under my chin and pulls me closer. Now, she waits for me to kiss her.

My heart feels like it's beating so loudly, I get self-conscious.

I try to gain courage and say, "I really care about you. I can't imagine not having you in my life. I like you as my woman. I…" A laugh nervously escapes as I struggle to complete my thought.

"Don't worry. I love you, too," Jess says.

Under her trance, I eliminate the distance between us.

Our kissing takes on a more fevered intensity. All other thoughts leave my body. Every pulse of my heart reminds me how much I need her. My only concentration is on Jess and how she makes me feel. Her hands explore my body and I take a sharp breath as I discover her intentions.

I freeze. "Are you sure?"

Rather than answer me with words, she moves her hips in a way that makes it very clear exactly what she wants. She leans in closer and initiates another kiss. It takes all the restraint I have to pull back from her.

A little breathless, I whisper, "With everything that has been going on, I want to make sure this is what you want."

I take another deep breath and open my eyes to look at her. She's pulled back and is staring deeply into my eyes. Used to her with some degree of guard surrounding her face, I'm surprised to see her completely open. Her gaze is filled with a type of love I didn't even know was a possibility.

"I don't want to move too quickly," I finish lamely.

She grabs her messy hair and pulls it behind her neck to place it on the side. My heart beats emphatically and reminds me of the importance of this moment.

"Elliot, there's just you and me right here. Forget everything else. For tonight, it's just the two of us and that's all the matters. That's enough."

She grabs my hand and places it on her heart. It threatens to burst out of her chest.

"Are you sure?" I repeat, my defenses crumbling down.

She responds nonverbally and gently comes forward for another kiss, silencing me from voicing any other questions. While our last kiss was more frantic in a need for each other, this one is tender and gentle. I run my hands through her hair. Slowly, I move them down her back.

I slip one hand under her shirt and she flinches. She smiles against my lips.

"Your hands are freezing, Elliot."

"Sorry," I blurt out and move my hand away automatically.

She leans back with another smirk. Her eyes light up in amusement.

"I didn't say I wanted you to stop," she clarifies as she replaces my hand on her back.

I smile back and use my other hand to lift her shirt off. Her hair flows down her shoulders and cascades down her chest.

With mischief in her eyes, she says, "Fair is fair," and places her hands on my stomach.

I lean forward so she can take my shirt off. Very deliberately, she leans back down and kisses the scar on my chest.

Her acceptance overwhelms me. Our lips meet again and I rotate her so I'm on top. She's right. It's just the two of us. Nothing else matters.

*   *   *

Afterward, once conscious thought returns, I kiss Jess on her forehead.

She rolls over and looks around.

"My book fell off the bed," she says. "I lost my place in it."

Her brown eyes stare at me in joking accusation.

"Please accept my most sincere apologies. I'll try my best to make sure that never happens again," I say.

She grabs her book off the floor and places it on the nightstand. She turns back into me and I wrap my arms around her.

"I guess I won't mind if it happens again," she says.

"What's the book about?"

"It's just a story. Honestly, I'd rather focus on reality right now. It's seemingly perfect."

"Yes, it is," I agree.

The two of us fall asleep intertwined, physically and emotionally. As my mind drifts off, I'm excited for what the new day will bring.

* * *

Sometime in the middle of the night, the sound of vomit hitting the toilet startles us awake. Jess and I look at each other in revulsion.

"The joys of pregnancy," Jess says. She automatically eyes the contraception package we opened a few hours previously.

I chuckle nervously at her apparent thought process and say, "She hasn't been sick in awhile. Should we check on her?"

"I could think of a couple other things we could do instead." Jess nuzzles closer to me.

I jump when her cold feet curl on my legs but pull her tighter anyway. Before I can kiss her, the sound of vomiting interrupts us.

Jess leans away and sighs. "I'll go check on her and make sure she doesn't need anything."

She smiles at my disappointed expression.

"I'll be right back."

I watch as she gets out of bed and puts a robe on. Right before she walks out of the room, she winks at me. I lean back on the bed. The memories of last night replay in my head and I can't help but smile to myself. After a bit, my eyes get heavy and I close them.

Jess's oddly calm voice brings me back to reality. "Elliot, come here, please."

I furrow my eyebrows at her tone. She probably just wants me to go grab water or something for Allison. I get out of bed, grab some shorts quickly, and join them at the bathroom.

My scar is visible, but Jess helped me work through that insecurity. In fact, she's helped me with almost all of them.

A much larger figure surrounds the toilet than I was anticipating. Allison whispers soothing words and rubs Matt's back as another round of nausea hits him.

Jess has put on her mask to hide her thoughts. My heart drops with worry.

I wait for Matt to get himself under control again until I walk closer. I pat his shoulder to let him know I'm behind him. Even with his shirt on, I can still feel the heat radiating off of him.

"What's going on, Matt?" I ask.

"Fancy meeting you here, brother," he whispers weakly. If I didn't see his mouth move, I wouldn't have recognized it as his voice. It's so hoarse and cracked.

"He wasn't bitten," Allison says. Her voice is tense and she speaks even quicker than normal. "I know that's what you're thinking, but he wasn't bitten or anything. You can check his body if you don't believe me. He wasn't bitten. He just has a bug or the flu or something. It happens all the time. He'll be fine once he gets this out of his system, but he wasn't bitten." She adds one more time for emphasis.

"We know he wasn't bitten. We just want to make sure everything is okay." I say.

I glance around the room in desperation for anything to do to help. With the four of us crammed into the small room, it's very crowded.

"Thanks, everyone, but you really shouldn't stay up for me. I'll be fine. I'm starting to feel better," Matt breathlessly says as he closes his eyes.

"We'll go get you some water and crackers."

I know Jess is trying to whisk me away so I nod and follow her across the house.

Once we're out of earshot, she says, "He looks exactly like my father did before he turned. He's infected."

Fear shoots through my body.

"He wasn't bitten. He could be just sick."

She shakes her head adamantly. "You have to trust me on this, he looks exactly like my father did."

"He also looks like my brother did when he had a stomach flu last year." I pull her into an embrace and say in her ear, "I know why you're worried, but he hasn't been bitten. Everything is going to be okay."

Jess pulls away and crosses her arms in stubbornness. "I can't ignore my gut feeling."

I run my hands through my hair. "What can I do to make you less nervous?"

She considers the question and then says, "Tie him up and help me keep Allison away from him."

"You want me to tie him up?"

My eyebrows shoot up in surprise. I glance around the room for inspiration on anything that would even work.

"You asked." The mask that was completely dissipated just minutes ago is in full effect and I can't get a feel for what she's thinking and how worried she actually is.

I sigh and nod at her request. I kiss her on the forehead.

"Let's go get the water and crackers and we'll talk to both of them. You get Allison away and I'll talk to Matt. She really should stay away anyway. I don't think any of us want a sick pregnant lady on our hands. Take her back to our room and I'll stay with Matt tonight."

"Be careful and let me know immediately if you need anything."

Jess kisses me one last time and walks down the hallway back to our friends.

I follow a couple steps behind her and contemplate the situation. He's just sick. I don't understand why Jess is so convinced he isn't. Whatever this disease is, being bitten transfers it somehow. I agree with Jess that Allison should keep her distance from Matt for the time being, but not for fear of him turning. He wasn't bitten.

Jess gently pats Allison's shoulder. "Let Elliot stay with Matt for a little bit. You need to get some rest." She reaches out to guide her away.

"What? No, I should stay with Matt." Allison shakes her head at the idea and continues to rub Matt's back while he hunches over the toilet.

"They're right. You should go get some rest. Go take care of our kid. I'll get some quality guy time with Elliot. It'll be fun."

Allison considers the offer. Despite her exhaustion, she doesn't want to leave Matt.

"It's best for your baby," Jess says.

Finally, Allison agrees. "I'll be right down the hall. If you need anything, come get me."

She leans down and kisses him on top of his head. Matt responds by dry heaving. With a look of concern on both of their faces, Jess and Allison leave. I sit down closer to Matt.

"Do you want any water or anything?" I ask him.

"Not now. I would just throw it back up. Maybe in a little bit."

Now that I'm closer to him, I can see him shaking. Sweat covers his body. I don't have any words that will make him feel better so I sit by his side in silence.

As I sit there, I begin to worry about the future. If Matt had gotten sick within a territory, he could have gone to a doctor, received treatment, and been fine shortly after. That's what happened to Dominic last year. If such a simple bug can leave someone like this, how are we supposed to deal with things more serious?

Allison's due date is getting close. She's about seven months pregnant now. What if the baby comes early? What if there is any sort of complication? Jess is our best chance at delivering the baby safely, but she had only just started her medical training. Almost all of her knowledge is from reading books. She's going to need all the help she can get.

My stomach drops at all of the uncertainties on the table right now. Once Matt gets better, Jess and I will have to go into a territory to find some medicine and get supplies for the delivery.

Matt is clearly on the same line of thought as he says, "We're going to have to go get some stuff for Allison. What if she goes into labor early?"

"I was just thinking the same thing. I can leave in the morning to go look for some medicine. Jess will come with me," I say with confidence. That's what Jess has become, my certainty.

"I appreciate it, brother, but I can't have you do that."

I expected Matt to react this way. "You would do the same for either me or Jess. You just need to focus on getting better."

A little bit of strength enters his voice. "You don't understand, you can't go off and leave me here."

He clenches his jaw in determination.

I take a deep breath and choose my words carefully. "I understand you want to be the one getting medication and the supplies for Allison, but we don't know how long you'll be sick and I'm not comfortable waiting any longer to start our search. With luck, Jess will be able to identify some medicine for you," I say. Now isn't the best time for his ego to be wounded.

Matt leans back against the pink wall and looks at me fiercely. "What did Jess want to talk about when the two of you went to the kitchen?"

The turn of conversation surprises me. "Why?"

"I saw the way she was looking at me. What does she think?"

I owe Matt more than lies.

"She thinks you might be turning. But Matt, you weren't bitten."

"I know I wasn't bitten. That's beside the point. What if I am?" Matt asks. I've never seen him scared before. It raises my own anxiety level in reaction.

"It's impossible. If the sickness were airborne, we would all have caught it. You just have a bug, but it'll get out of your system soon."

"What if it isn't though? What if the two of you leave and when you come back, I have turned and killed Allison and our child?" His voice breaks.

"And what if tomorrow you feel completely fine?" I say.

Matt studies me as if trying to decide if I'm being genuine or not.

"I hope you're right. I'm so worried that you're not. I need you to promise me something."

I nod in agreement and he continues. "If anything ever happens to me, I need you to protect and look after Allison and our child—just as if she were Jess and your child."

"Of course, Matt. I promise." I'm relieved that's what he needed a reassurance on. I thought that went without saying.

Matt smiles weakly at me. "One more thing. If I do turn, take care of me as well. Don't let me hurt anyone."

"You're not going to turn, Matt, there is no—"

"Promise me."

I hesitate before agreeing. He lets out a deep breath and clearly looks relieved.

"Maybe I'm starting to feel a little better. Can you help me back to my bed?"

I nod again and stand up, offering him a hand. He stumbles up and the two of us walk down the hallway.

"Wow, Matt," I say when he places more of his weight on me so I can help support him. "You need to lose some weight."

"I'm working on it. Give me a couple more days of this new diet and I'll be bikini ready in no time."

I chuckle under my breath. Matt startles me by stopping. He takes his weight off of me and opens the closet door and starts rummaging.

"What're you looking for?"

He ignores me and continues his search. He finally pulls out of the closet. He holds something in his hand, but it's too dark for me to make out what he's carrying.

"What's that?" I hope for a response this time.

Instead of answering, Matt grabs my arm with his free hand and motions for us to keep walking. It must be something important, so I support him as the two of us make it to the doorway of his and Allison's room. No one is in there. Jess must have taken Allison to our room.

"I thought Jess would keep Allison out of here," Matt says.

Our short walk has exhausted him. His breathing is shallow and quick.

I reach over to turn the lamp on so we can see better. I block the light from hitting Matt.

His face is in a shadow so I can't see his expression as he says, "Tie me to the bed."

In his hand is a coil of rope. I'm glad I don't have to be the one to bring it up. I merely help him into bed.

His eyes get really big and his hands go to cover his mouth. Quick on my feet, I rush over and grab a trashcan to hold under him. He dry heaves for a while before expelling some bile from his stomach.

Matt leans back, fatigued, and closes his eyes. "I'm sorry," he says.

"Nothing to apologize for." I gently grab his left hand and tie the rope around it. "Is this too tight?"

"Tighter," he says through his teeth.

I frown and tighten the rope. I don't want to hurt him. I make sure I can slip a finger under the rope and once I'm satisfied he's going to be able to maintain circulation in his hand, I tie the other side to the bed. I give him enough slack so he can be comfortable.

"I left you enough extra rope so you can lean down and grab the trashcan if you need to. Don't throw up on yourself—that'll be your baby's job when he or she gets here," I say, trying to lighten the mood.

"I can't wait." He pauses for a beat. "Thanks for helping me get into bed. I'll feel better knowing if worse comes to worst, I can't hurt anyone."

"Nothing's going to happen, but I'm glad you feel safer in here."

"Talk to me for a little bit to take my mind off of things," he says.

"What do you want to talk about?"

Matt's eyes are still closed, but he smiles as he says, "Did you have a good time with Jess earlier? I heard the two of you."

"What? Well, I mean…" I stumble and am unable to articulate my thoughts. What did he hear?

Matt opens his eyes and an echo of his normal laugh escapes him. "I was completely messing with you. I didn't hear anything, but we'll catch up on that later." He sighs and it's so obvious how poorly he feels. "Protect her and keep her safe, no matter what."

"I can't imagine not having her in my life. She's the part of me that I never thought I would deserve," I say. "I don't know what's going to happen in our new world, but I know that she will be with me and that's enough."

Matt takes in my words. "Remember your promise to me. That feeling of protectiveness you feel with her, please make sure to extend it to Allison and our child if anything happens to me."

"Of course. No matter what. And likewise for you."

"Don't worry, if the Hungry come for Jess, I'll just throw up on them and they'll be so disgusted they'll run away."

We both chuckle quietly and Matt says, "Do me a favor and go check the barriers. I missed the last round when I got sick."

"Are you sure you don't want me to stick with you?" I told Allison I would stay with him, but the barrier does need to be checked.

"I feel a little better after that last episode. I'm going to try to get a little rest. Don't sacrifice the group's safety just because I'm sick. I'll be here when you get back."

"Don't tell Allison I left. I don't want a pregnant lady's wrath upon me." I cringe in mock horror.

Matt shudders. "I wouldn't dream of it."

CHAPTER TWENTY-THREE

I grab a flashlight and long knife and head over to let Jess know I'm heading out. Allison's head is resting on Jess's lap while she strokes her hair. I go into the room, careful not to make any noise, and grab my shirt off of the floor to put it back on. Jess offers me a questioning look. I hold up the flashlight and weapon. She nods in understanding.

I head outside and the cool air greets me. Away from the smell of sickness, breathing in seems so much fresher. I close my eyes and recollect my thoughts. Even though Matt is sick, everything is going to be all right. I enjoy another deep breath and open my eyes.

It's a full moon tonight so I walk through the patio without my flashlight on. My eyes adjust enough for me to see fairly well and I make my way to the fence.

The sound of insects fills the air and the solitary moment is actually quite nice. My body turns to head down the trail, but my mind remains back in the house.

I know Matt doesn't want Jess and me to leave him alone, but I don't feel comfortable waiting much longer to get supplies for Allison. Honestly, it's something we should have done earlier. We just always thought we would have more time.

He hasn't been bitten, so I'll talk to Jess once she's calmed down to see what she thinks. I figure our best bet will be to go while Matt is sleeping. Hopefully, we'll be able to find some medicine for him.

A smell assaults me. There must be some of the Letum around. I frown. This is the second group today. With every step, the smell gets stronger. I sigh and finally turn on my flashlight.

Trying to get past our barrier is five of the Letum. Three of them are walking mindlessly into the fence while the other two stumble into their dead companions. They react to the light with a horrible chorus of moaning and gurgling. They all clamp their broken teeth down, snapping. Dried blood covers their chins. One of them has a knife stuck through its cheek. Someone missed.

Ensuring I don't repeat the same mistake, I grip my weapon harder and climb over the fence. I hit the ground and swing at the one with a knife in its cheek, finishing the job the last person couldn't. Either I'm getting better at destroying them, they're getting weaker, or some combination of the two because it's an easy job. The remaining four come slowly toward me and I take them out, one by one.

I scan the area with my flashlight and once I'm certain I'm alone, I grab the arm of one of them to drag it farther away from the fence. My grip rips the skin off of its arm and I exhale in disgust. I try again, this time hoisting it by its shoulders, and have more success. I automatically turn my head away in an attempt to avoid the smell of their decomposing bodies. I make quick work of moving the other four. They still need to be burned, but my lack of sleep catches up with me once the adrenaline leaves my body.

I hop back over the fence with my new knife and continue to walk the line. To pass the time, I hum a tune Jess taught me. I instinctively reach for the photograph of my mother and am disappointed when I remember it was left at Andrew and Chris's house. I haven't thought of my mother in a while, but truth be told, I have been so engulfed in the happiness that I've found with Matt, Allison, and most importantly, Jess.

There's a hitch in my step at the realization I have accepted all of the recent deaths. I no longer struggle in a sea of grief at the thought of their names.

As I think more about it, though, my mother would've been happy for me. How proud she would be of who I have become. She always told me I was more and I finally understand that.

I reach my starting point and walk toward the house. I take my shoes off in the patio so I don't track anything in.

Just as the air smelled a lot fresher once I left the house, I cringe when I walk in and smell the recent vomit. I head to the kitchen to wash my hands and pour myself a cup of water. I drink it quickly and set it back down on the counter.

I turn around and curse when I see a figure standing in the doorway. It takes a step closer into the light and Jess stares back at me.

"You're funny when startled," she says.

"I do it on purpose. I just want to amuse you," I say in a half-hearted attempt to make a joke.

"Ha, ha."

She gives me a light smile that doesn't quite conceal the tension in her eyes.

"I snuck out of the room once she fell asleep and checked on Matt." Her gaze examines mine. "He's tied up."

"I didn't even have to bring it up. It was his idea. He's worried and doesn't want to hurt anyone."

"That's good."

I frown. "Jess, he wasn't bitten."

Jess doesn't respond.

"Do you want any water?"

She shakes her head. "I want you to hold me and tell me everything is going to be okay."

I walk to her and take her in my arms. "Everything is going to be okay."

I pull back so I can look her in the eyes.

"I know you're worried and I understand, with everything that has happened with your family. This isn't that situation. Matt is just sick."

I kiss her forehead.

"Come on, let's sleep out on the patio tonight. It's a pleasant night and honestly, it smells nicer out there. I just did a sweep and the fence is clear of the Letum."

I kiss her again gently and the two of us separate. I grab some extra blankets out of the closet and meet her on the patio. She holds pillows for us. We spread one of the blankets on the ground and place the other on top. Jess plops the pillows down and we climb in.

Jess says, "This is going to be good for my back."

I chuckle and she joins in. The tension from the night leaves us. Even though we're lying on the floor, we're together.

"Come here," I say.

There are times for comforting words and at other moments, physical closeness can speak more meaningfully.

* * *

My first thought when I hear the screaming is that I'm still in a dream. As the desperate wailing continues, I fumble my way back to consciousness.

"Wake up, Elliot. Something's wrong."

Jess's words bring me back to reality and I open my eyes in time to see her rush inside. I run toward the source of the screaming, the scent of sickness assaulting my senses.

Jess is ahead of me and gets to Matt and Allison's doorway first. Her guard shoots up immediately. Wanting to do anything else, I look into the room.

Allison is in the corner screaming, tears streaming down her face. Matt, with one hand still tied to the bed, is lunging for her, blood flowing down his chin.

Allison echoes my thoughts. "He wasn't bitten."

I immediately scan her body, but it doesn't look like the blood is coming from her.

"He wasn't bitten. He wasn't bitten. He wasn't bitten," she cries in an endless loop.

Although I see what's happening, I can't grasp it. How is it possible?

Matt, the guy who could always make us laugh, is gone and replaced by a mindless monster that wants to hurt everything Matt cared about, starting with his love and unborn child.

Careful to avoid him, I hold Allison as she collapses into my body. I maneuver her so she can't see Matt and I can still keep my eye on him. His glazed, yellowing eyes follow the motion of our movements without recognition.

"He wasn't bitten. He wasn't bitten," she continues her infinite chant.

She's right, he wasn't bitten. He wasn't exposed in any way that the three of us weren't. All of his and Jess's worrying I just dismissed because it wasn't logical. If we can turn at any time, what does that mean for us?

"I know he wasn't bitten, Allison. I know he wasn't," I say to her.

Her chanting stops, but she continues to shake with sobs.

I look up in desperation at Jess. Her mask is back in place. She stares at Matt with no feeling. I swallow my frustration at her seemingly emotionally checking out of the situation. She shouldn't leave me alone right now. I thought we were past this.

"Jess." I say her name to get her attention. She glances my way and focuses on Allison. She walks out of the room.

Wondering where she went, I automatically pat Allison's back and watch Matt's awkward movements.

Back in school, they used to show us videos of the past to demonstrate how lucky we were to be where we are today. Like the majority of the clips, one focused around the importance of genetic engineering. It showed footage of people suffering from a neurodegenerative disease. I can't remember what it was called. Though with genetic engineering, it's now irrelevant.

There was a woman who it centered around. She had been suffering from the disease for a little over a year. Every movement was a struggle to get her muscles and body to listen to her mind. It was so impactful then because the woman was still so young, even though she looked around the same age as my mother. She had lost control. Now, looking at Matt and the similar motions, it's even more devastating.

Jess comes back through the doorway with a long knife in her right hand. I tense up at her intention.

Moments ago, I was sleeping peacefully and now the world has broken again. Allison senses the change in my body language and wheels around.

Before I can stop her, she lunges at Jess and screams, "HE WASN'T BITTEN!"

Matt, attracted to the noise and movement, reaches toward Allison with renewed interest. Its moans reveal a thick tongue, heavily flopping past its broken bottom lip to push more blood down its chin. Watching the red spread down its shirt, as it agonizingly bites its own flesh in a desperate attempt to hurt Allison, I'm painfully aware that Matt is gone.

Jess drops her weapon so she can hold Allison to steady her. "I know he wasn't bitten. That doesn't matter right now. Matt is gone and the thing that took over his body wants to kill you and your baby. Think rationally."

This seems to break her haze and she says, "Think rationally? Rationally, I don't see a reality where Matt doesn't exist. Rationally, he wasn't bitten so he shouldn't have turned. Nothing about this is rational. Don't you dare touch him."

Throughout this whole exchange, sounds of teeth gnashing and moaning spread through the room. My focus shifts to the Letum. Its movement is awkward and jerky, yet full of determination. It's sickening how quickly this happened. Matt was joking around with me hours before.

"That isn't Matt anymore, Allison," Jess whispers patiently and calmly. "I know it's horrible, but Matt is dead and you have to worry about keeping you and your baby safe. What would Matt want right now?"

She looks bitterly at Jess. "Matt would want to be healthy right now. Matt wouldn't want us to give up on him," she says.

"It isn't a matter of giving up on him. There's nothing we can do," Jess says. "Matt not being here is unthinkable and unimaginable. The world went to shit and fell apart and now you're going to have to be stronger than ever."

"Don't touch him," she repeats.

This time, it's Jess who looks to me at a loss for words. Jess is right, not having Matt is inconceivable and we need to take care of him. But she's also wrong. There is something we can do for him, something almost as unimaginable as not having Matt anymore. He may be gone right now, but what if we can get him back?

I shock even myself as I utter the words I never thought I would say again. "I need to find Dominic."

CHAPTER TWENTY-FOUR

With the exception of the Letum gurgling in the background, silence covers the room. Jess stares at me in disbelief. Allison's battle stance relaxes and she turns to me, face full of questions.

It seems like my voice is coming from another body when I elaborate. "The last we heard, he was working on finding a cure for the Letum. Say what you want about my brother, but he's determined and brilliant. If there's a way to recover, Dominic will know."

Allison's eyes narrow in skepticism. "I thought your brother was dead," she says.

"I never said he was dead. I just said he wasn't with us anymore," I say.

"Then why did you let me think he was dead?" Allison looks angry at this small deception. One look toward Matt, however, and she drops it.

"Because he's a dangerous person and can't be trusted," Jess says for me. Her jaw is clenched.

Allison doesn't care anymore that my brother is now suddenly alive again. All that concerns her is Matt. "You really think he knows a way to turn Matt back?" Allison asks desperately, full of hope.

I choose my words carefully. "If there is a way, Dominic could possibly find it."

"No," Jess says and shakes her head passionately. "We're not going to Dominic. Not if he 'could possibly' help. He's dangerous."

"Jess…" Allison says.

It makes a renewed attempt to hurt Allison and she jumps automatically. Her eyes well up and she wordlessly pleads for Jess to reconsider.

Jess takes a deep breath and gently takes Allison's hands in her own. "I'm sorry, but we're not doing it."

Allison jerks her hands away and looks imploringly at me.

A bigger part of me than I'd admit is relieved to hear Jess make such a statement. The idea of voluntarily going back to Dominic is absolutely terrifying. The sound of teeth clamping brings me back to desperation.

I turn and look at what used to be Matt. His eyes were always full of light and humor. Now, a blank stare returns my gaze. What if there is a way to turn him back?

I swallow hard and gain my courage. "You don't have to. I do. It's our only option. Dominic is staying at the genetic testing site in Potentia. I know how to get there." I'm afraid I sound harsh, but I need my point to come across. "Matt would do it for us."

Sensing this is an argument between Jess and me, Allison simply nods, tears running down her face, and watches the situation unfold.

"He tried to capture us last time he saw us. He wanted to run experiments on you. Have you forgotten about Andrew and Chris?" Jess squares her shoulders and raises her voice.

Her last question stings. "No, I haven't forgotten about them. Losing them was something I don't want to have to go through again. I should have fought harder for them." I take a deep breath and lower my voice. "And Jess, what if Andrew is still alive after all this time, waiting for us to come rescue him?"

Jess's shoulders slack and her voice lowers with it. "He's too dangerous. It isn't worth the risk."

Allison joins in the conversation. "Matt 'isn't worth the risk'?" She sounds absolutely disgusted. "After everything Matt did for you? After he saved your life—remember that? He isn't worth asking someone for help?"

Rather than defend herself, Jess asks, "Would Matt want you to risk your life and the life of your child on a harebrained scheme to maybe bring him back?"

"I'm not asking her to put her life in danger. I'm going to do this by myself," I say. Dominic is capable of horrible things that I can't expose Jess or Allison to.

It makes another renewed lunge at Allison and she can't help but scream. She collapses on the ground and cries at a faster rate, taking shallow breaths in quick succession.

"You need to calm down, Allison," Jess says as she sits on the floor with her. "You're going to hurt the baby. Let's leave the room and take a break."

"You…just…want….me…to…leave…" Allison says between each breath, "so…you…can…kill…Matt…"

She stares accusingly at Jess.

"No, we'll all leave the room together. We don't need to make this decision now. We'll close the door and leave…Matt…alone." She stumbles on saying his name.

It's clear, for me at least, that she's accepted Matt as gone.

"Promise?" Allison hiccups through her emotion.

Both Jess and I nod and Allison accepts our assurance. I help Jess up and the two of us steady Allison on her feet. She takes a couple of steps closer to the Letum. Jess's mouth opens in objection. Before she says anything, Allison stops just out of his reach. She holds her hand out and it reaches out to her.

Allison's expression is full of love and longing whereas the Letum's is one of hunger and madness.

Allison says, "I love you. I'm going to get you back."

Fresh tears spill down her face.

I look at Jess, pleading wordlessly for her to reconsider, but she shakes her head and grabs Allison's other hand to guide her out of the room. I follow them out and take one look back.

This can't be the end for Matt. He did everything right and still got infected. I don't accept what happened. I close the door, determined to get him back.

His disgusting noises are still coming from the room, so I go to the closet and grab extra sheets to stuff under the door. Satisfied that I can no longer hear him, I walk into the living room.

Jess has her arm around Allison. Both of them sit on the couch. I take a seat across from them.

It's ridiculous how much has changed in such a short time. Less than twelve hours ago, everything was fine. We were all laughing on the patio. Everyone was happy. How can we recover? How can Allison get through this?

When I made my promise to Matt last night, I didn't think I would have to follow through with it so soon. It seemed like such an abstract idea. How could someone turn without being bitten? Regardless of whether I understand it or not, it still happened. Ignorance doesn't prevent misfortune. It just slows down your reaction.

Over time, Allison's breathing slows down into a temporary respite of sleep. I expect Jess to leave but instead, she lets Allison sleep on her and looks up at me.

"We need to take care of Matt. He can't stay like this. You saw Allison. She doesn't understand he's gone. What happens when she goes to visit him without either of us and gets herself killed? He's a liability and we need to protect her."

"What if he isn't gone? What if we can bring him back?" I throw back at her.

"We don't have the luxury of living in the land of 'what-ifs.' If we don't focus on reality and what's in front of us, we're never going to make it," Jess says.

"Allison needs him."

"No. She thinks she does. We can protect her and the baby. She will survive. We all will." Her response is cold.

I furrow my eyebrows while I take in her last statement. The comment seems heartless. The fact that she comforts Allison proves how much she cares.

"Allison will never forgive us if we don't try and seek answers. I owe it to Matt to at least try," I say.

"I don't understand how you seem to be placing a blind eye to all of the horrible, terrible things your brother has done. He abused you, both mentally and physically, your entire life. He's never proven trustworthy. Why are you so willing to risk all of our lives?"

"Because I refuse to accept this is what the world has become. My brother still has the potential to do great things and maybe this is his redemption. He has the opportunity to fix everything. And no matter what you think, he did let me go at the lake. He hesitated."

She opens her mouth to object, but I speak before she can interrupt me. "Besides, I'm not going to risk all of us. I'm going by myself."

"Whether you accept it or not, this"—Jess motions widely with her arms to encompass the whole situation—"is reality. Your perception doesn't change how things actually are."

I shake my head. "I can't ask you to come with me. To be honest, I don't want you to."

Jess scoffs and I continue anyway. "Even though you don't agree about going to seek out Dominic, we do need some supplies for the delivery of the baby. I can get those items as well."

"So you expect me to stay here and let you run off and hope you come back?" Jess asks. Her tone is full of hurt and I suspect she views this decision as me choosing Matt over her.

After last night, I can't stand to have her look at me this way. I soften my tone. "I'm not trying to get away from you. I simply refuse to put you in a situation that has the potential to be dangerous. You're the most important thing to me. But we can't live in constant fear. There's hope. I intend on going for it."

Jess studies me, expressionless. "So you admit that this is a stupid idea? You're acknowledging that seeking out Dominic, after all it took to get away from him, is dangerous?"

"I know there's a strong possibility that it could go poorly," I admit.

"You're so willing to die and leave me?" she asks.

I look back at her pleadingly. I'm desperate for her to understand my viewpoint. "I'm not asking you to agree with me, Jess, I'm asking you to support my decision. If I sit here and do nothing, I'm not the person I want to be. You have to understand," I say.

Defeat takes over her face. "When do you want to leave?"

I let out a breath of air. "Thank you, Jess. I'll leave as soon as I can. I just need to gather some supplies."

"Okay, let's let Allison rest for a little longer. I really am worried about all of the stress that she's putting on her body and baby."

"She doesn't need to wish me good-bye, I'll be back soon." I stand up and stretch and stare toward the direction of Matt.

"Nobody is saying good-bye to anyone."

I look quickly back at her. "What?"

"I'm not letting you go off without me. I can't stand the idea of not knowing if you're going to come back. We can't very well leave Allison here to her own devices. Even if she manages not to get too close to the thing in her bedroom, she could go into early labor with all of this stress. We can't leave her alone."

"You think you're coming?"

"I'm not happy about it and I don't agree with you." She takes a deep breath. "We're not going to get separated. We need to stick together."

"No." I shake my head. "You're not coming."

"I'm not letting you go by yourself."

I try to stand my ground. "I won't let you come." For the first time since I decided to ask for Dominic's help, I'm truly afraid. Putting myself in danger is one thing, but to drag Jess and Allison into it? That's unthinkable.

Jess clenches her jaw and I flinch. "You won't let me come?"

"You're right. It isn't safe. I can't bring you and worry about you the whole time."

"We're in this together, Elliot. Plain and simple. If you go, I go," she says.

I sigh. We both know she's won. A small, satisfied smirk appears on her face before she hides it.

Three important words float around my mind and I want to express to Jess how much she means to me, but a very loud bang from Allison and Matt's room ruins the mood and Allison jets awake. Her eyes scan the room for the noise and focus on the door to her bedroom. Emotion floods through her face.

"Keep relaxing here. We're going to get everything ready," Jess says to Allison.

"Get ready for what?" Allison's eyes dart to Matt's room.

"We're going to try and find my brother," I say. Saying those words still seems unreal to me.

Hope radiates through Allison's face. "Thank you."

CHAPTER TWENTY-FIVE

The ride back to Potentia passes without much conversation. Allison has rested her head in Jess's lap the entire ride, leaving me alone in the front seat. Because their vehicle was for a government official, it can travel at higher speeds and we make great time. Almost too soon, I see the outline of Potentia's skyline.

My eyes widen as the walls come into view. After months of being away, they seem bigger than I remember. The barrier that was built years ago—in the event of an attack from Acroisia—has been enacted, completely sealing the territory. In school, they always spoke about how it was a last option resort, as it cuts Potentia off from the rest of the territories. This definitely qualifies.

Even though I fought to come back, my stomach turns at the thought of seeing my brother again. I cling to the hope that he will be able to help us. If I've changed since the last time we met, surely he has had the opportunity to change as well. He could've shot me when I was escaping into the forest. He chose not to. I have to believe this.

I push the commands to stop the vehicle just outside the walls of the territory. Very smoothly, it halts. I exhale. This is it.

"Are we here?" Allison asks.

"Yes," Jess says, scanning the high walls with apprehension. I look at my old home and try to imagine going back to that life. Nothing is the same anymore.

I steady myself. "You two stay here and I'll be back as soon as I can." I have little faith that it will work. I have to try, though.

"That's not happening and you know it." Jess's tone softens as she addresses Allison. "You should stay here."

I nod in agreement.

"I'm not missing this. I need to hear from him if there is something we can do to bring Matt back," Allison says. Her eyes dart between me and Jess, waiting for us to argue.

I sigh in frustration. They're forcing me to do something I promised myself I would never allow. I'm about to expose them to my brother.

"There's no time like the present," Allison says.

She's clearly anxious about meeting with the genetic engineers. I share that unease. Everything is riding on this.

I open the door and gasp in shock. I hear similar responses from Jess and Allison when the smell hits them. Dominic did not exaggerate. I thought it was horrible with a small group of them, but this is simply unbearable. Death has marinated and seeped through. I can almost see it oozing through the air. I throw up in the grass by the car, with Allison gagging behind me.

I recover slightly and stand up straighter. Jess comforts Allison and pats her on her back while she throws up. Jess looks to me with an expression full of disgust.

I toss my hands up in resignation.

"I imagine the smell is only going to get worse as we get deeper into the territory," I say.

Allison's hands cover her nose in an attempt to hide some of the smell. "Hopefully we'll get used to this."

"Is this really something we want to get used to?" Jess eyes the intimidating wall. "Let's get this over with."

Jess supports Allison while they walk toward the giant barrier with me following closely behind them. Dominic didn't disclose how they found him when he came back here after our mother died. I scan the area but see no signs of life. It's startling that Potentia is void of the busy scurrying of life I grew up with.

"Hello?" I call out.

I'm astounded when I get a response.

"Get back in your vehicle and leave. There's no more room in our safe zone," a female voice says.

I look for the source of the voice and have no success.

Allison pushes past me to get closer to the wall. "No, we need to get in," she cries out.

"We're at capacity," a deep male voice says. "There's nothing we can do."

Although I would never admit it to Allison, I'm thankful we're being turned away. Facing Dominic is one of my biggest fears and I'm relieved that I might be able to avoid it. That being said, I still have to do everything I can to bring Matt back to us.

"I'm here to see my brother, Dominic. Can you at least let him know I'm here?" I say in desperation.

"What's your name?" The female voice excitedly asks.

Her head appears at the top of the barrier. She's wearing some sort of mask. Jess stiffens beside me.

"My name is Elliot Greer, brother to Dominic Greer," I respond, apprehensive toward her sudden, obvious interest.

A beep echoes through the air and the barrier shifts slightly. A hidden staircase appears to our right.

"Come up and we'll take you to him," she says.

I automatically push forward, but Jess holds me back and asks, "I thought you were at capacity?"

"Family is a different situation," the male voice responds evenly.

Jess turns to me and gazes into my eyes. "We should get in our vehicle and drive away right now before it's too late. They're looking for you."

Before I can respond, Allison marches toward the stairs and begins her climb. I rush forward to follow her lead. No matter what Jess fears, we can't let Allison go by herself.

The three of us make it to the top of the wall. The two strangers are wearing masks that make it impossible to determine any physical attributes, with the exception of their height and obvious strength.

The woman holds out masks for us. "This will help with the smell," she says.

The relief is instantaneous. It doesn't eliminate the smell completely, but it makes it tolerable.

"Thank you," I say. I'm not sure how long I could have lasted without it. The respite allows my other senses to strengthen.

I take advantage of the high vantage point to study the territory. On the streets where there used to be a steady hum of traffic and vehicles, the slow, awkward movements of the Letum cover the ground. The female's voice brings me back to the top of the barrier.

"I remember the first time I smelled it without a mask on. It's dreadful," she states. "My name is Jocelyn. I'll take you to your brother."

"I'll stay here and keep guard on the wall," the male mumbles through his mask.

Jocelyn leads us away after a quick nod to acknowledge his comment.

Jess walks slowly behind her, eyes narrowed in her mask. "Where are you taking us?" she asks.

"Aren't you a guarded one?" Jocelyn asks. She deliberately pauses. "We're going to the main building where Mr. Greer will be. It's a short walk from here. You're lucky you came from this side."

The shadows of the living quarters where I began my life are just visible in the distance. My home from another life.

"Did Dominic find a cure?" Allison asks, her voice is so full of hope and fear.

"Dominic is an absolute genius. He's so amazing," she says. I roll my eyes. My older brother has placed his charms on her.

She leads us down another staircase. I know Potentia well enough to recognize where we are. The education building looms just down the road. We're going into the training facility where my brother studied with the other genetic engineers before the epidemic.

"Did he find an antidote?" I remind her of the original question. I'm not in the mood to hear about how perfect my brother is.

"I don't know if I would call it an antidote, but yes, he did discover a way to bring the Letum back to themselves," she says just as we reach a big door. She taps in a key code and it opens for us. Once we step inside, Jocelyn takes off her mask. We follow her lead and do the same.

Jocelyn turns toward us to make sure we get inside. The heavy lines on her face give evidence of her age. She must be at least fifteen years older than I am. Her earlier comments of admiration are surprising. She isn't Dominic's typical type.

She's led us to a very large, grey room with a high ceiling. Our footsteps echo off of the walls. I'm very insignificant and small in here.

I look back to Allison and Jess. The same excitement coursing through my body is replicated in Allison, whereas Jess looks anxious. A familiar voice calls out from a speaker on the wall.

Dominic's voice rings out. "Jocelyn, why are you back early? I am too busy right now for another one of our getaways."

Jocelyn has the grace to blush and at least appears to be embarrassed.

"I have Elliot and two of his companions with me," she says. She puffs her small chest out in pride.

"Are you sure?" he breathes through the system.

I announce to the speaker, "It's me, Elliot."

No response comes from the speaker system. My heart pounds in anxiety over our reunion. I twitch my fingers to expel some of my energy.

Finally, a door opens up and Dominic enters the hallway along with three other people in lab coats.

"Elliot, I never thought I would see you again." His voice is so full of relief. "And you brought Jess and…" He pauses when he gets a better view of Allison. "How far along are you?"

"I'm around seven months pregnant. That's why we're here, in fact. You see my baby's father just turned and—" Allison says.

Dominic interrupts her. "Was he bitten?"

"No. That's why it was so sudden. Please, I need your help. We left him tied to a bedpost—safe. Jocelyn mentioned you found a way to bring him back. Can you help? Please, my child needs a father," Allison begs.

"Of course, I can help," Dominic admits. "I have been working on this for the last few weeks. We actually just recently made great progress."

One of the men claps him on the back. His movement draws my attention. It's Phillip, the man who was with Dominic the day they killed Chris and Andrew. Jess tenses next to me, making it apparent she recognizes the same man.

"So it's possible to bring him back? He can be himself again not some mindless creature?" Allison asks and breaks my train of thought.

Dominic smiles at her desperation. "Yes, it is possible."

"Will you help us then?" Jess asks.

Dominic considers her. A small smile plays at his lips. That look brings back memories of him taking advantage of me and tormenting me over the years. This is the man who killed my two best friends.

"First things first. It is about time we finally get past the mistakes both of us have made." He reaches out to me with one hand extended for a handshake. Despite the small seed of rationality present in my mind, I return his handshake without question. There's a small prick in my neck. I pull away in confusion. Dominic looks very pleased with himself.

"You bastard," Jess screams at him. "What was in that syringe?"

"Something to help him relax. He seems a little stressed," Dominic says and shrugs.

Jess runs toward him in anger. Phillip pulls a gun and points it at Allison's stomach. Both of them freeze.

The world loses focus and it becomes increasingly harder to concentrate. I should care that he just injected something in me, but all I want to do is sleep. The drug tugs at my awareness. It would be a lot easier to just give in and let the darkness take me.

"Take him to room B6." Dominic's voice sounds like it's coming from far away even though I know he's right in front of me.

The two strangers drag me out of the room and I struggle to remain conscious. My vision narrows at an alarming rate. I focus all of my energy on raising my head to get one last glimpse of Jess.

Just as I'm able to finally lift my head up, we pass the corner. My head drops and I give in to the unknown.

CHAPTER TWENTY-SIX

I find my way back to reality very slowly. It feels as if a huge weight is on my chest. After an unknown amount of time passes, I gradually become more aware.

I lie on a lumpy mattress. The more I focus on that, the more uncomfortable the bedding becomes. A wire pokes out and jabs me in the side. I attempt to move and am unable to. This worries me greatly. Even though I tell my body to move, it won't cooperate. I'm too heavy.

I wonder if I can open my eyes. The effort turns out to be a major struggle. Much to my relief, I'm finally able to accomplish this simple task. The room I'm in is completely dark. I impatiently wait for my eyes to adjust.

Before they're given a chance, a door opens and light floods into the room.

My brother's voice greets me. "I thought you would be coming out of the effects of the drugs around now." His voice echoes slightly. I don't know if it's from the drugs in my system or the room or the high ceiling.

His footsteps bounce off the walls. Each one is louder than the previous.

He appears in front of me so I can see him. He looks so smug. A wave of frustration hits me. How could I have led everyone here? Why didn't I listen to Jess?

"Because we are family, I am going to give you two choices. Blink so I know you understand." After a moment's hesitation, I blink. "Good. In my pocket, I have two syringes. One of them will put you back out. It is the same drug that I gave you already. The other one will let you regain some of your strength. Notice, I said some and not all. Blink once for the first one and twice for the second option."

The idea of escaping, at least mentally, is appealing. But I know I need to focus. If I'm going to have any chance of getting us out of here, I need to have as much function as I can. I blink twice.

"So you still have hope," Dominic mutters, amused. "That will change once we get started." He pulls out a syringe from one of his pockets. "As promised." He waves it tauntingly in front of my face.

The medicine leaves my field of vision. I focus on Dominic's face. His expression reminds me of the time he came back from the hill. He looked just as arrogant then as he does now. It isn't that surprising, though. He won then and he won now. He got what he wanted.

There's a small prick in my neck as the medicine enters my body.

"It will take about thirty seconds for it to hit its full effect," my brother states.

First, the weight lifts off my fingers and toes. I tell my finger to move and it obeys. This continues throughout my body. The process of the medicine working is very short, as promised, and when the thirty seconds is up, I'm much more in control. However, the motion of sitting up is still tiresome. While I'm able to move everything, it still feels a little heavy. It's as if I'm swimming in my winter clothes.

"You bastard," I say to Dominic. My voice cracks and sounds much weaker than I would like. I cough. "I came to you for help. I gave you a chance for redemption."

Dominic laughs. "First of all, you are much closer to a bastard than I am. I was genetically engineered. Mother and Father actually wanted to have me."

Despite all that has happened, his comment still bothers me.

"Secondly," he says, "I do not need redemption. That implies I have done something wrong and I have not. Everything I have done has been to help society and bring balance back to the world. In addition, I saved your life when I got you out of the territory so you owed it to me anyway."

"You killed Chris and Andrew," I say. I don't see how he can rationalize this.

"In the grand scheme of things, their lives are meaningless. In fact, we were able to get some good information from Chris's biopsy that helped with our testing on Andrew," Dominic says.

I look at him in revulsion.

"You have no remorse for what you did to them? No remorse for what you're going to do to the three of us?"

Dominic shakes his head. "Of course not. The work I am doing here is going to save everybody. You should feel thankful you are finally able to contribute to society."

In my mind, I lunge out at Dominic and hit him square in the jaw and knock him backward. What actually happens is completely different. My movement is very slow and Dominic knocks it away easily. He pushes me back harshly and my head knocks against the stone wall. The result is pain, dizziness, and confusion.

"I suspected you would attempt to do something like this," Dominic says. I hear him rummage in his pocket. Another prick hits my neck. Instead of the feeling of weightlessness the previous drugs brought me, this one brings me down and my chest feels heavy again as it spreads throughout my body.

"Just know that every time I have to put this medicine in you, you are losing what little time you have left," he whispers in my ear.

Even if I had words, I'm not sure I could say them in an intimidating manner. The heaviness overtakes my entire body. I fight it and struggle to stay awake. Dominic's arrogant face zooms in and out of my vision while I attempt to remain conscious.

"There is no point in struggling, Joe," Dominic says. His voice sounds like it's coming from rooms away as opposed to right in front of me. "It will not change anything." I fall back into nothingness.

*   *   *

The first thing I become aware of as the drug wears off is pain in my neck. My head is at an awkward angle. Someone moved me to my stomach with no regard for the position I ended up in. From far away, the door opens and someone approaches. A familiar prick in my neck and I wait for my mind and body to clear.

Once I'm able, I roll over. My lower back aches. I reach back and touch a bandage. I sit up fully in alarm. Jocelyn stares back at me.

"What happened to my back?"

"Don't talk to me." She thrusts a plate of food at me along with a cup. She motions for me to eat.

I hesitate as they might have drugged the food or water, but if they wanted to, they could easily do it at any time.

I take a bite and follow it with a sip of water.

"I'm not going to waste my time watching you eat and drink your water. I'm leaving in one minute and whatever is left is coming with me," she says.

I eat the food as quickly as I'm able and swallow all of the water. She seems satisfied and takes the plate and cup away from me the moment I'm done.

"What happened to Jess and Allison? The people who came in with me?" I ask even though I don't expect her to respond.

She pauses slightly in her exit and makes no other indication that she heard what I said. Without a glance back, she exits the room. The beep, followed by the clamping of metal, signals that the locks are enacted.

Even though I just ate, I'm still hungry. I've completely lost track of time. There are no windows in my cell. I have no way of determining even the time of day or passage of time. I frown.

This is the end for Matt. Without us to bring back some miracle cure, he's going to remain tied to the bed until someone unknowingly finds him or he decomposes into nothingness. He doesn't deserve to go out like that. Matt was a genuinely good person.

I force myself to stand up and examine the room. The dull ache in my lower back remains constant, but it isn't crippling. I pace the area. My cot is against one wall with a flimsy blanket on top of it. Right next to my pathetic sleeping arrangement is a toilet and sink. I try the handle on the sink and am pleasantly surprised when some water comes through. I cup my hands to transfer some water from the sink to my mouth. I take another handful to rinse off my face.

The cold water takes me back in time to my mother cleaning off my face when I was young after Dominic pushed me in the mud. I don't remember what she said to me, but I recall the overall soothing effect they had. My mother was always encouraging me to choose my own destiny. And I can. I just have to get out of this damn room.

My self-pity is replaced by fresh determination to escape and get Jess and Allison to safety. I utilize some of my newfound energy by walking in circles around my room. I can't shake the nasty feeling of anxiety about their fate. I need to get answers about what's going on. I have to figure out a way to get us out of here.

The sound of a dead bolt moving interrupts my thoughts. Dominic enters. He looks tired. It must be late.

"You are nice and lively today, Joe," he says. "Unfortunately, I cannot say the same about your two companions."

"What did you do to them?" I say in an attempt to demand an answer.

"Nothing either of them did not deserve," he replies.

"They don't deserve to be in here. Jess has done absolutely nothing and Allison is pregnant. How can you be so heartless?"

"I am not being heartless, just rational," Dominic says. "All of you have your uses to me and as soon as you are worth more to me dead, you will be."

"And when will that be?"

"Soon," he says.

I let out a deep breath in annoyance. "Will you at least tell me why my back hurts?"

"It hurts because I took some cerebral fluid from your spine. I wanted to run some tests on it." Dominic shrugs as if it's no big deal.

"Find anything interesting?"

"I did. To be honest, though, I want to rerun the test. That is why I came back. I need more of the fluid." He raises his hand and shows a needle. It's much bigger than the ones he's been using previously. This one is enormous.

"You didn't get enough the first time?" I ask, backing up automatically.

"I do not have to explain myself to you. I brought more of the medicine to sedate you," Dominic says.

There are battles that are worth fighting and some that aren't. Even if I struggle, he will get his way. It's better if he thinks I have given up.

I make myself act like the submissive younger brother from our childhood and walk toward Dominic. I let him puncture my neck with the smaller needle to reintroduce the drugs to my system. As soon as he removes the needle, I make my way back to my cot while the weight fills my body. I collapse into the table and, for the first time, don't fight the medicine's effects.

Just before the drug completely takes ahold of my body, Dominic says, "I am glad you have finally relearned your place."

* * *

The next time I become aware of anything again, it's at a much quicker pace. One moment, there's nothing and the next, weight leaves my body. I open my eyes to see Jocelyn staring at me in disdain. I find my strength to sit up on my cot.

"What are you doing here?" I ask.

Instead of replying verbally, she shakes her head and thrusts food in front of me. I take it and study her. She looks as if she would rather be anywhere else than in here with me.

"Eat," she repeats.

I follow her order. It looks like less food than last time. Knowing she will leave once I'm done, I stop with a couple of bites left.

"What's going on with the two women who came here with me?"

She shoots me an annoyed glance.

"Please, just tell me if they're alive."

She looks significantly at the food.

"The thought of either of them being gone from our world is absolutely terrifying, especially since it's all my fault they got into this situation. I brought us here hoping we could bring back our friend who turned into one of the Letum. I know what type of person my brother is and what he's capable of, but I still led them here." My voice breaks in emotion at the end of my plea.

"They're alive." Her response is no more than a whisper. "Now eat the rest of your food so I can leave."

"Thank you," I say. I finish the last of my meal in appreciation of her answer.

She grabs my plate and cup. Right before she leaves the room, she looks back. Her expression is full of pity. Without a word, she exits the room and engages the lock.

I sigh and alternate between pacing the room, drinking water, going to the bathroom, and sleeping. The only forms of distraction available to me are my own thoughts and fears for the future. An unknown amount of time passes by. At some point, my female visitor stops coming to give me food and instead, every once in awhile, a flap I didn't know existed in the door opens and food pushes through it. It's the only way I can gauge any passage of time. But even the meals seem to come sporadically.

A couple days could have passed, a couple weeks, even a month. Time has lost all meaning to me. At every moment, worry over the fate of Allison and Jess courses through my body.

I lie and stare at the ceiling in boredom.

My endless passage of time is interrupted when lights come on in the room. Dominic walks toward me quickly.

When he gets close to me, I can't help myself. I say, "What happened?"

He looks absolutely exhausted. His right eye twitches from stress. "Stop talking, Joe. I'm really busy and I have some questions for you. I'm not here to play games. I just need information."

I raise my eyebrows in surprise. Right now, he needs me. I have something that he can't forcibly take from me. I sense a slight power shift. I suspect he does as well because he looks absolutely furious. But behind his anger, fear is at play.

"For every answer I give, you give me one," I say in negotiation.

His fingers drum in the air. "I told you, I'm not here to play some game with you."

I refuse to back down. "Those are my terms."

He studies me for a moment. "Fine. I'm going first."

I nod in agreement.

"Your friend, the one you all came here to help, are you positive he was Planned?"

"Yes. Are Jess and Allison alive?"

"Yes. Was he bitten before he turned?"

"Not that I'm aware of. How long have I been in this room?" I ask.

He pauses while he calculates. "You all came here twenty-three days ago. Have you met anyone else besides the two people you were staying with?"

"No, we haven't. You could get this information from either Jess or

Allison. Why are you asking me?" I look at him curiously.

"Because I know you well enough to know if you're lying to me or telling the truth." "What have you done to Jess and Allison?"

He narrows his eyes at me asking out of turn, yet still answers.

"All we have done with Allison is some blood work. I don't want to put any more stress on her while she is pregnant. It's important this baby is born healthy so we can learn from it. She has been kept very comfortable."

"And Jess?" I'm anxious for his response.

"Some basic genetic testing, similar to what I've done to you," he says.

I let out a sigh of relief. If all he's done is what he's been doing to me, she's fine. Bored out of her mind, but okay.

"I also taught her her place," Dominic says.

"What does that mean?" My mind races at the possibilities.

"It's my turn to ask the question," my brother says. "Do you still wish you were Planned?"

His question and tone take me by surprise. I really consider his question.

"I'm not sure. I genuinely don't know. What did you mean when you said you 'taught her her place'?"

Instead of answering, he turns around and heads to the door.

"Where are you going? You owe me an answer," I say.

"I don't have any more questions for you," he says. Dominic slams the door closed behind him. I sit down at the sound of the locks engaging.

I replay the scene in my head over and over again. Every motion he made, every tone he used, and every word he said. I come up with one conclusion. Something's very wrong.

I scream in frustration at being so out of control. There's nothing I can do right now to protect Jess. I can't even protect myself. Remaining on the cot, I lightly punch the wall.

The hopelessness threatens to encompass everything about me. In anger, I punch the wall again, a little harder. The pain in my knuckles is a welcome distraction from my thoughts. I punch again and welcome the hurt.

When the ache starts to go away, I yell again and hit the wall even harder, angry tears escaping. The pain sears through my hands and breaks through my skin. Blood spreads on the wall and starts to drip down my hand.

What am I doing? Punching a wall isn't going to do me any good. I take a deep breath in an attempt to steady myself.

My right hand is already swelling from the recent abuse. For some reason, the blood dripping down my wrist is funny. I chuckle in amusement. How did I think this would help me at all? Now, on top of everything else, I'm bleeding.

My chuckle turns into an uncontrollable laughter. As I struggle to get enough air in past my almost hysterical laughter, my breathing hitches and my sides ache. Here I am, locked in a room, and I try to punch my way through the cement. Who do I think I am?

I breathe one last humorless chuckle and stop laughing. My attention returns to my throbbing hand.

Dominic's voice echoes through my memory, "I also taught her her place."

What has he done to her? But also, what can I do about it? I'm hopeless, unable to do anything to protect the one I love. In this room, I'm useless. Just like when my mother died, when my friends were killed, when Matt turned. And right now, I can't do anything to help Jess.

If only I had known Death would become one of my closest companions, I would have spent more time appreciating all that was good in my life while they were still with me.

Ever since the world fell apart, I've been pushing down the pain, as best I can, to numb myself from all the hurt. It's how I've really been able to survive—by going forward. But there's no running from it anymore. Grief has caught up and forces itself to be acknowledged.

I lower my head into my hands and finally let myself feel everything. It almost breaks me.

CHAPTER TWENTY-SEVEN

Once again, I'm subject to an endless passage of time. I've only received one meal since I last saw Dominic and my stomach tells me it was a long time ago. I hate everything about this room. I just want it all to be over, one way or the other. This waiting game is slowly driving me insane. I suspect this is Dominic's intention.

With nothing better to do, I pace the room. I know the room's dimensions well enough by this point that I close my eyes and pretend I'm somewhere else. Sometimes I have Jess, Allison, and Matt walking with me. Other times, I'm with my mother. I even fantasize about laughing with Andrew and Chris. The most heartbreaking moments are when I allow myself to daydream about it just being me and Jess together.

When I return to reality, my heart breaks every time. I wish I had some physical evidence that they existed and were part of my life.

But no matter where my daydream takes me, I'm never alone. In my fantasies, someone I care about is always with me. There used to be a time when I savored my time by myself. But now, all I want is someone to talk with. I want this endless solitary confinement to end. I wonder if Jess wishes I were with her as much as I want her beside me.

A beep followed by the lock retracting fills the room. I jump up and run over to the door. I'm going to try to tackle Dominic and overpower him. I hope if he's surprised enough he will not have time to put his guard up. The door creeps open. I plant my right foot so I can get a good push off the ground. A shadow appears at the door. I hold my breath in anticipation.

A weak voice echoes off the walls. "Elliot?"

I exhale in shock. I never thought I would hear that voice again. "Is that you, Andrew?" My voice cracks with disuse.

Andrew turns on the lights. It blinds me and I have to wait for my eyes to adjust. Andrew steps closer to me and my shock at discovering him alive is overpowered by the overall dramatic transformation in his appearance.

He looks like he's aged about twenty years. He's lost too much weight and almost all of his hair. What's left is flaky-looking. His eyes appear to have sunken into his head. The difference in his skin is more subtle. I can't think of a better way to describe it besides overall unhealthiness.

He notices me gaping and attempts a pained smile. "I know, I don't look good. You can say it. We can address the elephant in the room."

"You've looked better," I admit. "What happened?"

"Hold on, let me take a seat," Andrew says.

He moves slowly to my bed and sits down. I join and eye him nervously.

He takes a few deep breaths before answering. "Well, the last we saw each other, I was runnin' toward Dominic after he killed Chris."

All of the suppressed guilt from leaving Andrew floods to the surface. "I'm so sorry, Andrew. I thought you were dead," I say.

"I've found myself wishin' he had killed me right then." Before I can ask him to elaborate, he continues. "He shot me in the leg and rushed back here so they could heal me. Once I was, they began their testin'."

I curse myself for being so naïve and believing Dominic let us go by not chasing after us. He just had to get Andrew back as soon as possible.

"Did they take fluid out of your back like they did for me?" I ask.

"That and a lot more. I was stuck in a room similar to this for...I don't know how long, to be honest. It felt like it was never-endin'," he says.

"I understand the feeling," I say.

"Anyway, one day Dominic came in lookin' more excited than normal and injected me with some medicine. It made me really sick. I was throwin' up constantly for a few hours."

"What happened next?" I ask though I know where his story is leading.

"The next thing I knew, I was tied to a bed and felt horrible. I was so tired and felt like I had a fever. I was surrounded by a large group of people cheerin' and shakin' Dominic's hand." Andrew looks at me significantly. "Elliot, they turned me into one of the creatures and brought me back."

"They actually found a cure?" My voice rises in excitement. No matter the terrible things Dominic has done, he has a brilliant mind and found a way to turn this whole mess around.

"They found a way to bring someone back, yes," Andrew says. A coughing fit takes hold of his frail body.

"Do you know where the antidote is so we can give it to one of our friends who turned?" I stand up in eagerness.

"I know where it is," Andrew says. His chest heaves as he struggles with another coughing attack.

"If they found a remedy, why are you so sick? What's going on with you?" I ask.

"Because in order to bring me back, they had to give me another illness."

"You're going to get better from this one, right?" I fear his response.

"There ain't a cure for what's in my body now," Andrew says, voice full of pain and hopelessness.

"How bad is it?" I ask.

"Honestly, it's the worst. They was giving me some medicine to slow down its progress, but it just makes me even more tired, nauseous, and then this whole mess," he says as he points toward his balding head.

"How long do you have?"

He breaks eye contact before saying, "Not much longer."

"I wish I could have saved you and Chris. It isn't fair that this would happen to you. He was only coming for me. I'm so—"

Andrew interrupts my apology. "You did what you had to do. I haven't blamed you for one second."

Hearing him say those words offers so much relief. I'm able to let go of some of the guilt that I've been harboring since the day he was taken. Soon, my overall feeling of gratefulness for having his company is replaced by general confusion.

"Don't take this the wrong way, Andrew. I'm obviously really glad to see you and have your company but…" I taper off as I try to phrase my question in a way that isn't offensive.

"What am I doin' here?" he asks for me.

I nod.

"I came to get you out."

"How?"

"A lot of people have been leavin' the compound lately. Everyone else is mostly sleepin'. It's just past midnight. I overheard a couple of the genetic engineers talkin' about their next transformation, so I had to make my move. I can't let this happen to any of you."

"What about Dominic?"

Andrew's eyes dart to his feet before he returns my gaze. "He left on an errand and won't be back 'til mornin'."

"Do you know where Allison and Jess are?" I eye the open door to my cell excitedly.

"I have the codes to get into their rooms. Jess is closest to us and then we'll grab Allison," he says.

My whole body fills with anticipation. "What are we waiting for? Let's get them out."

Andrew doesn't match my energy and remains resting on my cot.

"I'm grateful I had you in my life. Always remember that." His voice is so soft I almost miss it.

"I've missed you so much, Andrew. You, Chris, and Carly were always like the siblings I should have had. But we're not saying good-bye yet. You still have time. Let's go rescue them and get out of here," I reply.

I offer him my hand to help him up. His weak grip encompasses my strong one and I pull him to his feet.

"I can tell this is hard for you. Thank you so much for finding the strength to come find me and help me get out of here."

"Don't thank me," Andrew says, voice cracking from the strain. "You're not out of here yet."

Andrew reaches the door first and walks right through. I pause. I'm finally leaving this room. Assuming everything goes well, this is the last time I'll ever have to be stuck in here again.

"You comin'?" Andrew asks when he notices I stalled.

"You bet," I say.

I take a step out of the room and then another. Every step further from the room takes away the overwhelming feeling of helplessness that it embodies.

"How far away is Jess right now?"

Even though I've waited weeks for this moment, I can't wait another second before we're reunited. It takes all of my patience to not start running down the narrow hallway.

"She's just down the next hall. Listen, Elliot. Before you go in and see her, there's somethin' you oughtta know," Andrew says.

Without breaking stride, I ask, "What did Dominic do to her?" The venom in my voice is unmistakable. "I just need to see her. I need to see that she's alive."

My strides lengthen when the lights on the wall shine dimly enough to show me we're getting closer to the end of the hall.

"Just prepare yourself," Andrew says.

"I don't need to prepare myself. I need to see her."

We turn the corner. There are rooms on both sides of the new hallway.

"Where is she?" I ask.

Andrew hesitates before pointing at the closest one on the right.

I rush forward and place my hand on the cold metal door. She's on the other side. I'm moments away from being able to hold her again. Andrew seems to be walking at half speed. He makes it to her door and punches in a code.

A familiar beep echoes down the hallway, followed by the clank of the dead bolt moving. Unable to wait any longer, I push the door open and quickly scan the room to find her. It looks very similar to the room I was kept in. She's lying in the fetal position facing the wall.

Her body moves in reaction to the door opening.

She's alive. We're together again. Everything will be okay.

"Jess," I say, my voice full of emotion.

I take a step forward toward her. She turns and faces me. I freeze as I take in her appearance.

Her right eye is swollen shut and her upper lip is cracked and bloody. A large bruise covers her left cheek. Her nose is at an unnatural angle. It must be broken. A blood trail starts on her scalp and runs all the way down her neck into her shirt collar. The visible parts of her skin are covered in scrapes and bruises.

"I'm fine," Jess says and continues to stare at the ground.

"Oh, Jess."

I'm at a complete loss for words. I take a couple steps to get closer. Her entire body tenses up. She looks up at me and I see something much more startling than the evidence of physical abuse she's endured.

Even before I really knew her, she inspired strength in me. When I discovered my grandparents were dead and my mother died, she helped get me through it. Throughout dealing with Carly's death, we supported each other. When Chris was killed and Andrew's fate remained unknown, she was my rock. She was even able to help bring Allison to her senses by bearing all of the strength that she carried with her all the time.

Looking at her now, I see none of the strength that has defined her as a person. Instead, she's empty. She looks broken.

"Please, Elliot. Don't touch me." Her head returns its gaze on the ground and her good eye fills with tears. I put my arms behind my back and take two steps backward. She relaxes slightly once I put the distance between us.

"What did he do to you?" I whisper.

She shakes her head. "Just get me out of this room."

All I want to do is help and comfort her, but I don't know how to do that. Instead, I nod and motion toward the door and walk out. Andrew waits outside the door. When Jess walks out, he stares at her with an expression that's so clearly filled with sympathy.

"I'm sorry I didn't get you out sooner. Before…," Andrew begins and Jess shoots him a panicked look. "Before it got worse. I'm gonna get you out of here."

Jess offers him the slightest of nods and stares blankly in front of her. I've never seen someone look so defeated.

"Right. Let me take you to Allison."

Andrew gives Jess one more look of despair and continues down the hallway. He motions for both of us to follow and Jess walks slowly after him. I can tell that walking is painful for her and it makes me sick to think that while I was in my room, relatively undisturbed, for the last few weeks she was being abused the entire time, all because of my brother's jealously. This is all my fault. Why did I agree to bring Jess and Allison with me?

At every corner, I expect to find somebody at guard, but it just seems to be the three of us. The only noise is our footsteps echoing off the walls and Andrew's painful wheezing. I get more and more nervous. Why isn't anyone trying to stop us?

"Up….ahead…." Andrew wheezes. This walk has drained almost all of his limited energy.

"Over there to the left?" I ask for clarification and Andrew nods.

He mutters the code to me. I give him a concerned look as I walk toward the door. We need to find him some medicine. He's in terrible shape.

I punch in the code for the door and find a completely different scene than when I opened the door to Jess's room. Instead of hiding in a dark corner, Allison greets me at the door in a warm hug. I stumble backward when her stomach pushes me. Despite everything, I allow myself a small smile.

"I heard your voice. Thank goodness you're okay. And Jess?" she asks and looks past me.

Her face falls when she spots Jess but instead of commenting on her appearance, she lets go of me and walks up to Jess and embraces her.

Jess does not stop her, but at the same time, doesn't hug her back. Jess's eyes stare blankly ahead. After a few moments, Allison steps back and spots Andrew for the first time.

"I'm Andrew. I was with Elliot and Jess at the lake," Andrew says and begins to tell his story.

"The one who was shot?" Allison was clearly not expecting to see him here.

Andrew nods and coughs.

I take over telling the story so he can save his strength. "Dominic and the other genetic engineers turned him into one of the Letum."

"But he's not one of them," Allison says with her voice full of enthusiasm. I look over at Jess and she appears uninterested.

"They turned me back," Andrew says and gestures toward his frail body.

"How? What does this mean?" Allison asks as she subconsciously rubs her very large stomach. "Can we turn Matt back?"

"We can try, but look at Andrew—" I start but get cut off by a squeal of pure joy.

I can't help but return some of her delight and look over at Jess to share in the moment. She looks forward blankly, bringing me back to reality.

"We can go into more details later. We need to get out of here now before anyone realizes what's going on. Andrew said he will show us where the medicine is to bring Matt back, but we need to get out of here soon."

"Elliot, think about it. We're going to get Matt back. He isn't just gone."

Andrew lightly touches Allison's shoulder and looks very anxious as he says, "He might not be gone, but he's not comin' back."

For the first time, I notice that even his fingernails look unhealthy. A cough takes over Andrew again. He leans over in pain.

Allison supports Andrew and says, "I know it won't be like it was before. There is hope that I can speak to him again and he can meet his child. That's more than there was ten minutes ago."

"But for how long?" Andrew asks as soon as he recovers some of his strength.

Abducted and forced to suffer through a terrible disease. Who had it worse: Andrew or Chris? I've been so happy just to see him alive again that I haven't really taken in the actual situation. Surely if they can give him this disease, they know how to get rid of it.

"You have to have hope, Andrew. Maybe Dominic and the team have an antidote or at least something that will help with the pain. There has to be a way to make you feel better," I say.

His eyes dart across the hallway. "You're right. We oughtta keep movin'. The lab is just around the corner with the medicine for your friend."

Jess hasn't contributed to the conversation so I quickly glance to make sure she's still with us. Her arms wrap around herself as if she's trying to hold herself together.

Instinctively, I step toward her but freeze when she tenses up. I don't know how to comfort her if she won't talk to me or let me get close enough to touch her.

The sound of coughing interrupts my thoughts. I motion for Andrew to lead the way.

He goes into a dark room and the three of us follow without hesitation. My eyes struggle to adjust to the dark.

I ask, "How do we turn the lights on?"

"What's the matter, little brother?" Chills run down my spine at his voice. "Scared of the dark?"

CHAPTER TWENTY-EIGHT

A sob escapes from my left and Allison curses from my other side.

"Don't play games, Dominic. Turn on the lights," I struggle to keep the fear out of my voice in the hope that I come across strong.

The artificial lights turn on and assault my eyes. We're in one of the testing laboratories. Just like every other room in the genetic engineering facility, it's grey and immaculate.

Dominic stands smugly in front of me in a raised section in the middle of the room. He holds something in his hand. I look over at Andrew. A tear falls down his face.

"I'm so sorry," he says.

"Do not apologize, Andrew," my brother says. "You did exactly what I asked." Dominic flashes him an insincere smile and walks closer to him.

I turn a confused look of betrayal at Andrew in time for him to repeat, "I'm so sorry," before my brother pulls up his weapon and shoots him in the head.

"No," Allison and I scream in unison.

His dead body hits the floor in an unnatural thud. I stare at the scene in shock. Dominic takes a step back to avoid the growing pool of blood around Andrew's head.

I painfully tear my eyes away from my friend's dead body and examine his killer's dispassionate face.

"Why?" I ask as soon as I'm able to speak.

"I needed something and he needed something, it was mutually beneficial."

"So you murdered him?" Allison asks, voice raised in shock.

"I wouldn't classify this as murder. He asked me to end his life. I did him a favor," Dominic says to defend himself.

"I've known Andrew my whole life," I say. "He would never have asked anyone to kill him."

"That may have been true for Andrew in the past, but not today. He was suffering and I promised to end his pain if he did one small thing for me."

The Andrew I knew would never do something like this. He wouldn't have let Dominic use him as a tool to get what he wanted.

"I don't believe you," I say.

"I do not really care what you believe. It does not change what happened," Dominic responds.

Allison's voice interrupts our argument. "How did you bring him back?" She's examining Andrew's body with a peculiar expression on her face.

Small evidence of emotion displays on his face as he smiles proudly at her question.

"Once I understood more about how the infection worked and how it was spread, I focused on the timing over everything. What caused this disease to take place at this point in history? Why now? I found the only thing that correlates with these deaths," Dominic says. He pauses dramatically. He enjoys the fact that he knows something we don't.

I lose patience with his game. "And?"

"For our generation, cancer was eliminated from the gene pool for the Planned. All along, cancer was an evolutionary defense mechanism that protected humanity from turning into the Letum. Every time an individual got cancer, it was the body's only defense against this virus. Once cancer was removed from the gene pool, our bodies could no longer fight it and turned into the Letum.

"The reason Unplanned with the ability to get cancer still turn is because the infection is too strong at the beginning and does not allow enough time for the cancerous cells to develop and metastasize to suffocate the cells infected with the virus," he explains.

How could something that historically had such a bad reputation actually turn out to be our society's biggest protector? Removing cancer from the gene pool was such a celebrated accomplishment of genetic engineering before I was born.

"Why did it take all this time for the infection to begin?" I ask.

"I am still working on that theory, but I believe it is related to brain development and hormones, as the brain is not fully developed until around twenty-five. I could go into more detail, but what is the point? You are not going to understand it," Dominic says.

I clench my fists and take a deep breath. Even though he's trying to get a reaction out of me, I refuse to take the bait and argue with him. I'm too focused on this information. All of this genetic planning to create the ideal population and all it led to was death.

"Try me," I say through clenched teeth.

He studies my expression before answering. "Do you recall learning about apoptosis?"

The term seems familiar. Before I can speak, however, Allison responds, "Programmed cell death?"

Dominic raises his eyebrows and nods.

Allison notices my confused look and continues, "Starting as embryos and throughout childhood development, certain cells are told to die. For example, this is how our fingers and toes get separated."

She looks questioningly at Dominic. "I don't understand how this is related."

Dominic opens his bag and puts his gun back inside.

While taking inventory of the items inside, he says, "Before an individual is fully developed, their cells are reproducing and dying very quickly. When the virus is introduced, without the cancerous cells to protect the body, cell necrosis occurs to further spread the virus, thus causing apoptosis to occur unchecked and new, healthy cellular reproduction to cease.

"The developing individual then has a host of rapid developmental problems that cause the brain, and individual, to die. That was the cause of the spur of children deaths recently."

Dominic considers for a moment and concludes, "Imagine a candle lit at both ends, if you will. They don't stand a chance—similar to you, Joe."

I bite back my retort. It seems like a lifetime ago that Ian was accusing the genetic engineers of causing his sister's death. He was right all along and the only one brave enough to challenge Dominic.

I repeat the new information back to myself to try and increase my understanding of how this virus works. "So once someone is fully developed, apoptosis ends, the body loses its last defense, and becomes fully susceptible to the virus?"

"Correct. And without the cancerous cells to spread and smother the virus, the Letum is created."

"That's what happened to Matt? Because he was genetically planned, his body no longer had the ability to protect itself from the virus by developing cancer. That's why he turned into the Letum even though he wasn't bitten."

"That's right," Dominic says as he zips up his bag and sets it on the table next to him.

My eyes widen at the implication. "That means everyone from our generation who is Planned can turn without being exposed to the Letum." I nervously eye Dominic and Jess.

"That took you less time to catch on than I thought, Joe. Well done," my brother responds.

I glare at his condescending tone and bite back my response. All of the questions about why everything has happened have finally been answered, yet it's somehow unsatisfying. It was all so avoidable. We did this to ourselves.

Allison glances down at her growing stomach and repeats her earlier question. "How did you bring him back?"

"I introduced a high concentration of cancerous cells into his body. The cells quickly spread and fought the virus until Andrew was able to regain control. Unfortunately, while we know how to prevent cancer from occurring via genetic planning, there is no cure. We could treat some of his symptoms, but not eradicate this new infection."

No longer able to stand the sight of Andrew's vulnerable body lying crumbled on the ground, I take one of the medical sheets off the nearest shelf and cover his body. The white sheet quickly turns red and I turn away in pain. I look to Jess for strength. Mentally, she's so far removed from the conversation. I rub my forehead, trying to make sense of everything that has happened tonight.

Allison interrupts my thoughts. "You could have gotten us out of the rooms yourself. Why did you need him?"

"To gain your trust and give you hope. If I had simply told you I had the power to bring someone back from this infection, would you have believed me?" Dominic asks us and then he quickly answers his own question. "Of course not. You would have thought I was scheming."

I look at him in disbelief. "So you're not scheming right now?"

"Of course I am, Joe, but that's not what you should focus on."

My eyes return to the sheet outline of Andrew. Dominic has now shot two of my closest friends right in front of me.

"And what do you gain from all of this?" Allison says.

"I can bring your unborn child's father back and have him hold your baby," Dominic states instead of answering. One glance at Allison and I know, without a doubt, whatever he wants, she's going to agree to it.

I look over at Jess to see if I can gauge her thoughts. She's still staring at the ground. I frown and look back at Dominic. He watches Jess with an arrogant look on his face and my hatred threatens to choke me.

Gathering all of my strength and courage, I run and catch him by surprise. Our bodies hit the ground when I tackle him. Dominic may be a lot stronger, but I catch him unaware and wrap my hands around his neck. My fingers tighten around his sensitive skin as I strangle him.

Allison screams while a blind rage consumes me.

He put me through so much growing up, always making me think I wasn't good enough for anyone. He murdered Andrew and Chris right in front of me and clearly damaged Jess.

My grip tightens even more and I notice with satisfaction that Dominic looks scared, his eyes bulging in alarm. His hands flounder against my chest, but he's getting weaker and weaker with each passing moment. Who's the strong one now?

There's a pressure at my side and I'm put off balance. This brings me back to reality and the sound of Allison screaming, "Stop it. Don't kill him. I need him. I need to get Matt back. Think of Matt. Please!"

Her voice finally resonates and I'm able to see the truth in her words. I relax my grip and slide off of Dominic. He rolls over and sputters. Unable to resist, I kick him in the side.

I back up a few feet and try to regain my breath. Allison grabs me in an embrace. She sobs, "Oh, thank you, Elliot. Thank you, thank you, thank you…" she continues irrationally.

I pat her back without taking my eyes off Dominic. He manages to get up on all fours and coughs nastily.

I shift my sight to Jess. She looks at Dominic, but it doesn't seem like she's actually seeing him. Her mind seems far away from the present situation.

I turn my attention back to my brother. At this point, he's made it to his knees and, somehow, smiles.

"You finally had your chance," he says in a taunt. His voice is hoarse and almost unrecognizable. "You had me, but you weren't strong enough to finish it. You are, and always will be, too weak."

"Stop talking," I say.

"Or what? You won't do anything. You just proved that. I've been miserable to you your whole life. I captured the only two friends you truly had growing up and killed both of them right in front of you. And there's what I did to Jess." He winks at her and I clench my fists. "But you won't do anything to me because you care too much. Simple as that. The people you love expose you and leave you even more vulnerable than you were in the first place."

"If you have it so figured out, then why do you need us right now? Why else would you have hatched this plan to get us here?" I ask.

A cackle escapes his mouth and he says, "You think you have the power right now? You need me. I have a semi-cure for your friend, a vehicle to get out of the territory safely to get to him, and medicine to help keep him as healthy as possible after he turns back."

Even if he gives us the medicine, we don't know how to administer it without him. "What are you getting out of it then? You're the most selfish person I know. There has to be something in it for you."

He pretends to consider the question. "Now that I understand what caused this virus, it is not safe to be in a location with a lot of Planned. I doubt it will be secure here much longer. There has already been desertion." He rubs his beard. "I want to go to Acroisia. Their population should be relatively unaffected by this outbreak."

I thought nothing he could have said would have shocked me at this point, but I was wrong.

Growing up, we were all told of the stories of savagery and the backward population. Acroisia is supposed to be full of lawless, dangerous individuals who don't understand reason. Can I expose Jess and Allison to this?

With my mind racing, I ask, "If you want to go there, why do you need us?"

Dominic sighs with impatience. "I cannot show up by myself or I will stand out. I need to bring you all with me so they'll be more likely to accept me in their group. In case you think you can just kill me and steal my medicine, I have special codes for the drugs that only I know how to administer. In addition, I have packed supplies to help with the impending birth of the child. Jocelyn was a doctor and I convinced her to teach me how to deliver a baby." He nods at Allison and concludes his argument.

"If she was a doctor, why can't we bring her with us?" Allison asks.

"Because I have the knowledge to assist you now. She's no longer needed," he states and grabs his bag. "Let's move out before this place crumbles. I got rid of the guards for the vehicles so we should leave before the next shift gets in."

He whistles so happily that it makes me nauseous.

"Please leave the room while I discuss it with Allison and Jess," I tell him in as calm a voice as I can manage. I know Allison has her mind made up, but I need to get the approval from Jess. I hope she will be honest with me.

Dominic smirks and walks toward the door. He pauses when he's next to Jess and her whole body tenses. He leans in close and whispers something in her ear. A sob escapes Jess's mouth. I quickly move toward her, but it appears Dominic accomplished what he wanted to do because he steps back and raises his arms in the air.

"Easy, Joe. I was just asking how she was doing. I did not mean to offend you by talking to your...ah..." He pauses and a smile plays on his lips when he finishes. "Whatever she is, no need to worry. She is all yours." He continues whistling and leaves.

I utter a sigh of relief the second he exits the room. I walk toward the far wall, away from Andrew, and motion for them. Once I reach the farthest point away from Dominic, I sit down and wait for them. Allison waddles and clumsily sits down next to me, with Jess on her other side.

Before I can speak, Allison says, "Matt."

"I know," I say.

"What's there to talk about? We need Dominic," Allison says.

I remain silent as I consider my next words. I need to be blunt, but I don't want to hurt her feelings. "There are several things to discuss. First of all, we don't even know if it will work and even if it does, how long will he be back? And at what quality of life? Would he want to come back just to get sick and weak? Do we want that for Matt?"

A silent tear falls down Allison's cheek and she grabs my left hand and Jess's right hand and places them on her stomach. There's a movement under her shirt and for a few seconds, the three of us sit there quietly as we feel Allison and Matt's unborn child shift positions.

"Matt would want to come back to meet his child. I'm not unrealistic. I know it isn't a permanent solution and it won't be like it was before. Dominic is giving us the opportunity for my child to meet his or her father."

"Jess?" I say in an attempt to get her to contribute to the discussion.

She jerks her hand off of Allison's stomach. "Whatever you guys want. It doesn't matter."

"Look at Jess, Allison. We can't bring Dominic with us," I say with clenched teeth.

Allison addresses Jess. "I'm going to be selfish. I have an opportunity to have my child know Matt and I need you to be okay with that. Please."

Keeping her eyes on the floor, Jess nods and Allison pulls her in for another hug. Jess flinches again, but lightly pats Allison's back before she pulls away and retreats back into herself.

"What about going to Acroisia? You've heard the stories. They're supposed to be very dangerous and unpredictable," I say to remind her of the full implications of bringing him with us.

Almost too quietly for me to make out her words, Jess whispers, "Look around, Elliot."

I examine the room. The evidence of all of the experiments is visible in every corner of the room with all the supplies and machines used for the genetic engineers' manipulations.

In my mind, a seemingly endless loop of devastating images takes over. Andrew's pool of blood, Matt's desperate attempts at hurting Allison, Chris's limp body falling, Carly being torn apart, the emptiness in my grandfather's eyes, my grandmother ripping into my mother's throat, the two men Dominic killed outside the territory. Our society did this. It's the problem.

I finally see clearly the society that I grew up in. With one more look at how damaged Jess is, a decision and plan lock into place. Dominic isn't going to use us to get to Acroisia. We're using him.

So, even though accepting my brother's help is one of the last things I want to do, I'm somehow forced, once again, to ask for it.

I walk toward Dominic. He comes through the door with an arrogant look.

I tell him quietly enough so no one can hear, "If you so much as look at her the wrong way, I don't care what you can do for Matt. I don't care that you're my brother." I let the rest of the threat hang in the air.

"Joe, who do you have left to protect you now?" Dominic taunts.

I let out a deep breath through my nose. "I don't need anyone else to fight my battles."

He considers me for a second, a smirk playing at his lips. "Don't worry, I like my toys shiny and new." He raises his voice to address the group. "Let's move out."

He heads back to the door. Allison follows him and Jess and I exit the room side by side. I take one last look at the shape of Andrew's body and take a deep breath to steady myself. I engrave the image into my mind so I never forget.

"Where are you going?" I jerk my attention toward the source of the familiar voice. Phillip is looking at Dominic in confusion, and under that, a small tinge of betrayal. "Are you leaving us?"

Dominic's fingers tap on his thigh. "You have to trust me right now. I need to get away, but I will be back for you as soon as I can."

Phillip's eyebrows furrow. "We're supposed to do this together. You can't leave."

He meaningfully eyes his weapon at his side. I stiffen at his apparent threat. I'm not sure who to root for. At least my brother is the known evil.

Surprisingly, Dominic smiles. "Phillip, we are in this together. I need you to keep everything running smoothly here. You are the only one I can trust."

Phillip plays with the holster of his gun, his teeth gleaming in the artificial light.

"If that's true, why were you going to leave without telling me? And what are you doing with them?" he spits out.

"I am asking you to have faith. Can you do that for me?" Dominic responds.

"You'll come back for me?" Phillip asks as he drops his hand. There's a flash of a desperate need for belonging across his face.

"Of course. I need you." Phillip smiles instantly at Dominic's words. "It would be beneficial for you to go away and pretend that you never saw us."

Phillip looks like he still doesn't want to leave Dominic, but clasps his hand in farewell anyway.

"I'll see you soon then?"

Dominic nods and Phillip walks down the hallway, shoulders slumped.

Once he is out of earshot, Dominic mutters, "Idiot."

Allison studies my brother. "Why didn't you just kill him?"

"He can still add value, just not with me. Lying to him had the highest likelihood of his leaving." Dominic takes a deep breath. "Let's keep walking."

We all keep moving down the long hallway. There's a bounce in Allison's walk. Her joy infectiously threatens to spread through the empty hallway. I don't blame her. The thought of hearing Matt's cheesy jokes again, leaving our prison, and getting back to where I was happiest makes it so tempting to give in to her hope. But I can't.

Without thinking, I make to put my arm around Jess for support. She automatically shrinks away. Jess looks at me in unbearable pain and shakes her head. She speeds up to be closer to Allison. Reality slams back into me.

I clench my jaw and try not to feel the pain of her rejection or imagine what happened to her. A look at Dominic's arrogant walk lets one small seed of hope plant itself. When the time is right, I'll rid him from our lives.

Dominic hands us all masks like the ones we received when we first came here. "It is in the middle of the night. The vehicle's headlights would attract the Letum, so we are going to drive without them through Potentia. The moon should be bright enough," Dominic says. He opens the large door to let us out of the building.

Darkness awaits us.

ABOUT THE AUTHOR

Originally from Plano, Texas, Robin is a graduate of Kansas State University and currently lives in Tulsa, Oklahoma with her dog, Juno, and plenty of bottles of wine. *Specious* is her debut novel, the first in a three-part series that explores the provocative and divisive theory of genetic planning.

For more information on Robin and her upcoming projects, visit her website at www.robinberkstresser.com.